The Wedding

BOOKS BY RUTH HEALD

The Mother's Mistake
The Woman Upstairs
I Know Your Secret

The Wedding

RUTH HEALD

bookouture

Published by Bookouture in 2021

An imprint of Storyfire Ltd.
Carmelite House
50 Victoria Embankment
London EC4Y 0DZ

www.bookouture.com

ISBN: 978-1-83888-226-6
eBook ISBN: 978-1-83888-225-9

For Lewis

PROLOGUE

The wedding day

The fresh cut on the side of my bare foot stings as it comes into contact with the wooden floor of the honeymoon suite, and the train of my wedding dress drags behind me, heavy with dirt and sand. The image of the bride in the mirror shocks me as I pass. My sleeveless silk wedding dress chosen so carefully, my dark curls manipulated into a long braid, flowers entwined in the plait. Me. But the woman in the mirror is from another life.

I am no longer a bride. I will not be a wife. Not now.

The reflection draws me to her, but when I get closer I see the real me. Mascara in angry black streaks down my face, tear tracks parting my thick foundation. A couple of the clips in my hair are tumbling out, half suspended between my head and shoulders, strands of dark hair breaking free. I run my hand over the soft silk of my dress, feeling the edge of the rip from earlier under my fingers, now sewn up so neatly it's barely noticeable. Not all scars can heal so beautifully, even if you can't see them any more.

What am I even doing here? I should have run away as fast as I could, away from this place, this hotel, away from her. But instead I've come back to this suite. It had felt like a safe haven, with the four-poster bed, the chaise longue and the jacuzzi in a glass-covered sun room. Not any more. Now the bed taunts me, reminding me that it should have been the witness to the start of my marriage, not the end of my relationship. The digital clock on the dresser glares out the time. It's later than I thought, the day creeping away from me. If things had gone to plan, I'd have already said my vows and kissed my husband. Now I'd be celebrating with my guests.

I hear a gentle whirring. At first I think the sound is in my head; a symptom of my unsettled mind. But it isn't. It's the jacuzzi. It shouldn't be on. No one's here. At least, that was what I thought.

'Hello?' I call out tentatively.

As I open the door to the room that houses the jacuzzi, I blink. Earlier the light had streamed through the floor-to-ceiling windows, but now it's completely dark, the blinds pulled down and the ceiling covered. I can't see anything at all.

'Hello?' I say again, curiosity quickly turning to fear, my heart pounding. Someone must be in here with me, their eyes already adjusted to the dark. Waiting, watching. I think I can make out the sound of someone breathing, steady and even, a contrast to my shaky and uncertain breaths. My chest tightens and I take a step back, jarring my shoulder against the tiled wall. Running my fingers along the tiles, I finally connect with the light switch.

It's a relief when the room reveals itself. Empty except for the jacuzzi, bubbling invitingly. My eyes dart around the space. There's no one here. I can't think with the bubbles whirring, the foamy water sparkling under the low-level lighting. I push my hand onto the red rubber off-switch, watch the bubbles subside.

As the water stills, dark hair floats up towards the surface.

I feel a rush of heat spreading through my body as my breathing gets faster. I grip the edge of the jacuzzi, my knuckles turning white. It feels like everything has been building up to this moment. She planned this.

A small, smooth, pale face bobs just under the surface of the water, hair fanning around it, glassy eyes staring, white material swathing its body.

It's a doll. Like the other one she left for me, it has long dark hair – just like mine – and is wearing a wedding dress.

Its matted hair wraps around my arm as I reach into the water to pull it out. Its white dress is torn, its body cut open.

This is it, I think. I can't escape her any more. She has won.

The silence is broken by footsteps behind me. I scream, but it's instantly stifled by a hand clamped over my mouth, small and strong. Another hand in my hair, fingers tangling in my plait. I see the flowers that had been woven in so carefully just this morning falling into the water. *An array of colour*, that's how the hairdresser described them.

The hands pull my head up by the hair as if it's me who's the doll, and then my face is being pushed into the water, fingers on the back of my neck holding me down.

I can't breathe. The water swirls around me and my head pounds. I fight desperately to break the surface, my arms flailing, hands crashing into the tiled seat of the jacuzzi again and again. I try to turn, to duck away, but the hand stays firmly on my neck. I push against it, needing to release my head from the water. I can feel it soaking through the shoulder straps of my perfect white dress, can feel my lungs burning.

Memories flash through my mind. Adam waiting for me at the end of the aisle. The elation I'd felt when I found out I was pregnant. Laughing with my parents at some juvenile joke, their faces stretched out into smiles. Then their expressions before they'd died: my mother panicked, my father determined, fighting to get back to her. Before they were both carried away by the current, disappearing under the water.

And then it hits me. I'm going to die here. I'm going to drown like my parents. On my wedding day. All because of her.

CHAPTER ONE

Lauren

2019: Three months before the wedding

Lauren picked up the first wedding invitation from the pile and opened it, her new fountain pen poised above the cream paper, ready to write the names of the first guests in the neat, cursive script she'd been practising. As she held the pen over the paper, a tear landed on it, spreading across the date of the wedding. She wiped her tears with the back of her hand as her cat, Misty, rubbed against her leg under the table. Lauren reached down and stroked her between the ears, for her own comfort more than the cat's.

It was not the time to be sad. Her own happy face beamed out from the engagement photo on the front of the invitations, and she tried to recall how she'd felt that day, with Adam looking at her as if she was the only woman in the world, his arms wrapped tightly around her.

'Are you alright? What's happened?' Adam's voice was etched with concern as he came up behind her, his broad shoulders casting a shadow over her. She gazed out of the window at the East London skyline and tried to stem her tears.

'I can't do it,' she said.

'Can't do what?' When she looked up at his face it was even paler than usual. 'You mean get married?' he asked, his voice barely a whisper.

'No, not that.' She managed to force a small smile. 'Of course not that. It's just the invitations.'

'What about them? Haven't they turned out like you want? You look beautiful in this picture.' He looked at her, studying her. 'But we could change them if you like.'

'It's not that,' she said, taking a deep breath. 'It's my parents.'

'Your parents?'

They'd drowned eighteen years ago, and although the pain wasn't as fresh any more, it was always there, lurking in the background, especially at moments like these. They should be at her wedding. She should have been writing the first invitation to them.

'Writing the invitations is just reminding me they won't be there, that I can't write one to them. I'll be walking down the aisle without my father's arm in mine, without my mother watching.'

Adam reached over and massaged her shoulders. 'I can't imagine how hard this is for you.'

Lauren stifled a sob and Adam sat down beside her and put his arm around her.

'We can make them a part of the day, find ways to include them,' he said.

'I'm going to wear Mum's silver bracelet,' Lauren replied. 'She wore it on her own wedding day. I've seen the pictures.'

Lauren's parents had married in the same church where Lauren and Adam had booked their wedding. She hoped that would help her feel like they were part of the celebrations.

'That's a brilliant idea,' Adam said. 'And we'll think of a way to include your dad, too. Maybe we could serve his favourite ale at the reception.'

Her dad had been a member of CAMRA, the real ale society, and he'd loved telling everyone he met about the flavours and textures of different British ales.

Adam squeezed her shoulders. 'Do you want to visit them?' he asked. 'Before you write the invitations? We could go to the memorial.'

'What, now?' It would be two hours before they got to the South Coast.

'Why not?'

They left ten minutes later. Her parents' memorial stones were just outside Bournemouth on a small grassy clifftop overlooking the ocean. The traffic was clear in their direction, the day trippers to the coast queueing to leave the seaside towns, while the traffic flowed freely into them.

Lauren used to come to the coast on family holidays, with her sister and her parents. Lauren's mother had been Adam's mother's closest friend and Adam's family had sometimes joined them. All the children would play in the sea together, followed by a trip down to Bournemouth pier to go in the arcades. Adam was older than them and he'd seemed so grown up. Even as a child she'd imagined marrying Adam, whispering to her sister about it in their bunk beds when they were supposed to be asleep.

When they arrived at the coast, Adam and Lauren sat in the car park on the edge of the cliff, staring out at the clear blue sky above the ocean. It was already early evening and the sun was low and bright. Adam reached into the back of the car and pulled out his briefcase. 'I wonder if it would help,' he said gently, 'if we wrote an invitation to your parents.'

'What do you mean?'

'I thought… it might be therapeutic for you to write the invitation and take it to the memorial stones. Help to make them feel part of the wedding.' He looked uncertain then. 'You don't have to, of course. It was just an idea.'

She nodded. 'Let's do it.'

He passed her an invitation and a pen and she hunched over in the passenger seat, leaning on his briefcase as she wrote their names.

For a moment she allowed herself to imagine another life. The excitement on her mother's face when she realised Lauren was getting married; her mother choosing her wedding outfit; her father practising his speech in front of the mirror.

She pushed the invitation into an envelope, sealing her love inside. Adam was right – she felt better.

When they were out of the car, Adam took her arm and they climbed further up the cliff to the memorial garden. A small sign on the gate said it had closed at four, but Adam paid no attention.

'I'll give you a leg-up,' he said. With Adam on one knee, she smiled at the memory of his marriage proposal, in their favourite local restaurant. But this time she stood on his knee, hoisting herself up over the wall. She fell down to the other side and then scrambled to her feet, brushing the dirt off the knees of her jeans. He followed easily, muscles well trained from the gym.

She went straight to her parents' memorial stones on the back wall of the graveyard. Most of the stones were weathered from the sea salt that blew in on the harsh wind, but the lettering on her family's was still legible, their names carved into the stones, one above the other. Her father had been five years older than her mother, but their lives had ended on exactly the same day. A bouquet of flowers had been left in a weighted-down glass, but now the petals had gone and only the stems remained.

With a heavy heart, she thought back to the day they'd died. The two families had been on holiday together in Thailand: six of them. Her and Adam, her sister Tracey, Adam's mum and her parents. But only her parents had drowned in the accident. Sometimes she thought that that was what had given her and Adam that unbreakable bond, witnessing that horror together, both wishing they could have saved them.

She thought of her sister, how close they used to be, how she'd always looked up to her. Tracey was two years older than her; nineteen when their parents had died. She'd been on an extended gap year. Lauren had expected her to stay in the UK after their parents' funerals, but instead she'd gone straight back to Asia and continued travelling. Eventually she had settled in Thailand, getting together with a fellow ex-pat and adopting a daughter. It was then that Lauren had realised her sister was never returning to the UK. Lauren still missed her. With her parents gone and Tracey in Thailand, Lauren had felt rudderless and alone. If it hadn't been for Adam, and his mother Sam, who'd welcomed her into their home, she didn't know how she would have coped.

Adam climbed up onto the wall that mounted the memorials and pulled Lauren up beside him. She rested her head on his shoulder as they gazed out. From their vantage point on the hill above the cliff they could see the sun was now touching the sea, its rays fanning out over the water. She could hear the waves below them crashing against the cliffs.

'It's gorgeous,' she said. 'It's so sad that they'll never see a scene like this again.'

'But *we* will,' Adam replied softly. 'We've got our whole lives ahead of us. They'd have wanted us to be happy.'

Suddenly Lauren could see things clearly. That by resisting writing the invitations, she was resisting starting a new life without her parents, resisting moving on.

As if reading her mind, Adam opened up his briefcase and pulled out the invitation. 'Here you go.'

Lauren gazed out at the sunset. There was nowhere to leave the invitation by the memorial. It would only blow away. So instead, she took a deep breath and opened the envelope that she'd only recently sealed.

She read out each word, telling the air the location, the time, the date, her voice getting lost in the wind that blew around her hair, and rustled the thick paper in her hands. Tears flowed freely as she sat on the wall with Adam's arm around her.

'Do you feel better?' Adam asked as she finished and wiped her eyes with the sleeve of her shirt.

She nodded. 'They'd just want me to be happy,' she said. 'And I'm happy with you.'

Her hands holding the invitation were damp from where they'd caught her falling tears.

She thought about tearing it up into hundreds of pieces and letting them scatter on the wind, falling like confetti. But she didn't want to litter the memorial garden, so instead she handed it to Adam, who put it back in the briefcase.

Then he pulled out a bottle of champagne and two glasses. 'Let's raise a glass to them.'

She hesitated for a moment, not sure how she felt about drinking champagne by their memorial stones. Then she thought of her mum's smile, and her dad's booming laugh, and she knew that if they could see her and Adam, they'd be happy. 'Sure,' she said with a grin.

'They can't be at the wedding, but we can toast them now,' Adam said.

She nodded, her face breaking into a smile. The sound of the popping cork was loud despite the wind.

As she sipped the champagne she realised that it was up to her and Adam to remember her parents, to find ways to include them in the celebrations. Lauren imagined their pride in her as she walked down the aisle to marry Adam. She closed her eyes and revelled in the feeling of family, of feeling safe and loved. She missed them both, but she was lucky. She was still safe, still loved, with Adam. When she got home, she vowed that she would write the rest of the wedding invitations. Nothing would stop her marrying him.

CHAPTER TWO

Lauren

Four weeks until the wedding

Lauren made her way through the bustling East London market, past the stalls selling artisan breads and cheeses and overpriced vintage clothing, to the meats, fish and veg section at the far end of the alleyway, where her mother used to shop when Lauren was a child. Lauren loved living in East London. Round every corner was a memory from her childhood. She hardly saw her sister any more, with her so far away in Thailand, but at least by staying in the area she grew up in she still felt connected to her family.

At the market, Lauren chose a whole sea bass and some oriental vegetables, picking up some fresh chillies and ginger to go with them. She'd loved Thai food ever since the holiday to Thailand with Adam and their families, when she was still a teenager.

On the way home she stopped at the off-licence and asked them for the best wine to have with sea bass, leaving with a bottle that cost twenty-five pounds, far more than she'd normally spend.

When she arrived back at her block of flats, she managed to ignore the lure of the lift and took the stairs up the fourteen floors, a habit she was determined to stick to as it got closer to the wedding.

Inside the flat, she found Misty in the spare room and stroked her. The cat had made the room her own since the lodger left, curling up on the pillow of the bed in a small patch of sunlight streaming in from the window. That was one of the nice things about being on the fourteenth floor. There was nothing to block the sun. This room was supposed to be the baby's room. The baby that would have been due in a few weeks' time, if she hadn't lost it. Lauren swallowed her tears. They were planning to start trying for a baby again after the wedding.

She went into the living room, sat down at her dining table and tried to work out the table plan for the wedding. It was the top table that was the problem. Who would be on it, where they would sit. Her sister would be beside her, standing in for her parents. On Adam's side, his mother, Sam, would be there, and his father, who'd finally confirmed he was coming. His presence would make things difficult. Adam's parents' divorce had been acrimonious and his mother wasn't willing to sit anywhere near his father. Lauren would have to shuffle everyone around, but she'd be able to keep them apart. Lauren would be next to her sister, with Adam's dad the other side of her, a few seats away from his mother, who'd be next to Adam. Lauren just needed to work out where she'd put Adam's dad's girlfriend. Perhaps he could go next to Ken, Tracey's husband.

She thought of her sister. The wedding was bringing them together again, helping to repair their relationship. After their parents had died, they'd argued over the sale of their flat. Lauren had wanted to take time to clear it out, but Tracey had wanted to sell it immediately to get the money in the bank. They'd hardly spoken for years when Tracey moved to Thailand, despite Lauren's efforts. But Tracey had softened towards her in the last couple of years, and now they chatted regularly. Last year, Lauren had finally made the trip over to Thailand to meet her niece and twin nephews.

Adam would be home in an hour, so she put away the table plan and then got to work on the sea bass, filleting it and then seasoning it with chilli and ginger. From next door, she could hear the sound of a pumping bass. Ever since their neighbours had started renting out their place on Airbnb there had been a steady flow of tourists. When the neighbours had lived in the flat they'd got on well, checking each other's flats when they went on holiday and watering the houseplants. But since they'd moved out, she'd given the spare keys to Adam's mother and her uncle instead, in case of emergencies. Adam had also given one to his friend Kiera, who worked with him and lived nearby.

Lauren ignored the gentle thump of the bass and put the radio on. Soon she was singing along to Britpop, reminding herself of the days when she and Adam were young, when he'd just been a teenage crush for her, before they'd embarked on their relationship. She smiled when she thought about how, back then, she'd had no idea that they'd actually end up getting married.

It had been weeks since Lauren had had a meal with Adam in the evening. Her shift pattern at the hospital's A&E department meant that they often missed dinner together, and even when she was working daytime hours, Adam was regularly late home from the GP surgery, meaning they either ate separately or had a rushed meal together.

Whizzing round the flat, Lauren checked it was tidy. She paused for a moment, looking into the sunny box room where Misty was curled up in the corner. The bed was covered in wedding paraphernalia: the cake stand, spare wedding invitations and her bridal shoes.

Lauren caught sight of her mother's jewellery box on the side. She went over and opened it, slipping her mum's silver bracelet over her wrist. The blue stone sparkled in the light. She thought of her mother on her own wedding day, wearing this bracelet; the cold silver that was now touching Lauren's wrist pressing against her mum's wrist all those years ago. She closed her eyes and smiled.

She pulled the door to the room half closed, leaving Misty enough space to get out if she wanted to, and then went to the kettle and switched it on to make a cup of tea. Unopened post had been put in a small pile on the kitchen counter and she picked it up and flicked through. Mainly junk mail – an invitation to try a new broadband supplier, a pre-approval for a credit card, a charity appeal. The final envelope was square and addressed to her with a typed label. It felt like a card. She looked at it curiously, wondering what it was for. It was ages until her birthday. Sliding her finger under the seal of the envelope, she pulled out the card. It was thick and shiny. On the front was a picture of her and Adam wrapped in each other's arms under a canopy of bare winter trees, the sun shining low through the branches. She smiled. It was the same as the photo displayed on their dining table, the picture she'd chosen for the wedding invitations. It was her favourite of all the engagement pictures her friend Zoe had taken because it captured the looks in their eyes, the understanding and the love that existed between them.

They'd been so happy then, no clouds on the horizon. There were other pictures, too, ones she hadn't put up. Of her touching her stomach and smiling up at Adam. Of him with an arm protectively around her waist, beaming. He'd proposed because of the baby, saying he wanted to commit fully to her, to be a family. They hadn't known that they'd lose the baby just a few days later.

But they'd try again. And whatever happened, they'd still be together, still have each other. That was what Adam had said when she'd lost the baby. The thought of being married to him made her feel warm inside, and she imagined their future together: swooning over a crying baby, sipping cocktails on a sun-kissed foreign holiday, and then finally retirement together, cosying up in slippers by the fire. They'd be good together, always. They'd known each other since they were tiny, grown up in and out of each other's houses. A part of her had always loved him. She could vividly recall drawing hearts on her school notebooks and writing their names neatly in the middle. Lauren and Adam. She'd only been about eleven years old, but her childish fantasy had come true. Now they'd been in a relationship for almost eighteen years. A lifetime already. And Adam was still the same kind, sensitive soul she'd fallen in love with all those years ago.

She opened the card, expecting to see a congratulatory message from someone in the family. For a second she stopped breathing.

Inside was a printed picture. It couldn't be meant for her.

It was a photo of a doll in a wedding dress, lying on a wooden floor, its hair fanned out around it. The doll had Lauren's dark, curly hair. Her piercing blue eyes. Her high cheekbones. It was as if it had been made specially, carefully crafted to resemble her.

The wedding dress was slashed, ripped into shreds by a sharp knife. And the doll's neck was cut, a clean slice through the plastic. Its body lay on its front on the floor, but its head had been twisted round at an impossible angle to face Lauren, its soulless eyes staring her down.

Lauren recoiled from the image.

There were just four words printed in the card, in such small lettering they were almost an afterthought.

He doesn't love you.

CHAPTER THREE

Adam

Adam looked at his watch: 6.30 p.m. He hadn't quite finished his paperwork, but he'd completed everything urgent. He needed to leave the surgery now to get back in time for dinner with Lauren.

He went past the reception on his way out and was surprised to see the lights on over the desks; Kiera was still sitting there, staring blankly at her computer screen. The receptionists usually left well before the doctors, although sometimes Kiera would wait for him and they'd have dinner in the pub together if Lauren was working.

'I can't do the pub tonight,' he said. 'Sorry.'

Kiera didn't answer and when he looked closer, he saw the tears running gently down her cheeks as she stifled a sob.

'Kiera…?' he said softly, coming round the back of reception and putting his hand on her shoulder. 'What's going on?'

'It's Carmelle,' she said. 'We've split up. I can't do it any more. I don't love her. You were right, it's all a pretence. I explained how I was feeling and now she's chucked me out.'

'I'm so sorry, Kiera.' Adam resisted the temptation to look at his watch. He wanted to help, but he was running out of time. He'd have more time tomorrow when Lauren would be working the night shift at the hospital. 'Why don't we go to the pub tomorrow after work? We can chat it through then. Work out a plan.'

Kiera shook her head. 'It's past that stage. She wants me to collect my stuff as soon as possible. I don't even have anywhere to go, but she doesn't care.' Kiera's sobs got louder.

'She can't just chuck you out of your home.'

'She owns the flat. I have no claim on it. I've given up so much for her.'

Kiera had met Carmelle when she was working in Asia. She was the person who had finally persuaded Kiera to return to the UK after fifteen years living abroad.

'It will be alright,' Adam said. 'I'll help you in whatever way I can.' He went back a long way with Kiera. She'd studied medicine for a year at university with him before she dropped out, and he'd got her the job as a receptionist at his GP surgery when she'd come back to England to be with Carmelle.

'I'm so sorry.' He sat down in the office chair beside her and gently stroked her arm.

Kiera looked at him. 'Is there any chance I can stay with you and Lauren? I know you've got that spare room.'

Adam swallowed. He was the one who'd told her to leave Carmelle, that she wasn't right for her. But he hadn't imagined Kiera moving into their small flat with them. Yet he couldn't say no, and he found himself reluctantly replying, 'Yeah, of course.'

'I would pay rent, obviously.'

'Don't worry about that.' It seemed churlish to charge her rent when they weren't using the room anyway.

'Thanks, Adam. I owe you one.'

'It's no problem at all.' He wondered what Lauren would think. He stole a glance at his watch. He needed to get back for dinner.

'Right, I think I'll come straight to yours. I can collect my things tomorrow.' Adam thought of all the stuff Kiera had acquired since she'd moved back to the UK. There was lots of space in Carmelle's flat. Much less space in Adam's box room.

'OK,' Adam said slowly. He couldn't mention the romantic meal Lauren had planned now, could he? Not without making Kiera feel awful and unwelcome. Lauren would understand, wouldn't she?

'Brilliant,' Kiera said. 'I'll just get my bag.'

'Let me ring Lauren and tell her you're coming.'

'It will be OK with her, won't it?'

'Yes, of course,' he said, sounding more sure than he felt. 'I just want to let her know.'

'I don't want to be in the way.'

'You won't be. I'll ask her to put on some extra dinner for you.'

'Are you sure?'

'Yeah, it's no problem. I'll just give her a ring now.'

He picked up his mobile and called Lauren. It rang and rang, but she didn't pick up. He was just going to have to hope she'd understand.

CHAPTER FOUR

Lauren

Lauren stared at the picture in the card in disbelief. The doll in the torn wedding dress, her neck cut. It looked just like her. It *was* her.

Bile rose in her throat and she swallowed it back down. She picked up her tea and chucked it down the sink, then went to the fridge and poured herself a large glass of white wine, making sure she chose a cheap bottle, not wanting to waste the expensive one she'd bought to go with the sea bass.

She needed to talk to Adam about this.

The words in the card echoed in her head. *He doesn't love you.*

Would he know who'd sent it? And why? She took a swig of wine, noticing its sharp taste as it slid down her throat. It sounded like someone who was jealous of their relationship. Or someone who was interested in Adam themselves.

Pacing back and forth across her living room, she tried to reassure herself. *It was just a piece of paper, just a photograph. It couldn't hurt her.*

She looked at her watch. Adam should have been home half an hour ago. Realising she was still wearing her mother's bracelet, she quickly went to the spare room and put it back on top of the jewellery box, wanting to keep it safe. She put the rice on, then rushed round the flat, setting the table and laying out candles. She wanted to talk to him about the wedding, confirming the table plans and the background music. Lauren had created a choice of playlists for them to consider, and she thought they could listen to them over dinner.

Misty meowed as she brushed Lauren's leg and Lauren realised it was time to feed her. She was so predictable and reliable. If only people were so easy to understand. Lauren watched as Misty devoured her cat food before slinking off back to the spare room.

As she rushed around the flat, Lauren couldn't shake off her fear about the card. She told herself that it was just someone trying to upset her. But whoever it was had her address. And access to her engagement photos.

Footsteps echoed in the corridor outside the flat, interrupting her spiralling thoughts. It sounded like Adam.

Thank goodness.

He was chatting to someone. Most likely the people staying in the Airbnb next door.

She turned the steamer on to cook the fish and vegetables, just as she heard his key turn in the lock.

'Hello?' Adam called out. 'Lauren?'

'Hi,' she said, as she came into the hallway.

She realised there was someone behind him. Kiera. Lauren forced a welcoming smile, trying to mask her annoyance. This was their date night. The only night in two weeks that they were having dinner together alone.

'I tried to call you,' Adam said quickly. 'Kiera's split up with Carmelle.'

'Oh,' Lauren said, smiling sympathetically at Kiera. 'I'm so sorry.' Kiera's face was unusually devoid of make-up and her eyes were puffy.

'I said she could stay here while she sorts out another place to stay.'

Lauren blinked back her own churning emotions as she thought of the plans they'd had for the box room. The baby's room. 'Sure,' she said, reluctantly. She had to let Kiera stay. She was Adam's closest friend. He had even chosen her as 'best woman' for his wedding, replacing the traditional best man. 'I'll get the bed made up in the spare room after dinner.'

'Don't worry,' Kiera said. 'I can do it myself. Dinner smells lovely, by the way.'

Lauren thought of the hours she'd spent researching how to prepare the sea bass exactly the same way as they did at Adam's favourite local Thai restaurant. She swallowed her annoyance and smiled at Kiera. 'Do you want a glass of wine? I've already opened a bottle.'

'I'd love one,' Kiera said.

'I'm so sorry about you and Carmelle. What happened?' Lauren asked, as she poured the wine.

'We've just come to the end of the road.' Kiera's face flushed and tears started to fall down her cheeks. Adam put his arm round her and Lauren winced. As much as she tried to ignore it, she'd never liked how tactile Adam was with his friend.

Lauren turned away, checking on the fish. She could easily split it into three without anyone being too hungry.

'She gets jealous easily. Of anyone I'm friends with. Female, male, it doesn't matter. Anyone who spends any time with me seems to be a threat to her,' said Kiera. 'Even Adam.'

Adam shifted in his seat.

Carmelle was jealous of Adam? Her mind went to the card. *He doesn't love you.*

She pushed the thought aside. The food was ready now and Lauren dished it up. As they sat at the table, Lauren saw Kiera noticing the two glowing candles.

'Oh,' she said, putting her hand to her mouth in embarrassment. 'Was this supposed to be a romantic dinner? Have I interrupted something?' She turned to Adam. 'You should have said. I could have gone to McDonald's and then come over later, after you'd eaten.'

'Don't be silly,' Lauren said. 'You're more than welcome to join us.'

Kiera looked at the fish and the small portion of potatoes and vegetables on her plate. 'Are you sure?' she asked.

'Of course.' Lauren managed a smile.

'Lauren – you've been so busy hostessing that you haven't even got a glass of wine for yourself,' Kiera said. 'I'll get you one.'

'Oh, I forgot,' Lauren said. 'I bought a bottle specially to go with the sea bass. It's in the fridge door.'

Kiera fetched the bottle and poured Lauren a glass, before topping up her own glass with it, mixing the expensive wine with the cheap one.

'How's your day been, Lauren?' Adam asked. 'Table plan sorted?'

Lauren thought of the card. She couldn't mention it. Not with Kiera here. 'Fine,' she said. 'And I've figured out how to sit your father away from your mother. Not quite sure where to put his girlfriend, though.'

Kiera laughed. 'Weddings are complicated, aren't they? I never realised how much organisation a wedding involved until my sister got married. Mum went spare trying to sort out all the details. She was in her element on the day, bossing the photographer about and telling him exactly what photos to take.'

Lauren swallowed, thinking of her parents. She imagined her mum in a carefully selected outfit, chatting with their wedding guests and checking everyone was alright. No doubt her father would have spent his time propping up the bar, glowing with pride that his daughter was getting married.

Adam reached for Lauren's hand across the table. 'Lauren's mother isn't with us any more,' he said. 'But my mum wants to help with all that side of things.'

Kiera looked at Lauren sympathetically and then changed the subject. 'I can't wait to organise your stag do,' she said to Adam, grinning. 'We're going to have the best time!'

Lauren felt a twinge of jealousy at the thought of them having fun without her. It was all very well Adam going out with the boys for a final night of freedom, but something about Kiera organising it made her feel uncomfortable. She'd be the only woman there, and even though Lauren knew she wasn't interested in men, it still felt wrong.

'I can't wait either,' Adam said. 'What have you got planned?'

Kiera tapped her nose. 'It's a secret. You'll find out on the night.'

Adam laughed. 'Should I be worried?'

'Maybe.'

After dinner, Kiera collapsed on the sofa, glass of wine in her hand. She turned slightly and picked up the framed engagement picture of Lauren and Adam from the shelf.

'This photo's just perfect,' Kiera said with a smile. 'It really captures your love.'

'Thank you.' Lauren looked over at Adam, thinking of the card, the same photo on the front of it. But he was busy in the open-plan kitchen, studying an old cocktail book they'd got for Christmas five years ago, trying to work out how to pull something together with the ingredients they had in the cupboards.

'Try this,' Adam said to the two of them, when he was finished. He handed them each a glass of lime-green liquid. Lauren took small sips of the strong drink as she watched Adam and Kiera down theirs.

'I'd better go and get your room ready,' she said to Kiera. She went into the spare room, and Kiera followed, helping her move the cake stand and wedding magazines from the bed and putting the sheets on.

Lauren caught sight of her mother's jewellery box on the side in the room, the silver bracelet that she was planning to wear to her wedding lying on top of it. She went over to it, running her fingers over the smooth silver.

'That's beautiful,' Kiera said, appearing behind her. Lauren quickly put it in the box and smiled at Kiera. 'I think the room's all ready for you now,' she said, before carrying the jewellery box into her bedroom.

Wanting to be fresh for her shift tomorrow, Lauren decided to go to bed and leave Adam and Kiera to the cocktails.

Adam came into the bedroom before she'd fallen asleep. 'How's Kiera?' she asked.

'Asleep on the sofa.' Adam slurred his words drunkenly. 'I've put a blanket over her.'

'I hope she feels a bit better tomorrow,' said Lauren.

'She'll get over it,' Adam replied. 'It's been on the cards for a while.'

'Oh?'

'We've talked a bit about it after work.' For a moment Lauren felt left out, imagining them together in the pub, having dinner. He probably ate more often with Kiera than with her.

'I need to talk to you,' Lauren said.

'About what?' Adam started to strip off for bed.

'I got a card in the post.'

'Hmmm...?'

'I'll go and get it.' Slipping out of bed, Lauren went into the living room and tried quietly to take it out of the drawer. But the drawer creaked when she opened it and Kiera stirred.

'It's alright, go back to sleep,' Lauren said softly.

She grabbed the card and went into the bedroom. But by the time she got there, Adam was already fast asleep.

CHAPTER FIVE

Adam

2001: Thailand

He saw her lying by the pool, her bright red bikini standing out against the white sunlounger. When he walked over to say hello, she smiled, putting her hand to her forehead to shield her face from the glare of the sun. She had the kind of smile that took you by surprise, one that transformed her face. He couldn't help smiling back.

'Enjoying yourself?' he asked, indicating the cocktail in her hand.

'Very much. It's like paradise. The kind of place you only dream of.'

He nodded, unsure what to say next. It was unlike him to get tongue-tied around girls. Usually the words flowed out easily, especially with her. They'd known each other since they were children, chased each other down the beach on family holidays in Bournemouth. But she'd grown up, and now when he looked at her he no longer saw the child he used to play with.

He'd noticed the chemistry between them on the ferry to the island. How her knee seemed to rest against his; how when she fell asleep her head slipped onto his shoulder. He hadn't moved it away, liking the feel of her long hair against his skin.

She picked up the book beside her and began to read. Feeling dismissed, he dropped his towel down on the sunlounger beside hers and then dived into the swimming pool. His body submerged under the cool water and then he glided smoothly up to the surface. As he swam, he could feel the hot sun on the back of his neck. She was right; this was paradise. While he was here he didn't have to think about the stress back home, how he was struggling with the work at medical school, how unhappy his mother had been when she was divorcing his father. His mother had been right to book this holiday to escape it all, to put it all behind them. Under the hot Thai sun the troubles of home were far away. The holiday was the perfect escape.

CHAPTER SIX

Lauren

When Lauren got up in the morning, Adam and Kiera had already left for work. Usually when she was due to start night shifts, she appreciated how considerate Adam was, making as little noise as possible to allow her to sleep in. But this morning, she'd really wanted to talk to him about the card. Now it would have to wait until she saw him later. There was no point texting him, he never had his phone on when he was working.

After breakfast, she studied the card again. Looking at the picture of the broken doll that resembled her so closely made her feel queasy. She reread the words inside. *He doesn't love you.* What did that mean? That he loved someone else? In the many years they'd been together, their relationship had always been plain sailing. No flirtations, no cheating, not even many arguments. Too good to be true, her friends had sometimes teased. But they'd only been joking. Hadn't they?

She closed the card, looking at the photo on the front, and saw her own face beaming at Adam, his grin in return. She'd loved that picture, but now it felt tainted. The back of the card showed the logo of the printing company. She pulled up their website on her phone and found a contact number. When she was placed on hold, she looked at her watch. She had half an hour before she was due to speak to Tracey about her visit to London next week. When the company finally answered, nothing would convince the woman on the other end of the phone to give her any information about who'd sent the card. She claimed data protection forbade them from telling her anything. Lauren hung up, frustrated at having wasted half an hour.

Lauren was caught off guard by a WhatsApp call ringing from her phone. When she answered, Tracey waved at her from the video call. Her backdrop was the twinkling lights of a hotel pool. Lauren smiled, thinking that she'd be in Thailand soon enough herself, on her honeymoon. She was planning to visit the five-star hotel Tracey owned with her husband while she was there.

'How's everything?' Tracey asked. 'All ready for the wedding?'

Lauren looked down at the card on the coffee table and wondered if she should tell her sister about it; whether she'd have any advice. Tracey had always been the first person Lauren turned to back when she'd been a teenager.

'Just about ready,' Lauren said. 'Just the table plan and the music to finalise.'

'There's always so much to do, isn't there? The wedding planners here are run ragged with the demands of the brides.'

'I'll bet,' Lauren said. Tracey's hotel offered expensive wedding packages, and the brides expected a lot for their money. Lauren's wedding was a more low-key affair. After the wedding ceremony at the church, there'd be a reception at a local pub, where she and Adam had gone on some of their early dates.

'Jasmine can't wait to come over and see you,' Tracey said. Jasmine was Tracey's daughter, who she'd adopted when she was just three years old after her parents had died in the 2004 Thai tsunami.

'I'm so glad she's visiting. I was so disappointed she couldn't make the wedding.' Lauren had invited Tracey's whole family, but Jasmine had a revision course for school and couldn't come. Instead she was visiting England with Tracey a few weeks before the big day.

'She needs the revision course to get her grades up at school. She's been difficult recently. I don't know what's got into her. Teenage moods, I guess.'

'It sounds hard,' Lauren said sympathetically.

'Look, Lauren, I need to tell you something… Ken won't be coming to the wedding either.'

'Oh.' Lauren thought of her table plan. She'd been hoping that Tracey's husband would be able to keep Adam's father's girlfriend company during the wedding, as neither of them would know anyone else. 'Is he OK?'

'He's fine.' Tracey sighed. 'It's just… we're getting divorced, and I don't think it's appropriate for him to be there. He's not living with us any more, he's moved to his own place a few miles away.'

'You're getting divorced?' Lauren asked, eyes widening.

'Yeah. Sorry to tell you just before your wedding, but it is what it is.'

'Are you alright?'

'I'm fine,' Tracey said, and Lauren wondered if her breezy voice was covering up her pain. 'It's been a long time coming.'

Lauren remembered when Tracey had married Ken. She hadn't been invited, and had only received an email from her sister when the wedding had already taken place. It had been a surprise. He was twenty years older than her and a cynical part of Lauren had wondered if the marriage had something to do with the chain of hotels he owned. But then they had adopted Jasmine together, and Lauren had realised that there must be more to their relationship.

'Jasmine's struggling with the divorce,' Tracey carried on. 'I think that's why she's acting out. She hasn't been herself for a while.'

'What do you mean?'

'She tells me she hates me. She goes off with boys from the island, takes drugs, gets into fights. She seems to be self-destructing. It hasn't helped that Ken has just washed his hands of her. He's said to me that he's not interested in her when she behaves like this. I think he's harsher on her because he's not her biological father. He seems kinder to the twins.'

'But you adopted her together.'

'I know,' Tracey sighed. 'And she doesn't even know that she's adopted. She thinks he's her real father, so his behaviour seems even more odd to her. But I can't tell her otherwise. Not now. We always agreed we wouldn't tell her.'

'It sounds so difficult,' Lauren said. She didn't know the first thing about teenagers, but she wasn't sure whether she thought it was fair not to tell Jasmine about her real parents. They'd both been European English teachers on the island. If she was Jasmine, she'd want to know all about them and her extended biological family. But Lauren bit her tongue. It wasn't her place to advise her sister. They'd only really connected again in the last couple of years, and Lauren wasn't willing to jeopardise their relationship.

'I don't know what to do,' Tracey continued. 'Maybe you can talk to her. I think you'll be able to relate to her better. I can't get through to her as her mother.'

'I can try,' Lauren said. At moments like these Lauren remembered the gulf between them, that at thirty-five Lauren was still trying to start her own family, whereas Tracey's daughter was nearly grown up already.

'Thanks. And I'm sorry this trip is so last-minute. Jasmine just booked her ticket without asking me. And I couldn't let her go on her own.'

'Don't worry. I have the weekend free, so we can go on the London Eye and see some of the other sights. Then you can both come to my hen night.'

'I can't wait,' Tracey said. 'But Jasmine will have to miss the clubbing bit. She's far too young, even though she's desperate to go. But she's excited to see you, and meet Adam. She's just sad to be missing out on the wedding.'

'I'm sad she won't be there too. But she'll get to see me at least. Adam will be at that medical conference I told you about.'

'Oh yeah. I forgot. Well, it's you who's most important. She can meet Adam another time. Besides, I think you'll be able to tell her more about all the wedding plans than he will. I don't remember Ken taking much of an interest in ours. I did everything.'

Lauren laughed, and then thought of her sister's divorce.

'Tracey,' she said tentatively, 'are you sure you're OK? About the divorce?'

Tracey smiled. 'I'm fine,' she said, but Lauren heard the tremor in her voice. 'Listen, I have to go.' And then the screen went blank.

Lauren stared at the phone. She promised herself she'd get to the bottom of what was happening with Tracey when she and Jasmine visited next week. In the meantime she had to figure out what to do about the card. It was still hours until she started her night shift.

She picked up the phone and rang Zoe, her best friend, hoping she could pay her a visit. Thirty minutes later, she was outside Zoe's house. Zoe opened her door, holding her son Harry in her arms, and reached out to hug Lauren.

'Sorry for the mess,' she said, as she indicated the scattered toys in the hallway.

'It's fine,' Lauren replied, carefully stepping over a toy truck. Before she'd had her son, Zoe had been a music producer, working for a major record label. As she'd got towards the end of her maternity leave, she'd realised it would be impossible for her and her husband to both go back to work and for her to manage her role's long hours, so she'd set up a business as a photographer. Most of her clients were mums with new babies, but she was thinking of moving into weddings and she'd taken Lauren and Adam's engagement photos.

'Do you want a cup of tea?' Zoe asked once they'd walked through to the kitchen.

'Yes, please. I'll put the kettle on,' Lauren said, going over to the other side of the kitchen. 'So, how's the business going?'

'I'm building it up slowly. I've had quite a few enquiries this week. People love the photos of you and Adam on my website. I've been getting more requests for engagement photos since I put them up.'

'You're so talented. I've had so many compliments on those pictures.'

'You both made my job easy. When people are in love, an energy radiates off them. It's just a matter of capturing those moments.'

'You certainly did that. Honestly, Zoe, I'll treasure them forever.' Yet already she couldn't think of the photos without thinking of the card, and the doll, its wedding dress and body slashed to pieces.

'Have you shown those pictures to lots of people?' she couldn't help asking.

'I'm trying to promote the business. I've put them on Facebook, Twitter, Instagram, plus my website.'

'Did you put our names on them?' Lauren asked, wondering if that's where someone picked the image up. Not a wedding guest, but someone else entirely.

'No. Why?' Zoe looked concerned. 'Is something the matter?'

'Something weird has happened, that's all.' Lauren hesitated for a moment, embarrassed. 'Someone sent me a card in the post with the engagement photo on and I was wondering where they got it from.' Lauren dug the card out of her handbag and showed it to Zoe.

'Gosh,' Zoe said, her hand flying to her mouth as she opened the card and saw the doll. 'Is that supposed to be you?'

Lauren nodded. 'Someone's gone to a great deal of effort to buy a doll that bears such a resemblance. Just to cut it up into pieces.'

Zoe peered at the card closer. 'I don't think they've bought that from the shops. It looks a bit like one of the baby props you get on set. You have to get them specially made to get that kind of detail.'

'So you think someone got this made specially?'

'I don't know. It just looks so realistic.' Zoe frowned. 'Have you thought about going to the police?'

'And saying what? It's hardly a huge crime, is it?'

'It's threatening.' The kettle boiled but they ignored it.

'Maybe it's just a joke,' Lauren said half-heartedly. She'd been hoping Zoe would reassure her, tell her not to worry about the card.

'What does Adam think? I mean, the card's about him, really, isn't it?'

Lauren tensed, recognising the truth of what Zoe said. The card said Adam didn't love her. Which made it sound like a jealous ex. Or maybe not an ex at all. Someone he was cheating with. Lauren shook the thoughts out of her head. Adam had always been faithful. There'd never been any hint of him playing away. And any previous relationships were far into the past. Adam had been with a string of women when he first started university, but they'd meant nothing to him. That phase of his life was long gone, ending when he'd got together with her, back when she had been a teenager.

'I haven't told him yet. I was going to tell him last night. But then he brought Kiera home with him. She's split up with Carmelle and she's going to stay with us for a while.' Lauren saw Zoe's brow furrow. 'Adam suggested it,' she clarified.

'They've always been close, haven't they?'

'Yes,' she replied, trying not to look worried. If Kiera was interested in men, her friendship with Adam would worry her. But as it was, she knew they were just friends.

'You don't have any idea who sent the card?' Zoe's eyes crinkled in concern.

'No,' Lauren said quietly. She thought of the photos of her on Zoe's social media. Suddenly she remembered something else. 'But I do have that picture as my profile picture on Facebook,' she said, wondering if that was where the sender had picked up the image.

Zoe sighed. 'I reckon someone would find it if they googled your name. Profile pictures aren't usually private.'

Lauren swallowed and typed her own name into Google on her phone and pressed search. Zoe was right. The engagement photo was one of the first results.

Lauren put her head in her hands and stared at Zoe. 'The photo's here,' she said. 'Anyone could have found it.'

CHAPTER SEVEN

Lauren

'Hi,' Adam called out when he got home from work the next day. Lauren had just got out of bed. She hadn't slept well after her night shift, preoccupied with the card. She'd gone through the shift on automatic, just waiting for it to be over.

'You're home early,' she said, smiling as she walked into the hallway and gave him a peck on the cheek.

'Yeah, I wanted to make sure I spent some time with you before your next shift. I left my paperwork at the surgery to do tomorrow. I'm sorry our romantic dinner last night didn't go to plan.'

'It's OK,' Lauren said. 'Where's Kiera tonight?'

'She's over at Carmelle's, collecting her things.' He dropped his rucksack onto the stool by the breakfast bar and pulled out some flowers from behind his back.

'What are they for?' she asked, smiling at the beautiful bunch of red carnations.

'I meant to buy you some on the way back from work yesterday, to say thank you for making dinner, but I got so caught up helping Kiera. So I hope you're happy to receive them today?' He smiled playfully.

'Of course I am,' she said with a grin. 'I'll put them in water.' She grabbed a vase and started to cut off the stems. Something Sam had said to her once flashed through her head. That when

Adam's father had bought her flowers, it had always meant he had something to hide. In his case, yet another affair.

'And thank you for letting Kiera stay,' said Adam. 'I know it's not easy.'

Maybe that's what he was feeling guilty about, she told herself.

Lauren thought of the box room, how in her mind it had been the baby's room for so long. 'It's OK,' Lauren replied. 'She's your friend, it's important we help her out.'

Adam's phone started ringing and he frowned down at it, and then swiped his finger across the screen to reject the call.

'Who was that?' Lauren asked.

'Just a junk call. I recognise the number. How was your shift?'

'Fine, thanks.' She knew she didn't have long until she'd have to leave again for her night shift and she needed to talk to Adam about the card. It had been niggling away at her ever since it arrived.

'Good. Shall I put some dinner on? I was thinking stir fry. It's nice and quick.'

'Great – but Adam, I need to talk to you about something.'

'Kiera?' he asked, as he took the onions out of the cupboard and began to cut them.

'No, not that. I need to show you something.'

'You're not…?' He glanced at her stomach, a glimmer of hope in his eyes.

'No, I'm not pregnant.' She hated saying the words.

'What is it then?' His brow furrowed.

'It's—' she swallowed, gathering her thoughts. Suddenly, she felt a bit embarrassed. The whole thing was childish and yet someone clearly disliked her enough to send it to her. 'I got a card in the post,' she said tentatively.

'A card? Isn't that normally a good thing?'

'Not this one. I'll show it to you.' Adam would know what to do. He might even have an idea who it was from.

She went to the living room, pulled it out of the drawer, where she'd returned it after seeing Zoe, and then handed it to him. He wiped his hands on a tea towel before taking it. 'This is nice,' he said. 'That's my favourite photo of us. You look beautiful.'

'Look what's inside.'

He opened it and saw the picture, his eyes widening in shock. 'Who sent this...? And why?' He looked from her to the card and then back again.

'It says "He doesn't love you". Does that mean anything to you?'

Adam's eyes narrowed as he looked at the card once more. He blinked rapidly. 'Why would anyone put that? Of course I love you.' He reached out and touched her arm.

Lauren smiled tightly, surprised by how much the card seemed to have got to him. 'I know you do,' she said.

Adam started pacing the room. 'Who would send this to you?' he asked, angrily.

'I really don't know,' Lauren replied. 'I've been racking my brain trying to think why someone would do this, but I can't come up with a good reason.'

'What's the postmark?'

'Leicester. But that's just the address of the printing company. It's completely anonymous. I've already rung the company. They couldn't tell me anything.'

Adam stopped pacing and stood next to her, his expression changing from anger to concern. 'It must have really freaked you out. Are you alright?'

'It did a bit. It scared me. Zoe – she thought maybe I should tell the police. It's threatening, isn't it?'

'I don't know...' Adam shifted from foot to foot uncomfortably. 'I mean, going to the police seems a bit much, doesn't it? It's just a card, it's not like anyone's done anything to you.'

'That's what I thought. But what does it mean?'

Adam went over to a pot plant on the windowsill and pulled off a dead leaf. 'Could it just be a joke? A cruel one, but still a joke?'

'A joke? They've gone to a lot of effort to match my exact hairstyle.'

'Yeah. They've taken it too far. Could it have been one of your friends? Part of the hen do, maybe?'

'I doubt it.' Lauren trusted her friends. And it just wasn't the kind of joke any of them would play. It was more like something Adam's friends might do. 'One of your stags, maybe?' she asked.

Adam smiled then, a smile of relief. 'Of course! It must be. You know some of the guys weren't too keen on Kiera being in charge of the stag do. Didn't think it was right. Jimmy mentioned they'd find another way to embarrass me if they couldn't on the stag do. Maybe this is his way of doing that.' Adam shook his head in disapproval. 'Not a great idea of a joke.'

'Jimmy?'

Jimmy was one of Adam's closest friends from school. They had both been big drinkers and both always had a new girl on their arms. But whereas Adam had grown out of that lifestyle, Jimmy hadn't changed. He was still a serial dater, still drinking like a teenager.

'Yeah, I reckon it's him. I'll ring him once you've gone to work, give him a piece of my mind. If he's done this, he'll never hear the end of it. He's just trying to make me panic before the big day. Seeing what I'm made of.'

Lauren smiled uncertainly. 'Are you sure? The card was to me, not you.'

Adam ran his hand through his hair, his bubble burst. 'Well, no. But I'll ask. I can't think of any other explanation.'

Lauren swallowed, still worried. She didn't think even Jimmy was capable of this.

Wrapping Lauren in a hug, Adam held her close. 'It will be alright,' he said, stroking her hair back from her face. 'We are going to have the perfect wedding, the perfect marriage, the perfect life.'

Lauren smiled. 'You're right,' she said. 'We've been through too much together to let anything stop us now.'

But even as she said the words, Lauren felt unconvinced.

'I'd better get on with this stir fry,' Adam said. 'Why don't you sit down and relax for a bit while it's cooking?'

Lauren nodded, and her fiancé glanced over at her.

'You look a bit pale. It must have been a shock for you. But honestly, I'm sure it must be a joke. I'll ring Jimmy tonight, ask if it was him. And if it was, I'll kill him when I see him.'

CHAPTER EIGHT

Adam

Adam listened to the door shut behind Lauren as she left for work. Once he heard her footsteps heading down the corridor and to the stairs, he let out a sigh.

He was supposed to be going to the gym tonight, but he'd have to miss out. He needed the time while Lauren was at the hospital to think. His heart was racing, adrenaline surging through him as if he was under attack. The words in the card came back to him: *He doesn't love you.*

Adam went over to the window and watched Lauren come out of the building and walk to her car. Her hair bounced in the light wind and she looked fragile as her slim figure crossed the car park. Pausing before she unlocked her car, she double-checked her handbag and pulled out her hospital pass, then climbed into the car and drove away.

Finally, she was gone. Picking up the card again, he looked at the picture on the front. He and Lauren looked so happy, the perfect couple. It had been just before they'd lost the baby.

She'd been different since. Quieter and more contemplative. Sadder. He'd wanted to make everything better for her, put everything right. They'd got engaged when they'd found out she was pregnant, and it had seemed like the right thing to do. He'd imagined them being a little family, the three of them. When she'd lost the baby just after, they'd booked the church and she'd thrown herself into organising the wedding. She hadn't stopped to grieve properly; she'd just changed her focus, planning their marriage and the rest of their lives together.

But if the person who wrote this card had anything to do with it, then he wouldn't be getting married at all. Not if she spoke to Lauren. He knew exactly who had sent it. She would have known he wouldn't be able to do much about it. He wouldn't be able to go to the police without being exposed. He was powerless.

As soon as he'd realised who it was, he'd tried to distract Lauren by suggesting it was a joke. But what if she followed up? What if she got in touch with Jimmy? It would be easy for Lauren to work out it wasn't him.

He released another sigh and grabbed his phone. He needed to speak to Jimmy to tell him what to say if Lauren called.

CHAPTER NINE

Lauren

As Lauren walked to the car after she'd finished her shift, her energy crashed. She'd tried not to top herself up with too much sugar overnight, relying on adrenaline to keep her going, but now the exhaustion was hitting her hard. It had been so busy at the hospital, she'd hardly had time to go to the toilet. She always felt jet-lagged after a night shift; as if her body was too heavy to carry around and her mind was treading water, struggling to stay awake.

But despite her fatigue, there was nothing like the buzz she got from being an A&E doctor.

She hadn't always wanted to be a doctor. Everything had changed on that family holiday in Thailand, when she'd seen her parents lose their lives and hadn't been able to save them. She'd promised herself that she'd never be in that position again, and when she'd got back to the UK, she'd put all her energies into working hard to get into medical school. She thought of what Tracey had said about Jasmine, how she wasn't concentrating on her studies. Maybe she just needed a sense of direction, too.

Lauren checked her phone. She'd expected Adam to text her to confirm that the card she'd received was from Jimmy, but he hadn't sent anything. She might as well ask Jimmy herself. She didn't have his phone number, but she was connected to him on Facebook, so she wrote him a quick message on there.

Hi Jimmy. Did you send me that card? If you did, you'll know what I'm talking about, and it was NOT funny. If you don't know what I'm talking about, just let me know!

Back home, she walked through her living room and sighed. Every corner of the flat seemed to be crowded with Kiera's possessions. Bags of clothes lined the living room, paintings and pictures were stacked up against the wall and bags of pots and pans littered the kitchen surfaces. She hadn't realised Kiera would have so much stuff. Peering into the spare bedroom, she saw there was no extra space to put her overflowing things. It was already packed floor to ceiling with boxes. She'd have to talk to Adam about it later. But for now, she just needed to sleep. In the bedroom, she let herself drift off, Misty lying beside her, stretched out over Adam's pillow.

She woke to the sound of rattling in the kitchen. Picking up her phone, she saw it was 3 p.m. No one should be home. Not Adam, not Kiera. Lauren rose slowly from the bed, bleary-eyed from sleep.

'Hello?'

'It's only me,' a voice called out from the kitchen. 'You didn't answer, so I let myself in.'

It took a moment for Lauren to place the voice. It was Sam, Adam's mother, soon to be her mother-in-law. And then she remembered. She had a wedding dress fitting this afternoon. Sam was coming with her. She'd insisted on helping her with all the wedding preparations, and Lauren knew she felt it was her duty to stand in for Lauren's mother, who'd been her closest friend. After Lauren had lost her parents, Sam had looked after her.

Sam made a coffee for Lauren while she showered, and then the two of them got into Lauren's car and drove to the wedding dress shop.

'Hello, Lauren!' the shop assistant exclaimed when she saw her. 'And your mother, how lovely.'

'This is my fiancé's mother, my future mother-in-law,' Lauren said quickly, shaking her head and feeling the familiar twinge of longing that her own mum couldn't be with her. Sam and Zoe had been so supportive, coming with her to choose the dress, but when she'd seen other brides with a gaggle of family around them, she couldn't help but feel envious. If she'd had her way, Tracey and her mother would both be with her now. Lauren had had to choose Tracey's bridesmaid's dress without her, sending her a picture to check it was OK. She reminded herself that she'd see her sister soon, and she'd be coming on the hen night. Considering she lived in Thailand, Lauren knew she should count herself lucky.

'Can I offer you a drink? Champagne, perhaps?' the shop assistant asked.

'No, thank you. I'm not drinking today.' Lauren wanted to be fresh for her shift later on.

The assistant raised her eyebrows. 'It's not long until your wedding,' she said. 'Do you expect your shape to change much more in the next few weeks?' She glanced quickly at Lauren's stomach.

'I'm not pregnant.' Lauren felt the surge of disappointment as she said the words. 'I'm just working a night shift tonight. I'm a doctor.'

'Oh, I see. I'm sorry. I had to double-check. We see more brides than you'd think appearing with a baby bump at the final fitting sessions.'

Sam laughed lightly, and then, seeing the expression on Lauren's face, she quickly changed the subject. 'There are so many gorgeous dresses here,' she said conversationally, running her fingers over the lacy material of the nearest dress. 'I love this one. I can just imagine it at a beach wedding on a summer's day.'

Lauren looked at the dress Sam was touching. It was a short, off-the-shoulder design, like the one the doll had been wearing in the card she'd been sent. She winced at the memory. Jimmy hadn't replied to her message yet.

'Here's your dress,' the assistant said, pulling it out from a cupboard.

Lauren had chosen a sleeveless silk dress that fanned out at the bottom, with a tight bodice laced up at the back. The assistant carefully laid it on the floor, spreading it out so that Lauren could step into it.

Sam watched intently as the assistant lifted the skirts up carefully to Lauren's waist and then began to lace up the bodice. Lauren felt a jolt of sadness that her mother wouldn't be around to help her get ready on her wedding day.

'We pull it very tight,' the assistant said, as Lauren tried to breathe in. 'The dress is designed to hold everything in.'

Lauren laughed. 'Will I even be able to fit the meal in at the reception?' They were having a five-course meal at a local gastropub.

The woman smiled. 'I wouldn't worry about that.'

When she was tied in, the assistant laid out her train so Lauren could look at herself in the mirror with the full dress on. She fetched her veil and put it over Lauren's face, then lifted it up over her hair.

'Stunning,' Sam whispered.

Lauren imagined walking down the aisle, her sequined train trailing behind her. 'Can you take a photo?' she asked Sam. 'I want to send it to Tracey.' Even though her sister hadn't been able to come to the bridal fittings Lauren had still tried to keep her involved, and had sent her pictures of all the different wedding dress options before she'd made her final choice.

'Sure,' Sam said. 'I'm looking forward to seeing Tracey. It's been years.'

Lauren nodded. Tracey and Sam's relationship had always been difficult. Tracey had shunned Sam's offer of a place to stay after their parents had died, and then Sam had taken Lauren's side when she and her sister had argued over the sale of their parents' flat.

'I'm so glad you two girls made up,' Sam continued. 'Sisters need to stick together.'

Lauren nodded. 'You're right.'

'Your mother would have been so happy to see you get married,' Sam said softly. Lauren felt herself tearing up, and Sam reached out and gripped her arm. 'I think of Debs all the time. Particularly while we've been planning this wedding. I imagine us laughing together at the reception, spinning each other round on the dance floor, just like we did at university, before we had you kids. We would have had such a brilliant time. She would have been so proud of you.'

Lauren bit her lip at the words. *Proud of her.* She hadn't done much to make her mother proud before she had died. Everything that was worth mentioning came afterwards: qualifying as a doctor, getting together with Adam, becoming an A&E consultant at the hospital. Lauren felt a familiar flicker of shame when she thought of how her parents had died. The accident should never have happened in the first place. In her mother's last moments, Lauren doubted very much that she'd been proud of her.

'Hey,' Sam said, reaching over and brushing a tear from Lauren's cheek. 'I didn't mean to upset you.'

'It's OK.' Lauren swallowed her tears and managed a small smile.

'Perfectly natural for brides to be emotional,' the shop assistant said calmly, putting a comforting hand on her shoulder.

Lauren nodded, sobs rising up inside her, making her unable to speak. All she could think about was her parents. How, if it wasn't for her mistake, they'd be here with her now.

CHAPTER TEN

Adam

Adam tapped his pen against his desk and looked at his computer screen. Two more patients to see today. If he could just get through them quickly, then he might get home before Lauren left for work. He glanced at the engagement photo on his desk. He used to love that picture, but now it made him feel nervous. Just like Adam had expected, Jimmy had confirmed that he hadn't sent the card to Lauren. He'd had no idea what Adam was talking about. But he'd still agreed to cover for him while he figured out what to do. At least that way Lauren wouldn't worry.

When Adam looked at his computer to see the name of his next patient, his heart sank. Amanda Jacobs. He stared at the name, working out if there was any way out of the appointment. But there wasn't. He was the one who was the doctor, the professional. He didn't have a choice. Reluctantly he pressed the button on his monitor, buzzing her through.

Amanda sashayed into the consulting room, dark glasses covering her face, her jet-black curls bouncing on her shoulders. She was in a green jumpsuit, belted at the waist, and heeled boots. She had the perfect figure for the outfit. Adam tried to stop himself staring, stop himself noticing how the jumpsuit clung in all the right places, how the colour matched her eyes.

'Hi,' he said. 'Come on in.' It was how he started all his consultations, no matter who the patient was. But even he could hear the tension in his voice.

'Long time no see,' she said with a wink. He ignored it. It had only been a week since her last appointment. No one could stop patients booking multiple appointments, especially if they were arranged long in advance. Amanda dreamt up a different ailment each time.

At first he had believed she was ill. There were conditions that had a range of symptoms, and patients who really suffered from them. Amanda had seemed sincere when she came in each week, first with headaches, then stomach aches, then chest pains. He'd made it his personal mission to find out what was wrong with her. He hadn't failed to notice that she was attractive. Very attractive. She had long dark hair, like Lauren's, cascading down her back, and she was open and friendly. He'd liked her back then, liked the way she'd smiled at him and asked him how he was, when most patients were so caught up in themselves that they forgot. He'd told her he wouldn't rest until he found out what was wrong with her. He regretted that now.

At her very first visit when she'd complained of headaches, she'd also had her arm in a sling. She'd claimed it was the result of an angry ex-boyfriend, weeks before. Adam had encouraged her to go to the police, but she'd said she couldn't as 'she'd given as good as she got'. He should have seen the red flags then, but at the time he'd simply thought she was joking.

'How are you?' she said now, picking up the picture of him and Lauren on his desk and studying it. He'd put it up recently, a warning to Amanda to back off.

'I'm fine, thanks.' Adam tried to sound businesslike. 'What can I do for you today?'

She leaned forward, giving him a view of her cleavage. He swallowed.

'I think I've found a lump,' she said slowly. 'On my breast.'

He felt queasy. He didn't want to examine her, to get pulled into her trap. With other patients he was able to completely switch off when he examined them. Whoever they were, they just became a body with a problem, whether it was a swollen ankle, a fever or a breast lump. But with Amanda it was different.

'OK,' he said. 'I'll need to take a look.' There was no other option. She smiled, her eyes sparkling, and he felt another flicker of irritation. How was it he always ended up dancing to her tune? 'But I need to sort out a chaperone first,' he continued. 'I'll pop out for a minute to see who's available.' At least he wouldn't be alone with her.

'You don't have to have a chaperone.' She grinned. 'I'll be safe with you.'

'It's just procedure, I'm afraid.'

He went out of the room and shut the door behind him, trying to calm his breathing. Amanda could ruin everything for him, if she wanted to. The waiting room was busy, full of patients looking expectantly at the screen, waiting to be called. He popped his head round the back of reception and told them he'd need a chaperone when one was available.

'Jane should be free in a bit,' one of the receptionists said. 'She's just with a patient, but I'll let her know between appointments.'

He sighed. Jane, the nurse, was always running late and was the biggest source of gossip in the surgery.

He paused for a moment, not wanting to go back to his room.

'Do you want anything else?' the receptionist asked.

'No, thanks. Just tell Jane to come through when she's got a moment.'

'Sure.'

He realised he didn't stand a chance of getting home to see Lauren before she left for her shift. This appointment would make him late. He went back to his consulting room reluctantly and Amanda tried to talk to him, asking him whether he'd seen any more episodes of the Netflix drama they'd talked about last time.

'No,' he said, trying to shut down the conversation.

'Why not?' she asked.

'No time.' He turned back to his computer, looking away from her, pretending to be studying her notes on the screen.

He was relieved when shortly afterwards the door swung open and Jane came through.

'Right,' he said. 'This is Jane, the nurse here. She'll act as chaperone as I do the examination. If you just go behind this curtain and take off your top and your bra, sit on the bed and then call me to let me know you're ready.'

He felt blood rush to his face. As he put on his surgical gloves, he could hear her unzipping her jumpsuit. The curtain moved slightly and he imagined her folding it and laying it on the chair, almost naked.

'Ready,' she called, her voice throaty. He glanced at Jane, but couldn't make eye contact. Then he drew back the curtain.

She was sitting in just her lacy black knickers, swinging her legs back and forth.

'So show me where you think the lump is.' He stumbled over the words he'd said hundreds of times before. He didn't dare look at Jane, standing at the other end of the bed.

'I don't *think* it's a lump. I *know* it's a lump,' Amanda said, self-righteously. 'It's right here.'

He swallowed. 'OK,' he said, putting his hand to her skin. Through the gloves he could feel its warmth. Her nipples were erect, but he tried not to look. His face was too close to them, but he needed to look at her skin, check it hadn't become orange-peel puckered, a sign of breast cancer.

'It's cold in here.' He could tell from her voice that she was smiling, that she sensed his discomfort. He just hoped Jane didn't sense it too.

'I'll be finished in a minute,' he replied. He was pretty sure the lump was just normal breast tissue but he needed to conduct a full examination just in case. He felt around the breast, focusing on identifying any abnormalities. There weren't any.

'I can't feel anything to be concerned about,' he said. When he looked up at her, he saw her eyes were twinkling.

'Thanks, Adam.'

He jumped at the use of his name, worried what Jane might think. But then he remembered that his first name was on the door of the room. Dr Adam Glenister. She could have got it from there.

'It's OK. You can get changed now. And once you're finished, come and sit down over here.'

He pulled the curtain back around Amanda, nodding at Jane to tell her she could go.

Once Amanda was dressed again, she sat in the seat in front of his desk.

'I couldn't see or feel anything to worry about,' he said abruptly, looking forward to the moment when she'd be out of his office.

'That's good,' Amanda replied. 'Because neither could I.'

'Why are you here then?'

She leaned towards him, her eyes meeting his. 'You know why. We're not over, Adam.'

CHAPTER ELEVEN

Lauren

The sun shone brightly through the stained-glass windows, patterning the floor of the cavernous building. Despite the warmth outside, the church felt cold and Lauren folded her arms around herself. She felt at home here. The church was a community where she always felt welcome.

That morning, Jimmy had replied to her message, telling her not to worry and that the card was just a joke. Relief and anger had rushed through her. It was such a horrible thing to send, trying to scare her just before the wedding.

She had been wondering if she should put the wedding preparations on hold, but now she could continue. She didn't need to worry about the card any more. She wandered down the pews, counting them. There were twenty on each side. She'd planned to hang white and blue bouquets at the end of every other pew, and she needed to let the florist know how many she needed.

The church was a part of her history. After Adam had proposed, she'd spent hours studying the faded pictures of her parents' wedding, seeing her mother gazing up at her father adoringly in her light and floaty seventies dress, wearing the silver bracelet Lauren was now planning to wear to her own wedding. In the photos she had seen the sparkle in her mother's eyes, how joyful she looked. She hoped she and Adam would have the same happy marriage her parents had. She could hardly ever remember them arguing.

She imagined standing in her wedding dress, Adam at the end of aisle, waiting for her. The room would be full of friends and family, the bouquets of white roses and blue hydrangeas lining the aisles. And she'd have her sister at her side, as her bridesmaid, to support her.

She felt a shiver of worry. Despite Jimmy admitting to sending the card, it was still playing on her mind. *He doesn't love you.*

Lauren tried to think what advice her mum would have given her. She closed her eyes and imagined her walking down the aisle towards her, the pew creaking as she took a seat beside her. She could imagine sinking into her arms, her mum holding her as if she was a child.

'Everything will be OK.' That's what her mother would have told her.

Except that everything wasn't OK. Her parents weren't here to share her wedding day. She could never forgive herself for how they had drowned. If only things had been different; if only she had been different, less immature. If only she could have saved them both.

Lauren snapped open her eyes and put her hands on the solid wood of the prayer book holder. She thought of her last memories of her mother and father. How generous they'd been on that holiday. After all the stress of her teenage years, the constant fights with her parents, it had felt like they were becoming closer again. They'd all been close, the two families; hers and Adam's. Lying on the beach together in the sun, talking and laughing and drinking cocktails from buckets in the evening. All she'd known on that holiday was that she felt free. Time had taken on that strange quality it does on a holiday, where at first it seems to pass so slowly that the days seem like endless pleasure, then speeding up until the holiday is almost over.

Everything had been perfect in Thailand, at the beginning. After years of fancying Adam from afar, he was finally noticing her. That had been the start of things. Thailand was where she'd fallen in love with him.

But then everything had changed. Her world had fallen apart the day the two families had gone white-water rafting. They'd all been looking forward to it. It was supposed to be the adventure of a lifetime. But instead she'd watched her parents drown, completely helpless.

'Please forgive me,' Lauren whispered into the silent church. She'd do anything to take back what had happened. If she could, she would have been a better daughter, a better sister. She wouldn't have let her anger take her over. But it was all in the past now. And she never got a second chance.

CHAPTER TWELVE

Adam

2001: Thailand

They sat on the back of the boat together, harnessed to the parachute. Beside him, she kept checking the straps to make sure they were still fastened.

'Nervous?' he asked, with a smile.

She grinned and shook her head. 'Of course not.' But she kept looking anxiously at the colourful parachute above them.

'Don't worry, it's perfectly safe, I've done it before,' he said, trying to reassure her. This had been her idea. She'd seen the parasailers flying over the beach yesterday and, over breakfast this morning, announced that she would try it today. He'd jumped at the chance to go with her, a way to get closer to her.

He reached for her hand, entwining his fingers with hers. Just then the man at the front of the boat shouted back to them. 'OK?' He put his thumb up and they put their thumbs up in return. Her hand left his and they gripped the straps.

Then they were off. He felt the breeze in his hair, as they gently floated up over the ocean. He turned to look at her. She was smiling now, staring out at the view.

It was beautiful. He could see for miles, the hotels dotting the coast, the hills beyond. Below them, the people on the beach looked tiny.

This had been his first chance to be completely alone with her, and every part of him was alert to her presence. Strapped in together, above the world.

'Enjoying yourself?' he asked.

'It's magical,' she replied, her hair lifting in the wind.

He was aware that he was close enough to touch her, almost close enough to kiss her, and his body ached with it.

When they descended back onto the boat, he felt a sense of loss. The moment was over; soon they would be back with their families, and he'd missed the opportunity to get closer to her.

'That was fun,' she said.

'We should do it again sometime.'

She laughed and he wondered how he could make things happen. He needed to be alone with her again.

He was relaxed here, for the first time in ages. Things were simpler out here, more straightforward. He thought worriedly of the situation at university, his low grades, the drunken mistake with Kiera.

He looked down at the deep blue sea, felt the cool white plastic of the boat beneath his feet. He wanted to stay in Thailand forever, but he knew he couldn't. He needed to enjoy every moment while he was here.

As they walked back towards the hotel, he took a leaflet from a vendor outside a shop, scanning through all the activities available: scuba-diving, paragliding, white-water rafting. He promised himself he'd do them all with her, make this a holiday they'd remember forever.

CHAPTER THIRTEEN

Lauren

Three weeks until the wedding

Lauren could hear echoes of laughter and chatter as she stood behind the heavy wooden church door. An usher appeared and smiled encouragingly at her, then pulled the creaking door open. The crowd hushed. She stood in her wedding dress, admiring her work on the beautifully decorated church. It had all turned out exactly how she had planned. The red carnations and white lilies that lined the pews perfectly complemented the white and yellow bouquet of lilies in her hands.

She studied the bouquet for a moment, struck by how strange it was that she'd chosen the same flowers as the ones at her parents' funeral. She'd been so sure she was going to go for white roses and blue hydrangeas, but in the end she must have been persuaded to change her mind.

At the end of the aisle, her groom stood in a perfectly pressed suit, facing away from her, an outline.

She felt an arm tuck round hers and turned to see her father. Her heart leapt. She could hardly believe it. Tracey stood behind him, smiling in her royal-blue bridesmaid's dress.

'Ready?' her father asked.

A feeling of pure joy spread through her. She nodded and looked down at the rows of guests before her. Her mother was at the front of the church, her beaming face turned towards Lauren, her hands clasped together in celebration.

Everyone was here. Her family. Her friends. Her baby kicked inside her. She adjusted her veil and prepared herself to step into her future.

But then a sharp pain stabbed through her like a knife. She doubled over and collapsed to the floor, her screams echoing around the church. Looking down, she saw she was bleeding, the red blood seeping through her white wedding dress. The baby. She was losing it, here in the church.

She felt someone brush by her, a shadow in white. The woman swept by her into the church, ahead of her. Wearing a wedding dress. Lauren crawled behind her, clutching her belly, clawing at the person's dress. It came away in her hands, torn and ripped. Lauren saw the blood beneath her fingers, then the woman turned round.

Glass eyes gaped at Lauren. A plastic face, torn to shreds. Dark hair cascading down her shoulders.

Lauren screamed and her eyes flew open, her heart hammering in her chest. It wasn't real. None of it was real.

'Lauren, Lauren. It's OK.'

She felt someone stroking her arm and she pulled it away, turning towards the voice. Adam. It was just Adam.

Disorientated, she blinked, looking around the room.

She was in the bed, the fabric of the duvet scrunched up in her clawed hands. She looked up at the familiar cherry-red curtains, saw her book on her bedside table, and loosened her grip on the covers. It was OK. She was at home.

'The nightmares are back?' he asked. 'Was it about the rafting trip again?'

He'd been there beside her for every nightmare she'd had since she'd lost her parents. He'd become used to them. But they'd been less frequent since she'd reconnected with Tracey, as if she was finally forgiving herself, moving on and escaping the past.

'No. It was about the wedding,' she said, breathlessly. 'The doll in the card. She'd come to life.' It sounded so ridiculous when she said it. She thought of the dream, her happiness at seeing her parents. She had been so full of joy. She should have known it was all a mirage.

'Oh,' Adam said. 'It sounds terrifying.'

Adam held her in his arms, her head against his chest, as she shook. Through his shirt, she could hear his heart beating and smell his aftershave. She felt herself calming. There was something about his mere physical presence that comforted her, made her feel safe.

Lauren wondered if she should tell Adam about the baby, too. The bump in her wedding dress. The blood. She knew what date it was today. She'd been dreading it. It was the day their baby had been due.

In the kitchen, they drank their morning coffees and Lauren thought of the weekend stretching out ahead of her. It was early, only 8 a.m., and Kiera was still in bed. The day ahead seemed endless. She'd blocked it out in the calendar when she'd found out she was pregnant, and she'd continued to turn down social engagements, even after she'd lost the baby. She hadn't known how she was going to feel, whether she'd want company or not. But now the weekend was here, she realised she would have been glad of a distraction.

Adam put his arm around her. 'It would have been today,' he said softly.

Lauren nodded. 'Or two weeks before or two weeks after, I suppose. Babies are rarely born on their due dates.'

'No, I guess not. Maybe we need to get out, do something. What about going out for brunch?'

Lauren smiled. They'd used to do that all the time when they'd first got together. They'd linger in bed at the weekends and then walk down to the high street where lots of little independent coffee shops had sprung up. She'd have eggs Benedict and Adam would have a full English. They hadn't done it in years, viewing it as an unnecessary expense once they were saving to buy a property and then for the wedding.

'It's odd to think of us, isn't it? In that different life. With a baby,' replied Lauren.

Adam nodded. 'Maybe that's why we should make the most of having brunch at a coffee shop now. I imagine that kind of thing will become more complicated with kids.'

'Not to mention more expensive.'

Adam smiled.

'I think kids might be more difficult than I imagined,' Lauren said, thinking of her niece. She'd be arriving in England soon, staying with Tracey at Lauren's uncle's house in Oxford before coming down to London. 'Tracey's having a really difficult time with Jasmine.'

'She's a teenager now, isn't she? It's supposed to be hard.'

'I'm going to try to talk to her when she's here. See if I can figure out what's bothering her. Pity you're not here to meet her too, and give her the male perspective.'

Adam grinned. 'It's a shame my medical conference is this weekend. But I'll get to meet her when we go to Thailand for our honeymoon. You know I'll be dealing with my own family drama at the conference.'

'Oh?'

'Yep – Dad's coming. On the second day. We're meeting for dinner. Without his latest girlfriend, for once.' Adam's dad had had a string of girlfriends since he'd left his mother, all closer to Adam's age than his own.

Lauren smiled. 'That's good. You'll get the chance to talk to him properly.'

As they got ready to go out for brunch, Lauren couldn't help noticing how silent the flat was, with Kiera still asleep. She thought how different it would be if they had a baby. She could almost hear its cries, imagine feeling needed by a small, defenceless human. The sheer joy she'd felt when she'd been pregnant had taken her by surprise. Despite the sickness, all she had felt was grateful and all she had wanted was to hold her baby in her arms. She'd bought all the books about pregnancy and babies and had known everything she should be doing. What to eat. What not to eat. What exercise to do and what exercise to avoid. She looked online to see how big her baby was each week, aware when it was growing from the size of a poppy seed, to a lentil, and then a raspberry. With each week the baby had seemed more real and Lauren became more attached to the idea of becoming a mother. And then suddenly, at nine weeks, it was all over.

'Just one of those things,' the doctor had said at the time, and when she'd looked up more about it she'd realised how alarmingly common miscarriage was.

For a few months, she'd felt an uncontrollable envy towards pregnant women, irritated by the way they showcased their baby bumps in maxi dresses, drifting through shopping centres, seemingly so unaware of their good fortune.

'Are you OK?' Adam asked, dragging Lauren away from her thoughts.

Lauren sighed. 'I'm just thinking of what might have been. We could have been a family now.'

'We'd have been happy,' he said softly. 'But we're happy now, too. And all that's to come in the future, if we want it.'

If we want it. She thought they'd agreed they'd start trying for kids again after the wedding. Turning her head, she faced him. 'You still want kids, don't you?'

'I think so,' he said. 'Yes, I think I do.'

She let out a little sob then, the emotion overwhelming her. She was angry with him for not feeling more strongly, for not knowing with his heart and soul.

'You'll have them?' she asked, tentatively. 'You'll have them with me?' She reached out and gripped his hand.

'If that's what you want,' he said quietly. He looked away from her then, a small frown creasing his features.

CHAPTER FOURTEEN

Adam

Adam put on his coat and locked up his room at the GP surgery. He had ended up overrunning, which meant that once again he wouldn't catch Lauren before her night shift. He checked his phone. Three missed calls from Amanda and a text. He read the message with a sigh.

Wanna meet up tonight?

He deleted it quickly. Surely if he kept blanking her she'd get the message?

'Fancy a drink?' Kiera asked him as he passed the reception desk on the way out.

'Didn't realise you were still here,' he said, smiling. 'It's gone seven.'

'I just had some paperwork to finish up. Filing patients' notes. If I leave it until the morning, I'll be so busy with the phones that I'll never get it done. But I'll be finished in a minute, so do you fancy grabbing a drink and a bite to eat?'

'Yes, please.' It would save them both from cooking.

'Pint?' she asked, when they reached the pub.

'Sure. But let me pay for it.'

She shook her head, going through the usual routine. 'I'll get the drinks, you can get the food.'

'Sure.' It was the way it always worked. He earned so much more than her now, but she always wanted to pay for something.

'Shall I order?' he asked.

'Yes please.'

At the bar, he found himself standing a few feet away from a tall, heavily made-up woman, her dark hair pulled back into a high ponytail. She was younger than the usual clientele at the pub, which catered mainly to retirees. 'Hi,' she said, nervously, pushing a stray strand of hair back behind her ear.

He nodded at her and she ordered her drink. He couldn't place her accent, which had an unusual twang.

'Having a nice evening?' the girl asked him, as he waited to be served.

'Yes, thanks.'

She stared at him, her eyes boring into him, and he couldn't tell if she was just a bit awkward and trying to be friendly or if she wanted something from him.

'Are you with someone?' she asked, indicating Kiera.

'Yes.' Maybe this was her clumsy way of coming on to him.

'Oh, that's a shame,' she said, her voice shaking. 'Maybe we can catch up another time.' It was a statement, not a question.

The barmaid handed the girl her lime and soda and she grabbed it and started to walk away.

'Hang on a minute,' Adam said, confused. 'Do I know you from somewhere? Are you a patient?' Maybe it was a mistake coming to the pub so close to his work. He should have learnt from the fiasco with Amanda. 'I'm not really supposed to speak to patients outside of work, you see,' he said placidly.

She turned back towards him. 'Look, now's not the right time. I wanted to talk to you, but we can speak later.' She nodded towards Kiera. 'When you're not with someone.' And with that, she turned away.

Adam watched her walk to a table and sit down, bemused. He thought of how Amanda had messaged him, wanting to meet up. Could the girl be connected to her? Amanda knew he went to this pub, she'd seen him here before.

'Bit young for you, isn't she?' the barmaid said, pulling him from his thoughts.

'Yeah,' he replied, glancing back at the woman. She seemed to be completely alone, with just the one drink. She was still watching him.

'That will be thirty-three pound twenty,' the barmaid said, and he handed over his bank card.

He returned to their table with a large glass of wine for Kiera, a pint for him and a wooden spoon with their order number painted on it in bright blue letters.

'How much for the drinks?' Kiera asked.

'Call it a tenner.'

She handed over the note and Adam stuffed it in his pocket.

'Making a friend at the bar?' Kiera asked. She never missed a trick.

'Not really.' Adam was still racking his brains to work out if he knew her. She hadn't looked familiar, but she'd seemed to know him.

'She was in the surgery earlier. Asking for an appointment with you. But she didn't have any proof of address, couldn't show she lived locally.'

'She wanted an appointment with me?' Adam raised his eyebrows.

'Yeah. You're popular these days, aren't you?'

'Did she say what was wrong?'

'No, she said it was confidential.'

'Then what?'

'She hung around in the waiting room for a bit and then just left.'

'And turned up here? Do you think she followed us?'

'I doubt it. If she was at a loose end, then this is the nearest pub, isn't it? Maybe she's meeting a friend here.'

Adam glanced over to the table where the girl was sitting on her own. 'Maybe.'

Just then his phone rang loudly and he looked at the screen. It was Amanda. He swiped to dismiss the call.

'Who was that?' Kiera asked.

'No one.'

'You clearly didn't want to speak to them. You rejected the call in a second.'

'That's because I want to spend the evening with you.'

Kiera narrowed her eyes. 'What's going on, Adam?' she asked, taking a sip of her wine.

'Nothing.'

'I saw Amanda was in to see you the other day.' Adam swallowed. Kiera knew him too well. 'Jane reported back from her chaperoning duties. Said you went bright red when you examined her breasts.'

'She makes me feel a bit uncomfortable. She's flirty.' Adam could feel himself blushing once again. He had no idea what to do about Amanda. He was sure she was the one who'd sent the card to Lauren, but he hadn't had the courage to confront her, afraid of how she might react.

'She keeps booking in to see you. Only you.'

'Yeah. It's getting a bit much, really.'

'I saw her in the waiting room. She's very attractive.' Kiera waited expectantly for confirmation.

'Don't tell me you fancy her?' Adam said, trying to get the attention away from him.

'No. And stop trying to change the subject.'

Adam gazed into his pint. A waitress appeared behind him and made him jump as she put their burgers down in front of them. Kiera started digging in.

'You know she's got a reputation, don't you?' she said between mouthfuls. 'Three of the other doctors have requested that the receptionists don't book her in with them.'

'Really?'

'Yep. And funnily enough, it's all the young male doctors. I could make sure she can't get an appointment with you, if you like. Say you're always busy.'

'She doesn't phone up for the appointments. Books them online. Ages in advance.'

'Hmmm… that's more difficult then.' Kiera grabbed a chip and took a bite.

Adam would have loved for Kiera to step in, but he knew Amanda would be outraged. And then who knew what she'd do? The card she'd sent Lauren had been vicious. He thought of the broken arm she'd had when he first met her, when she said she'd given as good as she got. What if that had been the truth? What if the threat to Lauren was real?

'I'm away this weekend, anyway,' Adam said. 'At a conference. I'll get a break from her.' He picked at his burger. He didn't feel hungry.

'Oh, is that the psychological therapies one in Barcelona? I saw the agenda. It looked really interesting.'

'That's the one.'

'You know, when I started med school, I always wanted to end up as a psychiatrist.'

'I remember,' Adam said.

Kiera sighed. 'Carmelle always said I was directionless, but I thought of myself as more of a free spirit. Now I'm starting to think she was right.'

'Ah, Kiera, you're fine the way you are.' Adam put a hand on her shoulder. 'I always admired your unwillingness to follow the crowd.' He moved his hand, placing it over hers.

The waitress came by, checking Adam was done with his half-eaten burger before she took the plates.

'Really? Sometimes it's hard to watch everyone else with their lives and their jobs sorted. I'm thinking of retraining as a psychiatric nurse.'

'Well, that sounds like a great idea,' Adam said.

'Glad you think so. I guess we'd better get back home. I promised Lauren I'd clear out a bit more of my stuff. I think I need to bin some of it. I've no idea how I accumulated so much.'

'I can help you,' Adam said.

As they stood up to leave, something made Adam glance over to the other side of the pub. He must have felt the girl's gaze on him, because she was staring right at him. Their eyes met and she didn't avert her gaze. He couldn't read her expression, a strange mix of determination and anger. Then she forced her face into a smile.

He turned away and walked out into the night air. Who on earth was she?

CHAPTER FIFTEEN

Lauren

Lauren woke to the sound of the alarm. She reached to switch it off, but then she realised it was on Adam's side of the bed, not hers.

'Sorry to wake you,' he said, turning it off and giving her a gentle kiss.

She rolled over towards him, groggily. Adam flicked the bedside light on and she blinked, catching sight of his packed suitcase on the floor.

She heard him get up, the sound of the shower running. She wished he wasn't going to Spain now, not just before the wedding. But the timing of the conference was the same every year, and he always went. She snuggled under the duvet, shifting positions again and again to get comfortable, but she couldn't get back to sleep.

Easing herself out of bed slowly, she went to the kitchen to put the kettle on, to spend the last half hour with Adam before he went away. Once he came back, they'd be in the final countdown to their wedding. Butterflies rose up in her stomach, a mixture of excitement and nerves.

She made two strong coffees and sat with hers by the window, looking out at the tower blocks stretching up above the tiled roofs of the houses below. Adam appeared from the bedroom, dressed in a crisp blue shirt and pressed trousers.

'That's a new aftershave,' she said.

Adam nodded. 'Thought I'd treat myself. Time to try something new after ten years.' He reddened slightly as if he'd said something wrong.

He came and sat beside her, wheeling his suitcase next to the sofa.

'I picked up some supplies last night for while I'm away. There's a chocolate cake in the fridge from the bakery and a few bottles of prosecco for your hen night.'

'Thanks,' she said, reaching up to kiss him, touched by his thoughtfulness.

He held her close to him, and with his strong arms around her, she felt safe. Then he pulled away, reaching for the handle of his suitcase and standing.

'I'd better be off. Have a great time on your hen night.'

She stood up and kissed him. 'I will. Enjoy the conference. And Barcelona. Can I have the details of your hotel, just in case I need them?'

A flash of surprise crossed his face. 'Sure, I'll write them down,' he said.

She watched him as he paused before he scribbled the name and address on the paper. He *was* going to the conference, wasn't he? He was in a new suit, wearing new aftershave… She frowned, shaking the thoughts out of her mind. They would be married soon. She had to trust him.

An hour later, Lauren got off the tube and walked along the South Bank to meet Tracey and Jasmine. The weather was drizzly and she carried an umbrella as she weaved her way through the crowds of tourists, cyclists and the occasional skateboarder. It was Jasmine's first time in London, and she supposed she might find the miserable weather disappointing after the glorious sunshine in Thailand. Grey clouds hung above the Thames and only a few hardy street performers were out, one pretending to be a statue with a silver-sprayed umbrella incorporated into his costume.

She chucked a bit of money in his hat as she walked by and he gave a robotic gesture of thanks. Lauren hurried on. She was running a few minutes late. When she got to the London Eye she didn't spot her sister and niece at first as they were obscured by a huge green golfing umbrella.

'Hello!' Lauren said when she saw them. She hugged her sister and then turned to Jasmine and embraced her too, their umbrellas clashing. Tracey looked older, her face etched with lines. The divorce must really be affecting her. But she couldn't ask her about it, not in front of Jasmine.

'Right, let's do this,' Lauren said, enthusiastically.

In the queue, Jasmine seemed excited and interested in what Lauren was telling her about the London Eye and the sights they would see, nothing like the surly teenager Tracey had described.

'It's so nice to have the opportunity to get to know you, Lauren,' she said. 'I really feel like I missed out on getting to know my British family when I was growing up.' She shot Tracey an angry look. Lauren swallowed. She would have liked to have got to know her niece, too, but Tracey had pushed her away after their parents died, and for years they'd hardly spoken. But she didn't want to say any of that out loud, not when her relationship with her sister had just started to recover.

'We can get to know each other now,' she said brightly. 'I'd really like that.'

'I just feel like we probably have so much in common. We've got the same blood.'

Lauren swallowed. That wasn't true. She wished Tracey had been honest from the start. She didn't understand why she hadn't told Jasmine she was adopted. Lauren couldn't help wondering if the disconnectedness Jasmine was feeling was because she was somehow missing her biological parents.

Lauren smiled at Jasmine. 'What do you like doing?'

'Mainly drinking and getting into trouble,' Tracey said with a laugh.

Jasmine glared at Tracey. 'I swim a lot,' she said to Lauren. 'To clear my head.'

'Adam loves swimming.'

Jasmine grinned. 'I can't wait to meet him. Mum's told me so much about him.'

'Has she?' Lauren was surprised. It was so long since Adam had seen Tracey. But then they'd all been close as children – they'd grown up together. 'He's not around this weekend, I'm afraid. He's at a conference.'

Lauren saw Jasmine's look of disappointment. She realised that her niece must have been desperate to connect to family. She must be so lonely in Thailand.

'Don't worry,' she said, reassuringly. 'You'll get to meet him when we're on honeymoon in Thailand. We'll pop in and visit you both.'

'Really, it would be so much easier if Mum just let me come to the wedding.'

'It's not that simple, Jasmine,' Tracey snapped. 'If you'd worked a bit harder at school then maybe you could have come. But as it is, you need to attend the revision course I've signed you up for.'

'Can't I go to a different one? In a different week of the summer holiday?'

'No, we've discussed this. That's the best one for you. And besides, you're in London now. I'm not paying for another visit in a couple of weeks.'

'But you're coming twice,' Jasmine shot back.

'Oh,' Lauren said. 'I thought you were staying now until the wedding?'

Tracey sighed. 'I wanted to, but I can't. It's Ken. I can't leave the boys with him for weeks on end. He won't have them. So instead I have to fly home and then come back again for the wedding.'

'That's crazy, Mum.'

Tracey glared at Jasmine. 'I'm only coming twice because I had to accompany you to London.'

'I didn't ask you to,' Jasmine shot back. 'I wanted to come on my own.'

Tracey gave a big sigh. 'I couldn't let you do that. I don't trust you not to do something stupid.'

Lauren put her hand on her sister's arm, trying to calm her. She didn't like listening to the two of them argue. Tracey shook her off.

'I don't trust you either,' Jasmine mumbled under her breath.

The queue inched forward. They were nearly at the gate now. 'Nearly our turn,' Lauren said brightly.

Soon they were in the air in one of the London Eye's pods with twenty other people. Lauren moved round, pointing out Big Ben, Westminster Bridge and Waterloo station to her niece and sister. Jasmine studied the pictures mounted by the glass panels, trying to match up the sights to the photos.

'Thanks so much for bringing me up here, Lauren. I'm having a brilliant time.'

'No problem.'

'I love seeing all the different parts of London. I want to live here one day.'

Lauren smiled at her, curious. 'You want to live in London?'

'Yeah. I might move after school. I'm not sure university's for me.' Jasmine threw Tracey a look and Lauren realised she was trying to wind her up. From the irritated expression on her mother's face, it was working.

'What are you thinking of doing here?' Lauren asked.

'Hotel work. I've done a lot of work in Mum and Dad's hotel, so I could do it easily.'

'I'm sure you'll figure it out,' Lauren said quickly, seeing Tracey shaking her head behind Lauren, signalling that she shouldn't encourage Jasmine.

'I will,' Jasmine said firmly. 'But that's for later. Now I want you to tell me everything about your wedding.' Jasmine smiled, linking arms with Lauren. 'I love weddings. I help out with them at the hotel sometimes. I have to know all the details.'

Lauren grinned and started to fill Jasmine in, telling her about the beautiful church, the flowers, the poems they were going to read out during the ceremony. And she told her about Adam, how she'd fallen in love with him.

'Sounds like you two were made for each other,' Jasmine said. 'I hope I have that one day. Someone who loves me. Who cares about me.'

'You have that now, Jasmine,' Tracey said. 'I care about you.' She sighed.

'And what about Dad? Funny you don't mention how he cares about me, isn't it? Or is it just because he doesn't?' Jasmine's voice rose and echoed around the pod. People were starting to stare at them now, their gazes turned from the view outside to the raised voices inside.

'I'm sure that's not true,' Lauren said, putting her hand on Jasmine's arm. She knew the divorce was difficult for her, but now wasn't the right time to discuss it. Jasmine shook her hand away, and went to the other side of the compartment, her arms folded.

'Is she alright?' Lauren asked Tracey.

'She'll be fine later,' she said. Despite Tracey's optimism, Lauren could see tears in her eyes. 'She often has these little outbursts. I've got used to it.'

'Do you think it's time to tell her about her real parents?' Lauren whispered, certain she was out of Jasmine's earshot. She could see how much heartache Jasmine was going through. Lauren couldn't help thinking that if she knew the truth it would make things easier for her.

Tracey shook her head. 'She'd never forgive me,' she said. 'I can't lose her. Jasmine and the boys are all I've got.'

CHAPTER SIXTEEN

Adam

Adam sat in the hotel bar in Barcelona, looking out of the window at the street teeming with people going out for the evening. The Spanish ate late, but everyone at the conference had already dined at the hotel, drawn in by the free dinner included in the ticket price. It had been a long day and he was tired. He was glad he wasn't meeting his father until tomorrow, as he could do with going to bed. The talks on mental health had been fascinating, but by the end of the day he'd been struggling to take it all in.

'So, how are you finding the conference?' He heard a familiar voice behind him.

'Kiera?' His eyes widened in surprise. 'What are you doing here?'

'I told you I was interested in this stuff, didn't I?'

'Yeah, but I didn't expect you to actually come to the conference. Why didn't you tell me?'

'It was a last-minute decision. I booked it on the spur of the moment, the other day. I'm only here today though. Too expensive to come for the whole weekend.'

'Oh, that's great. You should have messaged me earlier. We could have gone to some of the talks together.'

'I went to some of the specialist ones, in the breakout room. There were sessions aimed at people restarting their careers.'

'Did you enjoy them?'

'Yeah. They were interesting. Lots to think about, and I felt like I learnt something.'

'Do you want a drink?' he asked, indicating the seat opposite him.

'It's too pricey here. Shall we go somewhere else?'

He shook his head. 'I'm tired.'

'Come on,' she said. 'When do we ever have this much freedom? We could relive our uni days. Back when we didn't care how tired we were. We just kept going.'

Adam remembered the late nights, the endless hangovers, the weekends when he hadn't got up until 4 p.m. 'I've got the next day of the conference tomorrow,' he said.

'And I've got an early flight,' she replied. 'We could be out all night, and then I could pick up my things from the hostel and go straight to the airport.'

'Is that a good idea?'

'I've done it before, when I was travelling around Asia. When I was trying to save money, some nights I wouldn't even pay for accommodation, just be out all night and get an early-morning bus the next day.'

'There's no way I'm going out all night. Let's just have another drink here. I'll get them.'

Kiera sighed and sank back into her seat. 'Fine, fine. If you insist.'

As he went up to the bar, he noticed how quiet the hotel was, with its staid and unexciting atmosphere.

He went back to Kiera. 'OK,' he said, relenting. 'Let's get one drink somewhere more interesting. And then I'm coming back here to get some sleep.'

They found a bar up the road, rammed with tourists and locals. They both ordered cocktails and stood in the corner drinking them, uncomfortably close to a group of men on a stag do, who were moving erratically and occasionally bursting into booming laughter. One of the guys suddenly got down on the floor and started doing press-ups. Adam looked at him doubtfully, thinking of his hands on the sticky floor, while Kiera clapped and cheered him on.

'Your stag do soon,' she said. 'I've been busy planning.'

'Nothing too horrible, I hope?' He thought of the card that he'd pretended was from Jimmy.

'You'll see,' Kiera said, smiling.

'I hope I don't end up doing press-ups on the floor,' Adam said, looking at the stag next to them.

'No, probably not,' she laughed.

'Chug, chug, chug!' the group chanted and for a moment Adam felt embarrassed to be British.

'How many of your wedding guests have you slept with?' one of the guys shouted, slapping the stag on the back.

'I don't know, I've lost count.' They all erupted into laughter.

Kiera smirked at Adam. 'That would be a good question for you too,' she said.

'Oh, come on, Kiera, not that many. I've lost touch with most of the girls from uni. They're not invited to the wedding.'

'You were quite the ladies' man back then,' she teased. 'Anyway. There's at least one…'

'OK, yeah, there's you. And maybe a couple of others.'

'Does Lauren know?'

'Of course not. She said she didn't want to know about any of that when we first started seeing each other. She was very clear about it. Said she didn't want to walk round the university noticing all the people I'd slept with.' He'd been relieved when she'd said that. It had meant that he'd never told her about Kiera. Or any of the others before Lauren.

'Fair enough. Still, it will make it a bit awkward at the wedding, won't it?'

'Maybe. But I hope not. It was all so long ago.' Once they'd set that marker in the sand, to never talk about their pasts, then it was difficult to go back. Sometimes he wished it had been different, that they'd both come clean at the very beginning, told each other everything. Because with each passing year, as their relationship got more serious, he would wonder whether there were some things that he really should have told her a long time ago. But to dredge it all up now would seem deliberate, as if it meant something, when really it meant nothing at all.

'If it hasn't come up so far, I guess it's unlikely to now,' Kiera said. 'Not that you don't still have admirers. Amanda, for one. And that girl at the pub. Who was she?'

Adam thought back to the woman who'd tried to make an appointment with him at the surgery, and then appeared at the pub. 'I don't know. I thought maybe a friend of Amanda's? The way she came to the surgery and then to the pub was just like Amanda. And Amanda had messaged me that day asking to meet up, and I hadn't replied. She could have sent someone to check up on me.'

Kiera looked at him doubtfully. 'Maybe,' she said. 'I hope you're not cheating,' she said seriously. 'It would be unforgivable.' And with that, she downed the rest of her cocktail and disappeared to the toilets.

When she returned, she went to the bar and got them more drinks.

'The night's still young,' she said.

'This is the last one,' Adam replied. He felt hot and uncomfortable in the suit that he'd worn all day at the conference, and he was worried that tomorrow the jacket would smell of alcohol and sweat. He yawned, exhausted now, and the bar seemed too loud and too crowded. He longed for the soft sheets of his hotel room, the huge comfortable bed.

Twenty minutes later they stumbled out onto the street, Kiera holding Adam's arm for balance. She leaned on him as they walked up the road, too drunk to stand up properly. She must have been drinking at the dinner, before she met him. For a moment, Adam worried about someone seeing them together, him propping her up, but then he relaxed. There was no one to judge them here. And besides, he could hardly let her fall to the ground.

'Can I stay at yours?' she asked, as he'd known she would. 'The sheets at the hostel are scratchy and I don't like sharing a room with other people.'

'You'd have to share with me.'

She punched his arm playfully. 'I don't mind that.'

CHAPTER SEVENTEEN

Adam

2001: Thailand

The holiday in Thailand was better than anything he'd ever imagined. He'd been diving almost every day, losing himself between the coral and the shoals of fish. Today they were all on the boat, the two families together, snorkels piled up on the side.

He felt alive here, scuba-diving and whizzing through the streets on a hired motorbike. He never felt that way at home.

The boat anchored in a tiny bay, waves rippling underneath a bright blue sky. They jumped into the turquoise water first, the two of them, snorkels in their hands. Under the water, he opened his eyes and he could see her bright red halterneck bikini, her body weaving as her legs pushed up to the surface. As they came up his arm brushed her breast and he felt a surge of lust.

She grinned at him, her eyes sparkling and her dark hair shining in the sunlight. The water lapped around her. She was beautiful. This was love. This was perfect.

They put on their masks as they trod water and then swam quickly away from the others, not daring even to brush hands, although his hand longed to reach out and touch hers. Underneath them shoals of multicoloured fish shimmied through the water, over the coral. It felt painfully intimate to be so close to her, to see her red bikini top, the curve of her breast, just out of the corner of his eye, but to be unable to touch her. Yet it felt amazing just to be under the same sky, the same water lapping around them, seeing the life below.

They swam away from the others, through the shallow waters, around a rock and to a secluded cove out of sight of the boat. Once they were away from the coral, they let their bare feet drop to the ocean floor and removed their masks. Hers fell round her neck, and she ran a hand through her messy wet hair. There was an indent around her eyes where the snorkel had been, surrounded by her freckles. His snorkel felt tight on the top of his forehead.

He grinned at her and she grinned back. The moment seemed to last forever, and he couldn't believe how lucky he was. She took a tiny step forward, and electricity bolted through him. He wanted to be closer to her; needed to be closer to her. He wrapped his arms around her, skin on skin, her body lithe and alive.

As his lips met hers, he lost himself entirely. He couldn't draw breath, couldn't pull away, her tongue around his, exploring each other. He could taste the salt in her mouth, the slight taint of plastic from her mask. When he finally pulled away, neither of them could stop smiling. He wondered if he'd ever be able to stop.

CHAPTER EIGHTEEN

Lauren

Two weeks until the wedding

Lauren ran a brush through her messy hair and grabbed her keys from the side in the kitchen. She was going to the hairdresser this morning, starting the preparations for her hen party early. She passed Kiera's closed door and remembered that she was away. She'd mentioned some kind of career training, which involved staying overnight. Lauren was glad she was thinking about her career again, starting to plan her future without Carmelle. But she'd made her promise that she'd be back in time for the hen do tonight.

As Lauren came out of her flat, she looked down and saw a bouquet of red and white lilies sitting on the doormat outside the door. It must be from Adam. As if he hadn't already done enough, surprising her before his trip. Smiling, she looked at the little card that was attached. *Two weeks to go xx*

Misty wandered into the hallway, observed her for a moment from the door, and then returned to the bedroom, uninterested. Lifting up the bouquet, Lauren breathed in deeply to smell the scent. She frowned, catching a whiff of something unpleasant. She knew there were lots of different types of lilies. Maybe not all of them smelt nice. Adam wouldn't have known when he ordered them.

Back inside the flat, she found a vase, one that Sam had bought her for a birthday a few years ago. It was one of her favourites, with swirls of blue and gold circling it.

The packaging of the flowers was clearly designed to help them survive being left outside homes for long periods, as it was heavy and bulky, presumably containing water at the bottom to keep them alive. As she peeled off the layers of brown wrapping, she caught a whiff of the fetid smell again. She gagged, her hand flying up to cover her mouth. It was a rotten smell, and it was getting stronger the more layers she took off. She held her breath and stopped, turning away from the flowers.

Something wasn't right. Perhaps there was soil at the bottom of the bag with the water. Maybe manure had been used as a fertiliser and some of it had somehow found its way into the bouquet by mistake. When Adam got back from the conference, perhaps they'd laugh about this, and he'd joke about using another florist next time.

But she could still salvage the flowers. She started to pull them out, one by one, arranging them carefully in the vase. A white petal dropped to the counter. She held it between her thumb and forefinger for a moment, feeling how soft it was before she crushed it between her fingers and threw it in the bin.

The smell was getting worse. There was definitely something in the soil. As soon as she finished removing the lilies, she'd take it down with her on her way to her car and put it straight in the outdoor bin.

She picked out another flower and something white dropped to the counter again. She looked down, assuming it was another petal.

It wriggled on the counter and she jumped. A maggot. How did that get there? She got a glass and trapped it underneath, sliding a piece of paper under to catch it.

She pulled out the last two remaining flowers and screamed, as more maggots dropped onto the kitchen counter, writhing around on the shiny worktop. One dropped to the floor. Another crawled down the edge of the vase. She stepped back quickly. They were all over the flowers in the vase, too.

And the smell. The smell was everywhere now, filling her flat. She felt sick.

She peered into the soil that came with the flowers. But there was no soil. Only more maggots, climbing up the packaging, trying to get out. A whole mass of them, crawling all over each other and filling the room with their stench.

CHAPTER NINETEEN

Lauren

Zoe arrived at the door laden down with decorations and bridal paraphernalia: sashes and T-shirts and penis-shaped straws. She pulled out a load of bright pink T-shirts from her bag, and proudly showed her *Lauren's Hen Night* emblazoned on the back of them. 'This way we won't lose each other,' she said.

Lauren grinned. 'That's true. You could spot these a mile off.' She gave Zoe a hug. 'Thanks for going to all this effort.'

'No problem. Where's Kiera? I could give her hers now.'

'She's with Carmelle. The rent's due on the flat and Carmelle's insisting Kiera hand back her key tonight, otherwise she'll charge her half the rent. Kiera's gone to give it to her and check she hasn't left anything in the flat.'

'Sounds stressful.'

'Yeah, I think it is.' Even though Lauren felt sorry for Kiera, she couldn't help hoping she'd find somewhere more suitable to live soon. She had too many things to fit in their flat and needed her own space to spread out.

Lauren started to decorate the flat for the hen do. As she attached a banner to the wall with Blu Tack, she noticed the rotten smell that seemed to linger from the lilies.

'Can you smell something off?' she asked apologetically.

'No…' Zoe said slowly, but Lauren wasn't sure if she was just being polite.

'I'm so sorry. It's from some flowers I got this morning.'

'Oh, right. Some types of flowers do smell odd.'

'It wasn't the flowers. The base was full of maggots.'

'Yuck,' Zoe said, her nose crinkling. 'You should complain. What company delivered them?'

Lauren frowned. She'd been so busy disposing of the stinking packaging that she hadn't stopped to look for the name of the florist. 'I don't know. They were just left outside. The delivery person didn't even knock.'

'How horrible…' Zoe paused for a moment. Lauren had known her friend long enough to tell that she was trying to think how to phrase something tactfully.

'What is it?' Lauren asked.

'I was just thinking of that card you got. You don't think the maggots might have been deliberate? It could be connected.' Zoe bit her lip.

'No, the card was from a mate of Adam's. It was just a joke.' But as the words came out of Lauren's mouth, she wasn't sure if she believed them.

'OK,' Zoe said doubtfully.

'The flowers were from Adam,' she explained. At least, she'd thought they were from Adam. Now she wasn't so sure. He hadn't yet replied to her text thanking him. 'The note with them said "Two weeks to go". Until the wedding. So they must have been from him.'

'Maybe it was a problem at the florist then.' Zoe didn't look convinced, but before they could discuss it further the doorbell rang. Soon the flat was full of people: Tracey and Jasmine, Adam's mother Sam, and Lauren's friends.

It wasn't long until they were all laughing and drinking. They started on the prosecco Adam had left in the fridge and Zoe proposed a toast to Lauren. When the pizza arrived, Lauren already felt drunk. She was going to need to slow down.

She glanced over at Jasmine. She'd been worried about her fitting in with all her friends, being so much younger, but she seemed to be getting on well with everyone. She was really making an effort with people, asking about their lives and their jobs. In contrast, Tracey was quiet as the celebrations went on around her.

Jasmine sat chatting to Sam on the sofa, and Lauren went to top up their glasses. 'Not too much for me,' Jasmine said. 'Mum's watching.' Lauren glanced over at Tracey on the other side of the room. Jasmine was right. She was watching them, her brow furrowed. Perhaps it was to do with her talking to Sam. They'd never got on.

'It's so lovely to have the whole family together,' Sam said to Jasmine. 'I haven't seen your mother for years. But you're just like her. In the way you speak, your gestures. You remind me of her when she was younger.'

Lauren bit her tongue. Sam didn't know that Jasmine was adopted, and she could see that Jasmine didn't like being compared to her mother.

'Sam was just telling me all about your dress,' Jasmine said to Lauren. 'Can I see it?'

'Sure,' Lauren replied, relieved to defuse the awkwardness. She led her to their bedroom and Misty jumped off the bed where she had been resting and scampered out of the room. She didn't like groups of people.

Lauren pulled the dress out of the back of the cupboard, unwrapping it carefully. Some of the others appeared in the room behind her, oohing and ahhing as it was revealed.

'It's beautiful,' Jasmine said, taking it from her and holding it up to admire the firm bodice and the simple, flowing lines of the skirt, then stroking the silk material. 'Are those the shoes?' she said, peering into the cupboard.

'Yep.' Lauren pulled them out. The colour of the silk open-toed shoes matched the dress exactly, and the small heel would elevate Lauren to just under Adam's height.

'You'll look amazing,' a voice said over her shoulder. Lauren turned towards it and saw Tracey. 'I just can't believe my baby sister's getting married.' Tracey squeezed her arm.

'I need to show you something,' Lauren said, taking Tracey's hand. She led her to the other cupboard and pulled out the jewellery box. 'I'm going to wear Mum's silver bracelet. The one with the blue stone that she wore when she got married.'

'I didn't realise she'd worn that on her wedding day.' Tracey leaned in closer.

'I have the photos. I can show you sometime.' Tracey hadn't had any interest in any of their parents' possessions after they had died; all she had wanted was the house to be emptied quickly so they could sell it. So Lauren had kept all the sentimental items, including all their photos and her mother's jewellery.

Lauren put the jewellery box on the bed, opened it up and handed Tracey the bracelet. Tracey held it in her palm and turned it over, admiring the dark blue stone, then slipped it over her slim wrist and fastened it. 'It's perfect,' she said, tilting the stone so it caught the light. She smiled, but it didn't reach her eyes. 'You're so lucky to have a reminder of her on your wedding day.'

Lauren thought of Tracey's wedding in Thailand, how she hadn't told Lauren about it until it had already happened. If Lauren had known her sister was engaged, she would have offered her their mother's jewellery to wear.

Just then Zoe bustled in. 'Right, I've tidied up a bit in the kitchen, but we really need to get going to get to the club for eleven. I've booked us a table in the VIP area.'

Tracey unfastened the bracelet and handed it back to Lauren, who put it on top of the jewellery box. After a few moments, they all filed out of the flat. As they did so, Lauren's phone beeped, and she saw a message from Adam. She read it, and a shiver ran through her body.

What flowers? They weren't from me.

CHAPTER TWENTY

Adam

Adam studied the menu as he waited for his father at the hotel bar. He was late, as usual, and Adam sighed. It reminded him of his childhood. His father had always seemed to have someone more important to see than his son. Adam considered leaving the bar and going to bed. His head was still pounding from his hangover, and more than anything, he wanted to sleep.

When Adam was little, he had admired his father, wanting to be just like him. Adam wouldn't have even gone to medical school if it wasn't for his dad's brilliant career as a doctor. When he was at university everyone seemed to have heard of his father, and whenever he said his name they asked, 'Are you Dr Glenister's son?' seeming both delighted to meet him and disappointed that his father had produced such an unremarkable son.

'Are you ready to order?' A waitress interrupted his thoughts, standing over him with a notepad. 'Not yet. I'm waiting for someone. I'll have a drink now, though. Can I have a pint of Coca-Cola, please?' Maybe the sugar would take the edge off his hangover.

As the waitress went away, Adam thought about how tense he felt. Ever since his parents' divorce, he hadn't known what to say to his father. He'd had a string of younger girlfriends who Adam struggled to connect with. He knew his mother was worried about who exactly his dad would be bringing to the wedding, and the truth was Adam didn't know. He hadn't kept track of the latest girlfriend, keen to avoid another awkward meal. And it seemed his father hadn't been inclined to tell him either.

Adam's Coca-Cola arrived and he took a huge gulp, craving the caffeine. He checked his phone impatiently, wondering if his father had messaged to say he was running late. He hadn't. The last text was from Lauren. She'd said the flowers had been left outside the flat and were teeming with maggots and his heart had sunk. He was sure it was Amanda again. She knew where he lived.

'Hello!' His father's booming voice crashed in on his thoughts as he gave him a big slap on the back. Adam stood up and greeted him.

'Brilliant conference, isn't it?' his father said. 'Are you enjoying it?'

'I am.' Adam nodded.

After they had sat down opposite each other and ordered food, Adam struggled to make conversation.

'Are you bringing anyone to the wedding, Dad?' he blurted out, not knowing what else to say.

'Just Donna,' his father replied.

'Your girlfriend?' Adam wanted to ask how old she was, but he bit his tongue.

'Yeah, my girlfriend. Don't give me that disapproving look. I'm allowed to have fun, you know. I'm not past it yet. Besides, she's gorgeous. You'll like her.'

'Dad…'

'Don't be so judgemental. I saw you with that girl last night… She wasn't Lauren, was she?' His dad tapped the side of his nose. 'Don't worry, I'll keep it quiet.'

Adam sighed. 'I'm not like you, Dad. I'm engaged to Lauren.'

'Didn't look much like that last night. I saw you taking her back to your room.'

CHAPTER TWENTY-ONE

Lauren

The music boomed in the club, vibrating through Lauren's body. In the VIP area, cordoned off by a dirty white rope, they had their own tiny bit of floor space. They danced in a circle, Lauren keeping an eye on their handbags at the small table next to them. Zoe had scattered shiny pink penis confetti on the table, so there was no way they could forget which one was theirs. Everyone had made it out except for Jasmine and Kiera. Jasmine had been told firmly by Tracey that she had to return to their hotel as she was too young, and Kiera was still caught up at Carmelle's. There were fifteen of them at the club in their bright pink T-shirts, and Lauren marvelled at the fact that after going to so many hen nights, now it was her turn to wear the bride-to-be sash. It felt unreal.

Kiera rushed in just before midnight, barging her way through the crowd and then lifting up the rope to the VIP area to duck under. She looked tense, her mascara smudged. 'Are you OK?' Lauren shouted over the music, as Zoe rifled through her bag to find the final hen night T-shirt.

'Yeah, just about,' Kiera said, her eyes watery. 'I just… I don't know. I thought we could have an amicable split. Part on good terms. But even though Carmelle asked me to leave, she's still wants to blame me for everything that went wrong.'

'You're better off without her,' Lauren said, aware it was a cliché, but also that it was true.

'I don't want to even think about her,' Kiera said, slipping the T-shirt that Zoe had handed her over her sparkly top, and forcing a smile. 'I'm so sorry I'm late. I'm going to get a round of shots to make up for it.'

Ten minutes later she reappeared, balancing a circle of shots on a teetering tray. Sam refused hers, but the rest of them knocked them back, even Tracey, who hadn't been drinking much. Afterwards, Lauren staggered to her feet. Her legs already felt as heavy as lead and she knew she needed to slow down.

'Let's go to the drum and bass room,' Kiera said.

Sam shook her head. 'I'm going to call it a night,' she replied, smiling. 'I think I'm too old for all this.' She embraced Lauren. 'Have a wonderful evening. You deserve to.'

'Thanks for coming,' Lauren said, feeling her vision blur as her future mother-in-law squeezed her tight.

After Sam had gone, the rest of the hen party made their way up the stairs to the small drum and bass room at the back. The rhythm flowed through the room, and soon they were dancing once more, lost in the mass of bodies moving erratically to the fast beats. It got hot and sweaty quickly, and Lauren realised that some of the group must have disappeared to the toilets or back to the main dance floor. She looked around and saw Kiera at the bar, leaning in close towards a man in a suit, and laughing at something he said.

A few minutes later Kiera returned with yet more drinks. 'Everything alright?' Lauren asked Kiera over the noise.

'Yeah, fine.'

'That man coming on to you?'

'A bit. I think he's quite fit, don't you?' Kiera gave the guy a little wave and he lifted his drink up in return.

'Oh,' Lauren said, confused. She'd only known Kiera to date women.

Kiera laughed at her expression. 'I wouldn't rule him out if I was on the lookout,' she said with a smile. She glanced back over at him. He was staring right at them both. 'He *is* hot, isn't he?' Kiera handed Lauren a plastic flute of fizz.

'I've only got eyes for Adam,' Lauren replied with a laugh.

'Good for you,' Kiera said, grinning. 'You lucked out there.'

The room was crowded now, heating up with sweaty clubbers. The DJ was good, but Lauren was tired of the pounding beat of drum and bass and she wanted to get out of the small, hot space and go back to the main dance floor.

'I'm going to head back to the VIP area,' Lauren shouted, clinging to her drink.

'I'll come with you,' Zoe replied.

They left Kiera and some of the others there. Outside the room the rest of the club had filled up, now heaving with dancing crowds. They had to squeeze through a sea of bodies just to get to the top of the stairs. Lauren felt thirsty and disorientated, the alcohol catching up with her. She glanced down at the dance floor below, at the writhing mass of people, and she wobbled on her heels. As she made her way down the steps, she clutched the handrail tightly, steadying herself against the tide of people coming up the other way. The hairs on a stranger's arm brushed against her skin. She could feel the pulsing beat through her heels, as fluorescent lights bounced over her. It made her feel slightly giddy. She should have eaten more before they came to the club.

Zoe turned round to talk to her. 'Look at the queue for the bar,' she said, indicating the crowd about six people deep that lined the bar below.

'Wow,' said Lauren. She felt the person behind her push her forward a little and she took her hand off the rail and nudged Zoe in return, encouraging her to keep moving down the stairs.

'Let's get some water,' she said to Zoe.

'What?' Zoe shouted back, turning her head. 'What did you say?'

Lauren shook her head. She'd tell her when they got to the bottom of the stairs, where it was quieter.

Then she felt them, hands on her back. She started to twist around to see who it was, but it was too late; she was already falling, into Zoe and then past her. Her phone flew out of her open bag and into the air, vanishing into the crowd at the bottom. Her plastic champagne flute fell from her grasp, covering the people in front of her in prosecco. She didn't see it land, distracted by the surge of pain from her wrist as it smashed into the edge of the metal stair.

CHAPTER TWENTY-TWO

Adam

2001: Thailand

He met her on the path just beyond the hotel. They'd both managed to get out of a trip to the swimming pool with their families; his excuse, that he'd wanted to go for a walk in the hills, hers that she had food poisoning. Instead they were hiring a motorbike and escaping the resort together.

On the open road, the wind coursed through his hair, her arms wrapped tightly around him, her laughter ringing in his ears. He could feel the hot sun warming his skin, the dust of the road in his lungs. He didn't really know where he was going, he was just following the road, and he loved that feeling of freedom. The man who'd rented him the bike had mentioned a little beachside fish restaurant down a dirt track on the left. He saw a sign coming up: PARADISE RESTAURANT.

He took the corner a little fast and the bike tilted unexpectedly. Behind him, she let out a yelp as their flip-flops ran along the dirt for a second, burning the soles. But then the bike righted itself and they bumped down the track at a slower pace. She erupted into laughter, and he grinned.

At the restaurant, they were shown to a table, the waves of the bay only metres away. It was beautiful, like everywhere on the Thai island. The white plastic chairs seemed to glimmer in the sunshine and the sea shimmered beyond them. He looked at her sitting across from him, tanned and happy. He imagined them always being together, that this was the first of many holidays.

'It's so stunning here,' she said, her blue eyes sparkling.

His sipped his beer, refreshing in the heat of the day. He beamed at her, aware of how peaceful he felt. Everything felt right in the world when he was with her.

CHAPTER TWENTY-THREE

Lauren

Lauren stopped rolling a few steps before the end of the staircase, her sash tangled round her body. Her wrist throbbed with pain, and she swallowed back tears. A few feet away her plastic champagne flute was being knocked around by clubbers' shoes. She scanned the floor for her phone but couldn't see it.

'Are you OK?' Zoe shouted, bending over her. Around her the crowd was getting impatient, stepping over her, blocking the people going the other way. Lauren needed to get up before she was trodden on.

Zoe held out her hand and she stumbled to her feet.

A bouncer appeared, parting the crowd.

'Right, you two – out.'

'But I fell. Someone—'

He wasn't listening to them. A voice boomed in his earpiece as he took each of them roughly by the arm, shoving them towards the exit.

'I need to find my phone,' Lauren protested as her wrist pulsed with pain, her eyes searching the crowd. She'd never find it.

And where was the rest of her hen party? She needed to find them, too.

'My phone,' Lauren repeated when they got to the door of the club and the volume was a bit quieter.

'She needs to find it,' Zoe said. 'So she can contact the others. She's on her hen night.' She pointed to the T-shirts, and the bouncer sighed.

'You need to leave,' he replied, shaking his head, as he manhandled them out of the door.

The people queueing to get in watched nonchalantly as Lauren and Zoe were pushed out into the summer drizzle. Outside the street lamps shone so brightly that Lauren had to cover her eyes. The shock of moving from the hot club to the cool night air hit her and she shivered.

Beside them another bouncer removed the rope of the entrance and let a young couple into the club. Minicabs honked their horns at the waiting clubbers.

'Are you alright?' Zoe asked.

'I think so.'

Zoe glanced down at Lauren's wrist. It had swollen to the size of a tennis ball.

'I think you need to get that looked at.'

Lauren could feel it throbbing, but the pain was numbed by the alcohol she'd consumed. 'I guess so,' she said. It looked like it needed an X-ray. She dreaded the thought of turning up at her own A&E department when her colleagues knew it was her hen night. She'd never hear the end of it.

'What about my phone?'

'I guess you'll have to get it in the morning.'

'Is everyone else still inside?'

'Yeah. I think so.'

'Can you message the others? Maybe they can ask at the bar for my phone.'

'Sure.' Zoe got out her phone and typed a message.

'What happened?' Zoe asked, looking at Lauren's wrist, concerned. 'Did you trip?'

Lauren tried to remember. Her brain felt foggy, her recollections shaky. She'd had too much to drink. And yet she didn't remember losing her footing. She remembered two solid hands on her back. 'No,' she said. 'I was pushed.'

CHAPTER TWENTY-FOUR

Adam

Adam woke to the ringing of his hotel phone. The sound echoed around the room, far more intrusive and unexpected than his mobile. He looked at the digital clock on the television opposite his bed: 2.42 a.m. At first he thought it must be a wrong number or a wake-up call sent through to the wrong room. The ringing seemed like it would never stop, so he picked it up to let them know it was a mistake.

'Hello?' he said.

'Adam?' The word was slurred, thick. Adam's brain was foggy, unable to place the voice.

Why would someone be calling him in the middle of the night? And then he remembered. It was Lauren's hen night. Was it one of her friends? He'd scribbled the number of the hotel down on a piece of paper and left it in the kitchen.

The voice on the other end was silent. Was this some kind of a joke the hens were playing? Some kind of punishment for the card Lauren thought Jimmy had sent?

'Hello?' Adam repeated.

'Lauren's had an accident,' the voice said slowly.

Adam's blood ran cold, Amanda's face flashing through his mind. Had she done something to Lauren?

'What's happened?'

'She's fallen down some stairs. She's in hospital. You need to get back home. Now.'

CHAPTER TWENTY-FIVE

Lauren

When they got to A&E, all the seats were taken, so they stood in the crowded waiting room.

'Must be strange for you to be on this side of the divide,' Zoe said.

'Yeah, it is a bit,' Lauren said, looking at a man lying passed out on the floor.

Zoe lifted Lauren's sash over her head and handed it to her. She'd forgotten she had it on. It was boiling hot in the waiting room, and Lauren was starting to sober up. She felt desperately thirsty, so she got up to buy a couple of bottles of water from the machine. A group of men hovered nearby. 'Good night, ladies?' one of them leered, spotting their T-shirts. Penis-shaped confetti fluttered off Lauren's handbag and onto the floor, and she flushed.

Lauren ignored the laughing men, taking the water back to Zoe. She could only carry it in one hand, and she thought with alarm about the impact her injured wrist might have on the wedding. Would she be able to hold the bouquet? Or manage the first dance?

Downing some more paracetamol, she looked at her wrist. The swelling had gone down a bit, but it definitely needed checking out, just in case it was broken. When they'd stood outside the club, they'd considered calling the police and telling them that Lauren had been pushed. But they'd decided it wasn't worth it. It had been raining and they didn't have coats, and by the time the police came, whoever had done it would be long gone. It wasn't an emergency, and Lauren had decided the best thing to do was to report it in the morning and request the CCTV from the club. She thought they'd take her more seriously when she was sober.

'I'm sure someone pushed me down the stairs,' Lauren said to Zoe. She played with the bride-to-be sash in her hands, running her fingers over the fabric. 'It was a proper shove. I'm going to follow up with the police in the morning.'

'Let me know if you want me to come with you. For moral support.'

Lauren shook her head. 'I'll be fine. I'm just wondering who would have done it.'

'Maybe they were just an impatient stranger wanting to hurry you along?'

Lauren nodded. She knew violent interactions in clubs weren't uncommon. It was probably why the bouncers had been so quick to act. She'd seen some of the results in A&E: injuries from a glassing – a retaliation for queue-jumping; head injuries from fights after punters had been ejected by the bouncers, and several serious sexual assaults. It was more than possible that a drunk stranger had been pissed off with her for going too slowly down the stairs.

But... she wasn't completely sure. Why her? Why not Zoe? Perhaps the bride-to-be sash she had been wearing had made her an easy target. Or perhaps it was someone who was targeting her specifically. She thought of the maggots in the flowers and the card with its vicious message.

'You don't think it's connected, do you? To the flowers I got?'

'You think the person who sent the flowers came to the club and pushed you down the stairs?' Zoe replied doubtfully.

'No, I guess not. That's silly, isn't it?'

'How would they even know where we'd gone?'

'They could have followed us.'

'They'd have had to wait outside your block of flats for us to leave and then followed our Ubers to the club. I doubt it…'

Lauren put her hand to her temple. 'Yeah, you're right. That does sound crazy.'

'Plus, we would have spotted someone if they'd followed us all night.' Zoe rubbed Lauren's good arm comfortingly. 'It's just the drink talking. I'm sure it was some random stranger who knocked into you trying to get down the stairs. Try to forget about it.'

Three hours later, Lauren left the hospital with instructions to rest her hand before the wedding. Luckily the X-ray had shown that nothing was broken.

By the time she got back to her flat, it was already daylight and Sunday-morning joggers were running along the pavements as she went past in a taxi.

She let herself into her block with her key fob, saying good morning to the security guard, who looked at her hesitantly. She was still clutching her sash and her hand was bandaged. In the lift, she saw her reflection in the mirror, mascara trailing down her face. She cringed when she thought of how she must have appeared at A&E, in front of her colleagues.

As she let herself into the flat and shut the door behind her, she breathed a sigh of relief, glad to be home. Around the living room were the scattered remains of the hen party: a half-full bottle of prosecco next to the sofa, empty glasses on every surface. In the kitchen, pizza boxes were piled next to the bin. Lauren shuddered when she realised that underneath the oily smell of the pizza, she could still detect the faintly rotten scent of the flowers.

She felt sweaty and dirty, but desperate to sleep. She would clear up later. She took off her dress and chucked it in the washing basket, then forced herself to go to the bathroom to brush her teeth. As she went past Kiera's room, she saw the door was wide open. No one was there. Perhaps she'd hooked up.

In the bathroom, her head pounded and the overhead light felt offensively bright. She was about to drag herself back to bed when she noticed something. The shower curtain was drawn around the bath. That didn't make sense. It was only ever drawn if someone was using the shower.

She frowned. She knew she hadn't pulled the curtain round. Her brain whirred, thinking of the empty space behind the curtain. A space big enough to hide in. She swallowed, and despite having cleaned her teeth, the taste in her mouth was still sour.

'Hello?' she said softly, feeling faintly ridiculous.

She didn't really think there was someone behind the curtain, did she? Someone who had remained still and quiet as she'd unlocked the flat, who had listened while she brushed her teeth.

She reached out towards the white plastic shower curtain and hesitated for a moment, the material between her fingers.

'Stop being silly,' she whispered to herself. Taking a deep breath, she tried to sweep the curtain back, but it was heavy and unwieldy, refusing to move smoothly. It was stuck at the bottom, caught in the water.

Something warm brushed her leg and she screamed. She looked down to see that it was only Misty, who fled at the sound of her fear before she could reach down to comfort her.

Shaking, Lauren turned back to the bath. It was full. She stared, unable to make sense of it. Only half the bath was visible. And the water she could see was red.

Lauren jumped back in shock. Was it blood? Was someone bleeding in there? Kiera?

No, she told herself, her heart racing. It wasn't blood. It couldn't be blood.

And besides, if someone was in there, she'd be able to see their body. Whoever had done this was gone.

She twisted her engagement ring on her finger nervously, and then peered round the edge of the curtain, her pulse galloping. But there was no one there.

She let out a shaky breath.

The bath was filled with pale red liquid and there were bright red smears on the inside of the shower curtain. It must be paint. Blood would have darkened and congealed, but this was still bright red.

As she reached in to pull the plug, she felt the small metal balls of the chain, but also something else. Hair. She pulled her hand away quickly and peered into the water. There was something there. A dark shape under the surface.

She held her breath, reached into the water quickly and pulled the plug.

As the water drained away the features emerged. Big blue eyes. A wedding dress stained red. Long dark hair trailing towards the plughole. A doll. Deep cuts through its dress and plastic body. The head severed so it was hanging off at the neck.

CHAPTER TWENTY-SIX

Lauren

Lauren ran into the bedroom, her heart pounding. Someone must have broken in, must have been in their flat while she was out. She dug around in her handbag for her phone, intending to call the police, but it wasn't there. Then she remembered. It had flown out of her bag in the club. Instead she pulled out her computer, went onto Facebook and messaged Zoe. Zoe lived a bit further away from the hospital than Lauren did and she would have only just got home. Lauren sighed with relief when she replied immediately. She was coming straight over.

Pacing up and down the flat, Lauren thought about the doll she'd left in the bathroom. It was the same doll that had been in the card. When she'd tried to lift it out it was heavy, as if its plastic shell had been filled with something to weigh it down. As if it had been drowned.

When Zoe arrived, she looked worn and exhausted, but she immediately took control.

'Have you rung the police?'

'No, I don't have my phone. I lost it at the club, remember?'

'I'll ring them now. Say you've been broken into.'

Lauren listened as Zoe spoke to them, explaining what had happened. When she hung up, she said, 'They won't be here for a little while. Do you want me to make you a coffee?'

'Yes, please.'

'I can't believe someone would do this. While you were on your hen night, too.'

'Do you think they knew?'

'Knew what?'

'That I was on my hen night. That that's why I wasn't in the flat.'

'I don't know… Can I see it? The doll?'

'They must have known… the doll's in a wedding dress.' Lauren felt tears pricking her eyes. She felt unmoored. It was just sinking in what this all meant.

Leading Zoe into the bathroom, she showed her the doll.

'It's… shocking,' Zoe said, lifting it up, trying to hold its head in place.

'I know.'

'It's the same one as on the card, isn't it? The one you got in the post.'

Lauren nodded. 'But Adam said Jimmy sent that. And Jimmy confirmed it himself.' Yet that didn't seem right, it couldn't be right. Not now.

'Did they steal anything?' Zoe interrupted Lauren's thoughts.

'I don't know. I haven't checked.'

'We should look, before the police arrive.'

Together they went round the flat, checking that everything was there. When they got to Lauren and Adam's bedroom, they spotted the jewellery box on the bed. Lauren stared. She was sure she had left her mother's bracelet on top of it before they'd gone to the club.

Her heart was pounding as she opened the box. Perhaps one of the others had put it back for her.

'Is everything there?' Zoe asked.

Lauren pulled out the pieces of jewellery, but she couldn't find the bracelet.

'My mother's bracelet. It's gone,' Lauren said, starting to sob. Zoe gently helped her sit down on the bed and put her arm around her. 'I don't understand how this can be happening,' Lauren said breathlessly. 'Whoever came into the flat only took the bracelet, and it's not even worth anything.'

Her head spun with it all. They must have known what it meant to her. She thought queasily about how she had shown it to all her hens earlier. It couldn't be one of them, could it?

'Was it at the top of your jewellery box? Maybe they just grabbed the first thing they saw and left.'

'Maybe.' But it seemed so unlikely. Not when everything else that had happened was connected to the wedding.

'I'm worried about you, Lauren. Do you want to stay at mine until Adam gets back?'

'He's not back for a couple of days.' She looked at her watch. It was eight o'clock already. She'd been up all night.

'Do you think it's all the same person?' Lauren asked.

'What?'

'The engagement card. The maggots. The doll in the bath.'

'It must be, mustn't it? It can't be two different people with the same idea.'

'And my fall down the stairs? Do you think the same person pushed me?'

Zoe's brow furrowed. 'Are you absolutely sure someone pushed you? Are you sure you weren't just drunk? Because if someone pushed you, then that would mean you're in real danger, that someone's actually trying to hurt you.'

Lauren ran her fingers through her hair, her mind galloping as she tried to make sense of it all.

The buzzer for the flat interrupted her thoughts, an angry growl disturbing the silence.

'I guess that's the police,' Zoe said.

CHAPTER TWENTY-SEVEN

Adam

Adam sat on the plane, watching the green fields coming up towards him as it descended to land. He was desperate to get off and get home. He'd tried to call Lauren before he'd left Spain, but she hadn't answered and neither had any of her hens or his mother. The person who'd called his room had hung up before she'd given him any more information about what had happened, and the hotel reception hadn't been able to give him her number. He didn't know what was going on.

He'd got the first available flight and spent the entire journey on edge. Every eventuality had flashed through his head. What if Lauren hadn't answered because she was unconscious in hospital? What if it was something worse? He hated being up in the sky without mobile phone reception, unsure if she'd called him back.

As soon as the plane's wheels hit the tarmac, he got out his phone. He was sure she'd have left him a message by now. But the only notification on his phone was yet another missed call from Amanda. His heart sank.

He remembered Amanda laughingly saying she'd given as good as she got to the boyfriend who had broken her arm, and he shivered. He ran through the terminal and jumped into a taxi, getting back home in forty-five minutes. As he waited for the lift, he tapped his hands against his jeans pockets nervously. He nodded to the security guard.

'Everything alright?' the guard asked Adam.

Adam shook his head. 'I don't know. Lauren's fallen down some stairs. Hurt herself.' It occurred to him she might still be at the hospital. 'Has she come back home?'

The security guard nodded. 'Yeah. The police have been here, too.'

Adam's heart beat faster. *The police.* What had happened? He pictured Lauren tumbling down the stairs, her head cracking on the floor. The police could only be here because someone else was involved. Bile rose in his throat.

'Is Lauren OK?'

'I don't know. She seemed a bit unsteady, but otherwise fine.' Adam felt sick with relief.

'Thanks.' The lift beeped and he stumbled inside. Digging his nails into his palms, he waited for it to rise to his floor. What was going on?

When he got to his flat, the door was open.

He peered inside and saw two policewomen coming towards him.

'Hello?' he said.

'Hi,' one replied. 'We're on our way out.'

'Is Lauren alright?'

'She's fine. Just had a nasty shock. Her friend's been looking after her.'

'Lauren,' he called out as he went inside. She appeared, her face tear-stained. Zoe stood behind her.

He wrapped his arms around her, stroked her hair back from her face. She smelt of stale sweat and alcohol, her eyes bloodshot. He released her to give her space to talk.

She looked up at him, her face full of questions. 'You should be in Barcelona.'

'Someone called me and told me about your fall. One of your hens, I think. Are you OK?'

'I'm fine. At least, I am now.'

'What happened? Why were the police here?'

'There was a break-in,' Zoe said softly.

'What did they take?'

'My mother's bracelet,' Lauren said. 'The one I was going to wear for our wedding.'

'I'm so sorry.' Adam hugged her again, his mind racing.

'But that wasn't the only thing they came for. They left something here,' Lauren continued.

'What do you mean?'

'It was a doll,' Lauren said, her whole body shaking. Adam took her arm and led her to the sofa, where the coffee table was covered with empty mugs. She must have been up all night.

'The police have taken it now for evidence,' Zoe said, coming over and holding her phone up towards Adam. 'I took a picture of it.'

Adam stared at the picture of Zoe holding the doll above the bath, water dripping onto the floor from its long dark hair. He recognised it from the card. It looked just like Lauren. And it had been torn apart.

Adam felt sick. Lauren must have realised by now that Jimmy hadn't sent the card. Soon she would put two and two together, realise he'd lied.

'It's horrible,' he said, stroking his fiancée's arm as she sat beside him on the sofa. 'How did they get into the flat?' He glanced back at the door; there was no sign of it being forced.

'I don't know. The police didn't think it was forced entry. They must have had a key.'

'A key?' Adam's blood ran cold.

'Or we could have left the door ajar when we went to the club, but I'm sure we didn't. And anyway, Kiera came back to the flat after we left… She would definitely have locked up.'

But Adam's mind was spinning. He'd never told Lauren about losing his keys, how he'd taken the spares to the locksmith and secretly got another set cut. He hadn't told her, because he'd lost them the night he'd walked back with Amanda. The night when his life started to unravel.

CHAPTER TWENTY-EIGHT

Adam

2001: Thailand

He ate breakfast on the terrace with his mother. As he gazed out at the ocean, he thought how, just last night, he'd been in bed with his girlfriend, listening to the same sea through the open window, discussing their plans for the future.

'It's beautiful here, isn't it?' his mother said.

He nodded. 'Perfect.'

'You know, all those years I was with your father, we never came anywhere as nice as this on holiday. He was always too busy working.'

He felt his body tense. He hated it when she made everything about his father. His father had a lot of faults, but he didn't want to be constantly reminded of them.

'It's wonderful here, Mum. Thanks for treating me.'

'We haven't seen so much of you lately.'

'Oh,' he said, thinking of all the times he'd crept away from the others so he could be alone with his girlfriend.

'I heard you last night, talking. And I've seen the two of you together.' He flushed, alarmed that his mother had found out. 'You mustn't rush into relationships,' she continued. 'I know you feel you know her well already. You grew up together. But that doesn't mean you need to hurry things along. Your father and

I got together too young, had children too young. I gave up so much of my life for him.'

'I'm not like you, Mum,' he said, unable to keep the bitter tone out of his voice.

'You're my son. I love you more than anyone else. And I don't want to see you making a huge mistake.'

'I think I'm falling in love with her,' he said, embarrassed to admit the depth of his emotions. His mother didn't understand how he felt.

She frowned at him, and then reached out and ran her hand through his hair.

'You don't know the first thing about love,' she said softly.

CHAPTER TWENTY-NINE

Lauren

After Adam had brought Lauren a much-needed coffee, he'd tidied up the flat, taking the empty pizza boxes and prosecco bottles down to the bin. The place looked normal again, but Lauren couldn't get comfortable. Someone had been in her home. Someone who wanted to scare her, possibly even hurt her.

Lauren leaned into Adam on the sofa, looking down at her wrist ruefully. It was red and swollen.

'Is it painful?' Adam asked, following her gaze.

'A little. Luckily it's not broken, just bruised. If I rest it the swelling should go down before the wedding day.'

'So what happened?'

'I fell down the stairs in the club. Well, I think someone pushed me.'

Adam's eyes widened, but before he could reply they were interrupted by the sound of a key in the lock.

They both jumped, but it was only Kiera.

'Hi,' Lauren said.

Kiera frowned. 'Adam – I wasn't expecting you back already.'

'I came back early because of Lauren's accident.'

'Accident?' Kiera replied, her eyes narrowing with confusion.

Lauren remembered that they hadn't managed to find Kiera before they left and without a phone, she couldn't text her. Now she could see that Kiera was still in last night's clothes. Lauren guessed she'd gone home with the man from the drum and bass room.

She glanced up at Adam, and noticed he was looking disapprovingly at Kiera.

'Lauren was pushed down the stairs, at the club,' he said.

'Really? I didn't know.'

'And someone broke into the flat. Lauren said you were the last to leave. Did you leave the door open?' Adam's voice sounded accusatory, and Kiera looked at him in surprise.

'No, of course not.'

'They've stolen my mother's bracelet,' Lauren said.

Kiera crinkled her brow in sympathy. 'I'm so sorry. I know how much that meant to you.'

'And someone left a doll in the bath,' continued Lauren.

'A doll? What are you talking about?'

'A doll that looked like me. Cut into pieces. In a slashed wedding dress. I guess it was supposed to be dead. The police took it away.' Lauren was still struggling to process what had happened. It was all so surreal.

'What?' Kiera's eyes widened in astonishment. 'Who would do something like that?'

'I have no idea.' Lauren shivered when she thought about it, her heart beating faster. It really could be anyone taunting her. A stranger. A friend. She just didn't know.

Kiera looked at Adam, but Lauren couldn't read her expression. 'They did it when you were away at the conference,' she said. 'Do you think they knew? Maybe they thought Lauren would be on her own when she came back to the flat. Wanted to properly scare her.'

Adam shook his head. 'I don't know.'

Lauren frowned. 'But they wouldn't have known I'd be on my own. You would have been with me, Kiera. If you hadn't hooked up.'

'Maybe they thought I was still at the conference too.'

Lauren stopped still. So that's where Kiera had been. She'd said she was doing career training, but she'd been at the conference with Adam. Why had neither of them mentioned it to her?

'I didn't realise you'd gone to the conference, Kiera? I thought it was just for doctors.' Lauren knew exactly what the conference was about. She was on their mailing list and had seen the email with all the details. It *was* targeted at doctors.

'I did go to medical school, Lauren, remember. I'm not too stupid to understand.'

'I didn't mean it like that,' Lauren said quickly, realising how it must have sounded.

'Kiera's planning to retrain to be a psychiatric nurse.'

Kiera reddened. 'I'm still thinking about it, trying to work out whether I can do it. I'm getting older. It seems a bit late.'

'I'm sure it's not too late,' Lauren said, trying to make up for her insensitivity. 'You just didn't mention you were at the conference.' Lauren looked over at her fiancé and saw his cheeks reddening. She didn't know why she was focusing on Kiera. Really it was Adam who should have told her. 'Neither of you mentioned it,' she said more forcefully.

'I just felt a bit embarrassed, that's all,' Kiera said.

Lauren looked from Adam to Kiera and back again. Was there more to this than they were admitting? Had they wanted to be alone at the hotel together? Why hadn't they mentioned it? The questions whirled through her mind.

Lauren looked at her watch. She'd completely lost track of time. It was already 2 p.m., and she still hadn't slept or showered since yesterday.

'Tracey!' she said suddenly. 'I was supposed to be meeting Tracey and Jasmine for coffee in Covent Garden before they fly home. I'll have to ring her and cancel.' Once again she remembered that she didn't have her mobile. She'd have to go back to the club later, try and find it.

'Can I borrow your phone?' she asked Adam.

He hesitated for a split second before unlocking it and handing it to her.

When Tracey answered, Lauren explained about the break-in, how their mother's bracelet had been stolen and apologised for not being able to meet today. Tracey was shocked and sympathetic and it seemed easier not to mention all the other things that had happened. Lauren didn't want to worry her sister before she flew back. She had enough on her plate with the divorce.

After she hung up, Lauren looked down at her swollen wrist and thought of all the things she needed to do. She wanted to get the locks changed on the flat. The police had said that there was no sign of a break-in and, unless they'd left the door ajar, the intruder must have used a key. She needed to ring the club to see if her phone had been handed in. And more than anything, she needed to sleep. She had been up all night and she needed to be in a fit state to go to work tomorrow.

She handed the phone back to Adam. 'Hey,' he said, looking at the screen. 'Did you see this text?'

'What text?'

'It must have just come through. Someone's messaged to say they've found your phone.'

'At the club?'

'It doesn't say.'

Her brow furrowed. 'But how did they know to message you?'

'They said they took your sim out and put it in another phone. I was the first person listed in the contacts. Stroke of luck, I guess. They wouldn't have known I was your fiancé.'

'I'm just so glad someone found it.'

'They want to meet you to hand it over. They live the other side of London. I've got the address.'

'Tell them I'll head over now.'

'OK, I'll come with you. I don't want you going on your own. Not after last night. It scared the life out of me when I got that call.'

They sat side by side on the train, rows of red-brick terraced houses flashing by, as Lauren thought through everything that had happened. First the card with the picture of the doll, then the flowers full of maggots, then being pushed down the stairs, while someone placed the mutilated doll in the bath and stole her mother's bracelet.

Someone was targeting her and it was all connected to the wedding.

One thing she was sure of was that Jimmy hadn't send the card. He'd lied to her, to protect someone. It could only be Adam. She looked over at her fiancé, her stomach churning. How could she trust him now?

'One thing confuses me…' she said to him.

'What?'

'It must be the same person who put the doll in the bath as sent the card. But Jimmy said he sent the card.'

She felt Adam stiffen beside her, but he said nothing.

'Jimmy didn't send that card, did he?' Lauren said, looking at Adam, anger bubbling inside her, her voice rising from a whisper to a shout. 'He lied to me. You lied to me.'

A woman opposite them in the carriage looked up from her newspaper curiously, as Adam ran his fingers through his hair. She'd always thought he was easy to read, that he wore his emotions on his face. But now she wondered if she'd been naive, if really he'd been keeping secrets from her.

He glanced up at her, and she could see he was nervous. 'There's something I need to tell you,' he said.

CHAPTER THIRTY

Adam

Adam took a deep breath and looked at Lauren, wondering how much he should say.

'I think I know who's been doing all this,' he said quietly.

'Who? And why didn't you say?' Lauren's eyes bored into him, challenging him. He watched the world flash by the train windows and wished he was anywhere but here.

'I should have said.' He rubbed the side of his head, feeling a headache brewing. 'I thought she was harmless. I had no idea she'd do anything like this.'

'Who is it?' Lauren's jaw had tightened; her lips were pursed.

'It's a patient. She's called Amanda. She has some... issues.'

'What?' Lauren looked baffled. This was a good start though, he thought. She wasn't angry. Yet.

He looked down at the dirty train floor as he tried to gather his thoughts, watching an old crisp packet float up in the breeze as the double doors of the carriage beeped open. 'She's got a bit of a crush on me. Well, it must be more than that. A kind of obsession.'

'Why didn't you mention it?' Lauren's voice cracked as it got louder.

'I didn't want to worry you. You've had so much on, preparing for the wedding.'

'You think she sent the card? Put the doll in the bath?' Lauren's eyes widened. 'Do you think she pushed me down the stairs, too?'

'I don't know…' It seemed like such a big thing to say. But from the moment Lauren had shown him the card, he'd been sure it was Amanda. She must have done everything else, too. Guilt rippled through him. This was all his fault and he needed to fix this, make everything OK for his fiancée.

'I'm going to speak to her. Do something about it.'

'It's a bit late for that, isn't it?' Lauren fiddled with her engagement ring. 'She's dangerous.'

'Don't worry,' Adam said, putting his hand on her leg reassuringly. 'Leave it with me. I'll fix it.'

'Don't you think it's a police matter? We should tell them.' Lauren wrung her hands together.

He nodded. 'I will. After I've spoken to her.' But he couldn't mention her to the police, could he? Not when she had something on him. Not when she could cost him his career.

'I don't understand. How would she even know about the wedding? My hen night?'

'I have our engagement photo on my desk. She asked about it once. I told her we were getting married in August.'

'Oh.'

Adam sighed. 'I wish I hadn't said anything at all. But I was just making small talk while the computer loaded.' He looked at Lauren, hoping she believed him.

She searched his eyes. 'Why did you lie to me, Adam? Why did you pretend the card was from Jimmy?'

'There was no point in worrying you. I really didn't think she'd do anything else. I honestly didn't think you were at risk. And I didn't want you stressed before the wedding.'

'So you got Jimmy to lie too, to tell me he sent the card?'

'Yeah. I thought it was for the best,' he replied, his cheeks flaming.

Lauren's gaze was fiery. 'But it wasn't, was it? It gave me a false sense of security, made me think things were OK. And then she pushed me down the stairs and drowned a doll in a wedding dress in our bath. She must be crazy.'

'I think she is.'

'You haven't done anything to make her think you're interested in her, have you?'

Adam tried to keep his face completely blank. 'No, of course not.'

'So nothing's happened between you?' Lauren blushed. 'I'm sorry, but I have to ask. You remember what the card said: *He doesn't love you.* Why would she write that?'

'You know me, Lauren. I'd never do anything like that. It's all one-sided. I thought I could handle her.' He gazed into her pale blue eyes. He hoped she believed him. He needed her to.

'You're obviously not handling her very well, if she's doing this to me. How would she even have our address?'

Adam's stomach churned as he tried to gather his thoughts. What was the explanation for that? A stalker. She was a stalker. That was partly true.

He put his head in his hands. 'She followed me home once.'

'Followed you home? Why wouldn't you mention that? Why didn't you report her to the partners at work?'

'At the time I thought we just happened to be walking the same way. That was what she said.'

'That seems a bit of a coincidence, doesn't it?'

'I suppose so,' Adam sighed. At least she believed him about Amanda following him home. That was a start. 'I was tired at the time,' he said. 'It just didn't cross my mind she might be interested in me.'

Lauren shook her head. 'So you really think she did all this?'

'I can't think of anyone else. Can you?'

Lauren shook her head. 'No, I can't. She must have broken in.'

'Maybe Kiera left the door ajar.' He prayed that his friend would forgive him for this. But he couldn't tell Lauren that Amanda might have a key – there would be no coming back from that.

'What are we going to do, Adam?' Lauren's eyes filled with tears and he put his arm around her.

'I think we just have to leave it with the police. I don't see what else we can do. I'll speak to them.'

'You need to get her off your patient list.'

'Of course,' he said. 'I'll speak to the partners.' But he had no intention of doing that. The only person he could speak to was Amanda herself.

Lauren looked up at him. 'I'm scared, Adam,' she said, and his heart ached for her. 'The doll – the way its neck was severed. What if she does something worse, something even more violent?'

Adam didn't have an answer for that.

'She doesn't want me to marry you. What do you think she'll do next?' Lauren continued, her voice growing more desperate. 'She pushed me down the stairs. What if she turns up at the church?'

'She can't do that. She doesn't know the date of our wedding, or where it is. Don't worry, Lauren. I know what she's doing now. I'll be watching and waiting. So will the police. I won't let her hurt you.'

CHAPTER THIRTY-ONE

Lauren

Lauren's head was spinning with everything Adam had said. He had known who had sent the card all along. And instead of telling her, he'd lied to her and got Jimmy to lie to her too. If he had lied about this, then what else might he have lied about?

'This is our stop,' Adam said, checking the directions on his phone as the underground train pulled into the station. 'Then it's just a short walk from here.'

Lauren nodded. She couldn't wait to get her mobile back. She hated the idea of being alone in the flat, defenceless, without even a phone to ring for help. She wished they'd set up a landline, but they'd never felt the need before.

Once she had her phone, everything would feel safer and more manageable, she told herself. She was also desperate to text Zoe, to tell her what Adam had said about Amanda, see what she thought.

'It's only ten minutes from here,' Adam said as they climbed the steps out of the station. They were in an unfamiliar part of London. A shiny new block of flats looked down on a road full of run-down charity shops and boarded-up pubs. The pavements were crowded and littered with black rubbish bags, pedestrians weaving in and out around them.

Lauren and Adam made their way down the high street and then turned into a residential road. Soon they were standing outside a whitewashed terraced house with a neat garden and bins with the number of the house embossed on them. Red roses peeked out from above the small brick wall which separated the front garden from the street.

'This is it,' Adam said, double-checking his phone.

Lauren walked up the path and knocked on the door.

A woman in her fifties eventually answered, and looked at the two of them suspiciously.

'Hello. Can I help you?' she said.

'We've come to collect my phone. Thanks so much for finding it.'

The woman's eyebrows crinkled in confusion. 'What phone? I think you must have the wrong address.'

'No, no, we don't,' Adam said quickly, as he saw the door starting to shut. 'This is twenty-two Whitstable Street, isn't it?'

'Yes, it is.'

'But I'm guessing you're not Hannah?'

'No.'

'Hannah sent me a text to say she'd found my fiancée's phone. In Vertex nightclub.'

'There's no one called Hannah living here. You must have the wrong address.' And with that, she shut the door in their faces.

They looked at the closed door in disbelief. Adam showed Lauren his phone. It clearly said the address and was signed off: Hannah.

'She wouldn't have got her own address wrong, would she?'

'No.' Lauren was at a loss. 'Maybe she typed in the wrong house number? Or there's another Whitstable Street in the area?'

'I'll ring her.' They went back down the garden path and stood on the pavement outside the house. Lauren saw the woman peering out of an upstairs window, watching them.

Adam held the phone to his ear. 'She's not answering.' He hung up and then tried again, waiting until he got to answerphone.

'Hi Hannah,' he said. 'We're at the house to pick up the phone. Number twenty-two Whitstable Street? But the woman who's here says she hasn't heard of you. I think we must have got the wrong place. Could you ring me back?'

He hung up and stared at the phone for a second, as if expecting it to ring.

'Pass it here,' Lauren said. She opened up Google Maps and searched for Whitstable Street. The nearest other road with the same name was over ten miles away.

'We haven't got the wrong one,' Lauren said, holding up the phone.

'No, she's even given a postcode.'

'Try calling her again.' Taking the phone, Adam called her but there was still no answer.

'Let's get a coffee while we wait for her to call back,' Lauren said. 'I could do with the pick-me-up.'

'You've been up all night,' Adam said, putting an arm around her, as they walked down the street to find a coffee shop. 'No wonder you're tired. How's your wrist?'

'Feeling a bit better now. I don't think it's as bad as it first looked.'

There was a tiny café at the end of the street and they sat down at a small table in a corner and ordered coffees.

As soon as the waitress brought them their drinks, Adam's phone started vibrating. 'That will be Hannah,' he said. 'Typical timing.'

'I'm sure she won't mind if we finish our coffees first,' Lauren said, taking a sip and scalding her lips.

Adam looked at the caller display. 'It's not Hannah. It's Kiera.'

'Hi,' he said, frowning as she spoke. 'What does she say it's about?' he carried on. Lauren watched his face turning redder.

'What's going on?' she mouthed.

He shook his head.

'Has she said who she is?' he asked. 'Just tell her to go. Hang up and don't let her in.' Lauren could just make out Kiera speaking to someone on the other end of the phone. 'Are you OK?' Adam asked Kiera. Then, after a pause, 'Hopefully she's gone for good.'

'What was that about?' Lauren asked when he'd hung up.

'Someone buzzing our flat asking to speak to me. They wouldn't say who they were or what it was about.'

'Amanda?'

'Possibly. I don't know.' Lauren could see the bafflement in his eyes. 'I really have no idea.'

CHAPTER THIRTY-TWO

Lauren

Lauren was half an hour early for work. It had been the same yesterday, her first day back after her hen night. She'd left before Adam and Kiera, not wanting to be in the flat on her own. Despite changing the locks, she still felt unsafe in her own home. Luckily she was going out tonight. Kiera was treating her and Adam to a meal at the pub to thank them for letting her stay.

Lauren had time to grab a coffee before she started so she went to the hospital café and ordered herself a flat white. She'd brought her laptop with her, so she could communicate with her friends if she needed to. Without a phone, she felt lost. When Hannah hadn't answered Adam's calls, they'd eventually realised that she was never going to return it. The whole trip to the other side of London had just been a ruse. Adam had thought that Hannah was really Amanda, and that she must have picked up Lauren's phone after she fell. Lauren had told the police what had happened, and they were going to look into it alongside CCTV from the club when Lauren had been pushed down the stairs.

She got out her computer and emailed Zoe to update her on what had happened after she'd found the doll in the bath. How Adam had confessed that he thought it was a patient of his who'd sent the card; how Kiera had told them that a strange woman was looking for Adam. She wanted to ask Zoe if she thought she could trust Adam, but somehow she couldn't seem to make herself write it down. It would sound like she was losing faith in her fiancé. It would be much easier to speak to her on the phone, explain everything properly.

After she'd finished typing, her injured wrist ached, and she realised she needed to take it easy if it was going to be better in time for the wedding.

Just then, a Facebook message popped up from Tracey.

> *I'm all settled back in Thailand now. Just checking in to make sure you were OK after the break-in?*

Lauren paused for a moment and then replied, *I'm fine.*

The computer started ringing then. Tracey was calling her on Skype. Lauren felt anxious as she pulled her headphones out of her bag, put them in her ears and answered. She didn't know whether she should tell Tracey everything that had happened. She wasn't sure if she felt comfortable confiding in her.

On the screen, Tracey was sitting in an outdoor restaurant at one of her hotels. 'I've been texting you to say what a great time Jasmine and I had, but you didn't reply,' she said. 'I wanted to check you were OK.' Lauren could hear the clink of cutlery against plates and could see a barman opening a bottle of wine for a couple at a table behind her. It was a far cry from the hospital café.

'I don't have my phone at the moment…' Lauren said, trailing off.

'Was it stolen in the break-in?'

Lauren didn't want to explain. 'No, I lost it in the club.'

'That's unlucky.' She paused. 'Lauren – is everything alright? You don't seem yourself.'

No, Lauren thought. *Nothing's alright.*

'What's wrong?'

'It's just Adam,' Lauren said, with a sigh. 'He's… well, he's had this patient interested in him, stalking him. She sent me a threatening card.' She couldn't bring herself to tell her sister about being pushed down the stairs, or about the doll in the bath.

'Really?' The sun was shining behind Tracey, casting her in shadow and making it difficult to read her expression.

Suddenly Lauren felt exhausted with it all. Could she tell Tracey her fears about Adam? She was her sister, after all... 'It's not just that, Tracey – he lied to me. He pretended someone else sent it – one of his stags. Because he didn't want me to know about her.'

'What did the card say?'

'"He doesn't love you",' she said quietly, looking round the coffee shop to check no one was listening.

'And he didn't want you to know it was her? Do you think... Look, I don't want to upset you... but do you think something might have happened between them?'

Lauren let out a strangled noise. 'I don't know,' she said. 'I mean, I trust him. I really do. And I want to believe it's all innocent. But he did lie to me.'

Tracey was silent for a moment. 'He was always a player, wasn't he, back in the day?' She sighed. 'But I thought those days were long gone.'

'I don't know what to do, Tracey. We're getting married in less than two weeks, and I feel like I don't know him at all. I mean, everything might be completely fine, but I don't know that. I feel like I'm going into this marriage with my eyes closed.'

'You don't have to marry him, you know.'

'I love him.'

'Have you thought about checking up on him? Looking at his phone to see if there's anything going on?'

Lauren shook her head slowly. 'I don't know,' she said. 'It just doesn't seem right to me.' It was something she'd told herself she'd never do. She believed that if you trusted your partner then you'd never check his phone. But this was different. He'd lied to her. And she needed to find out the truth before the wedding.

'OK, fair enough,' Tracey said. 'It would just be one way of getting to the bottom of this.'

Lauren looked at her sister. She'd known Adam for as long as Lauren had. They'd all grown up together.

'Would you trust Adam?' she asked.

Tracey laughed lightly. 'Not in the past,' she said, and Lauren thought of the string of girlfriends he'd had when they were all at school. 'But I don't really know him any more. You're the one who knows what he's really like, not me.'

After her shift finished, Lauren put her make-up on in the staff toilets in A&E and then got the tube to meet Adam and Kiera. She felt the solid oak door of the pub under her palm as she pushed it open. They were sitting in a corner, at a small round table, heads bent towards each other, deep in conversation. Adam had a pint in front of him and she had a glass of white wine. If she didn't already know them, Lauren would have mistaken them for a couple.

They didn't look up until she was standing right above them. Kiera saw her first, jumping up and giving her a hug. 'Lauren!'

'I'll get you a chair,' Adam said, and pulled one from the nearest table.

'Thanks.'

'What do you want to drink? White wine?' asked Adam.

Lauren nodded. 'Yes, please.' She tended to avoid alcohol on weekdays, but today she could do with a drink.

'The Sauvignon's nice,' Kiera said, swirling hers round her glass.

'Do you want another?' Lauren asked.

'I'll get them,' Kiera said. 'It's my treat. And should we order food now? I'm starving.'

'Me too,' Adam said.

'Your usual?' Kiera asked him with a smile.

'Yes, please.'

Clearly they came here a lot more often than she'd thought, Lauren realised as she watched the exchange.

'I'll come with you to the bar,' Lauren said. 'I need to see the menu.'

'How are you doing today?' the barwoman asked Kiera.

'Yeah, great thanks. How are you?'

'Alright. Bit quiet tonight.'

'I'm sure it will pick up later.'

'So what are you having? Two cheeseburgers?'

Kiera grinned. 'Yeah, two cheeseburgers. And Lauren's just deciding.'

Lauren's eyebrows drew together. How often did Adam come here with Kiera, that the barmaid knew their order?

'Make it three today,' Lauren said.

'I love that ring,' the barmaid said to Lauren as she poured the pint. 'It's beautiful.'

'Thank you.'

'I've been married three times now. I hope you've picked a good one.'

'He's just over there,' Lauren replied, pointing Adam out.

'Oh,' the barmaid said. 'Ohhh…' She glanced from Kiera to Lauren, then back again, a small frown knotting her features. 'I always thought… never mind. Congratulations. When's the big day?'

Lauren shifted her weight from one leg to another, annoyed.

'In a week and a half,' she said, with a forced smile.

As the barmaid went to pour their drinks, Lauren turned to Kiera. 'So, how are things at work?' she asked.

'Yeah, fine. Busy as always.'

'You know Adam thinks it's one of his patients who broke into the house – Amanda.'

'Really? Gosh. That's serious. She does have a reputation, but nothing like that.'

'What kind of reputation?'

'Just a bit flirty with the younger doctors, that's all. A few of them have requested not to see her.'

Flirty. Lauren wondered if Adam had ever been tempted by her.

'Here you go,' the barmaid interrupted, handing them their drinks before Lauren could ask any more. Kiera paid and they carried them to the table.

'I needed this pint,' Adam said. 'It's been a crazy day. Flu going round.'

'We were just talking about Amanda,' Lauren said. Adam raised his eyebrows and glanced at Kiera. It was clear he didn't want to talk about it.

'Adam thinks she's been following him,' she said to Kiera.

'You didn't mention that.' Kiera tilted her head in Adam's direction, a question in her eyes.

'I thought I had it under control.'

'Is it common?' Lauren asked. 'Patients stalking doctors?'

Adam laughed lightly. 'Only for us good-looking doctors.'

Kiera laughed too. 'Adam does have a few admirers. Mainly over seventy though.'

The cheeseburgers arrived, and Adam dug in.

'This is delicious,' he said. 'You can't beat it.'

'Do you remember that time when they brought you a second cheeseburger by mistake, and you just ate it?' said Kiera with a grin.

'Yeah,' Adam said, cringing. 'We were so drunk that night. I think I thought it was a gift from the pub because we came here so often.'

'It wasn't. It was an order for another table,' Kiera explained to Lauren, laughing. 'He was so embarrassed. He went bright red.'

'I just wasn't thinking. They put a burger in front of me and I didn't think twice about eating it.' He shrugged.

Lauren bit her lip nervously. She didn't remember him coming in steaming drunk. When was this?

'It was a Friday,' he said, as if reading her mind. 'We didn't have work in the morning.'

'I don't remember you coming in late.'

'You were on nights.'

'Wasn't that the evening you stayed at mine anyway? You couldn't find your keys,' said Kiera.

The table was suddenly quiet, and Adam looked up, meeting Lauren's eyes. He'd never mentioned that he'd lost his keys to her, never mentioned staying at Kiera's. Lauren tried to think back. There had been a Saturday morning when she'd returned from work and he wasn't there. She'd assumed he'd gone out to the gym or the shops, but she could vaguely remember something feeling off. Usually when she got back in the morning from a night shift, she could smell Adam's deodorant in the bedroom and his shower gel in the bathroom. But none of the normal scents were there. And there were no crumbs on the work surface from Adam's breakfast toast, no dirty plates in the sink. But then, exhausted from her shift, she'd gone to sleep and forgotten all about it. By the time she'd woken up he was home.

For the first time, Lauren realised how easy it would be for Adam to cheat on her. She looked over at Kiera, thought about how close they were, so close they had seemed like a couple to the barmaid. So close that he'd crashed at her flat when he lost his keys and not mentioned it to Lauren. Had there been other days when she hadn't been able to smell his deodorant, hadn't sensed his presence? She couldn't be sure.

Lauren couldn't possibly know where Adam was when she was working nights. He could be anywhere with anyone, and she'd never know. Suddenly she felt sick. She had always been so certain of their relationship, but now she was wondering if it was all built on lies.

CHAPTER THIRTY-THREE

Adam

Adam looked at the picture of him and Lauren on his desk, running his fingers over the mottled wood of the frame. His phone was ringing again.

Amanda. She still called several times a day.

He never picked up.

But now he had to. For Lauren's sake. It was his job to protect his fiancée, and he needed to tell Amanda to back off. He couldn't afford to worry about her reporting him to his work any more. Any consequences were his to face. He just needed her to stay away.

He took a deep breath before answering. 'Hello, Adam speaking,' he said, keeping his tone formal.

'Adam… oh hi!' Amanda's slightly breathless voice suggested she hadn't been expecting him to pick up. As if she just kept dialling his number on autopilot, not really caring what effect it had on him. She sounded like she was in an office, a click-clack of keys in the background. 'I'm just at work. Let me go somewhere private.'

'OK.' He listened to her footsteps, then heard a door open and shut.

'I can talk now,' she said, her words coming out in a rush. 'You never normally answer your phone. I mean, I know you're busy, but it's rude. All I want to do is talk to you.'

Adam thought of all the hurtful things she'd done to Lauren. How could she act so innocent after all of that?

'Listen… Amanda… you're going to need to back off.'

'Sorry?'

'You really need to stop. Now.'

'Is this about that romantic moment we had together?'

Adam flushed at her words. He was glad she couldn't see him sweating.

'No, of course not. It's about what you're doing to Lauren.'

She didn't seem to hear him. 'I really thought it was the start of something special. I know you're my doctor, but I don't think that matters. I think we can make it work.'

'Just stop, OK? It all needs to stop. And the appointments with me, too. I can't see you as a patient any more.'

'Yeah, that's what I'm saying. I know you're worried about your job. I understand that. If I wasn't your patient, we could see each other properly.'

'We wouldn't be seeing each other. I'm engaged. You know that.'

'But what about that night?'

'It didn't mean anything.'

He heard her sharp intake of breath. 'I thought you cared.'

'I do care. I care about your health. But that's all.'

'You shouldn't have done it then, should you? You shouldn't have led me on.'

Adam swallowed. He needed to calm her down. 'I don't think I led you on. But I'm sorry if I hurt you.'

'You're sorry? I bet you're sorry. You shouldn't have flirted with a patient like that. You're my GP. I could report you.'

'Look, Amanda. You don't need to report me. I've said sorry. But now all I want is for you to leave me alone. You need to stop tormenting Lauren. Otherwise I'm handing your name over to the police.' And with that he hung up.

He looked up then, saw Kiera standing in the doorway.

'What's going on?' she asked. 'That was Amanda, wasn't it?'

'Yeah. I told her to back off.'

'You called her? Why didn't you just report her to the partners? Tell them you thought she'd broken into your flat. They'd take her off your list immediately. You wouldn't have to see her again.'

'I didn't call her, she called me. And it's not as simple as you think,' Adam said, putting his head in his hands. He hoped that Amanda had understood what he'd said, how serious he'd been. He couldn't let her ruin everything: his job, his career, his life.

'Why not?'

'I messed up, Kiera.'

'She was at the pub that night, wasn't she?'

'What night?'

'The night you stayed at mine.'

He sighed. Had Kiera known all along? 'Did you see her?'

'No, not at the time. It's just, when we were speaking to Lauren the other day and you mentioned the night you lost your keys… When I thought about it, I remembered seeing you from the bus. Talking to someone on the street, walking along with them. I was so drunk, I'd forgotten. But the more I thought about it, the more I realised that the person was familiar. And then I realised she was a patient. Amanda… you went home with her, didn't you? I've been thinking about it all day. You must think Amanda took your key, because otherwise how would she have got into your flat? You were with her that night.'

Adam was shaking his head. 'No – I didn't take her home. I just walked her home. When we got to my flat, I didn't have my keys so I called you.'

He had noticed Amanda as he was leaving the pub, and recognised her immediately, felt the buzz of attraction that he'd felt when she'd first come through the door of his surgery. When Kiera had left to get the bus, Amanda had come over to him and told him he looked familiar but she couldn't think why. They'd both known exactly who the other was but they'd both pretended otherwise.

Kiera was frowning at him. 'You walked her home to *your* flat? Don't you normally walk someone home to their own place?'

Adam looked at his shoes. 'My flat was on the way. At least, that's what she said. I'd mentioned where I lived, and she said she had a friend who lived in the same block, just a few floors up from us. She said she had to walk past it to get home. She was already heading my way and she didn't want to walk alone. She said that she was scared walking on her own at night. So I walked with her.'

'How gentlemanly of you. But she's your patient. And you're engaged. What were you thinking?' Kiera's eyes were fiery.

Adam put his hands to his temples. 'I was drunk. I wasn't thinking straight.'

He remembered how Amanda's eyes had sparkled in the moonlight as they'd met his. He didn't seem to be able to break away from her gaze. And then imperceptibly she'd moved in until she was so close he could feel her breath on his face. He must have moved forward a bit too because then she was standing on her tiptoes and he felt her lips brush his. It had taken all of his strength to pull away.

'She tried to kiss me,' Adam said. 'Outside my block of flats. I admit I was tempted. But I didn't kiss her back.' He looked into Kiera's eyes and could see that she wasn't sure if she believed him. 'Honestly, nothing happened. Nothing worth mentioning. I had my arms round her. We nearly kissed. That was all. She wanted to come up to my flat. I told her no.'

'And then what happened?'

'She kept trying to persuade me, to kiss me, to force her way through the door to the flats. I blocked her. I told her about Lauren.' He'd put the engagement photo of him and Lauren on his desk at work afterwards, to make it clear he wasn't interested.

'And?'

'Then she seemed to collapse, have a kind of panic attack. She sat down on the floor outside. I put my coat round her, helped her. And then I ordered her an Uber from my phone. I gave her my number in case she was ill in the taxi, then watched it drive away. Afterwards I searched in my pockets for my keys, looking in my work bag, but I couldn't find them anywhere. So I called you.'

'So you think she took the keys and then broke into your flat later?'

'She must have done.'

CHAPTER THIRTY-FOUR

Lauren

In the two days since Tracey had suggested Lauren check Adam's phone, Lauren had managed to resist the temptation. Before her new phone had arrived yesterday, she could have easily asked to borrow Adam's and checked his messages. But now she no longer had the excuse of not having her own phone. If she wanted to look at his now, she needed to do it without him knowing.

Lauren looked across at her sleeping fiancé. He looked so peaceful, so innocent. She'd been tossing and turning all night. It tore her heart apart that she didn't know if she could trust him.

It was 6.30 now, and Adam's alarm would start ringing in ten minutes. She lay beside him in bed, anxiously waiting until it went off. Pretending to be asleep, she listened to him plod across the hallway to the bathroom and then reached for his phone, her heart racing. She quickly typed in his PIN. It was his birthday. He hadn't changed it. Surely that was a good sign? He couldn't have anything to hide. She felt a tiny worm of guilt work its way into her head. She shouldn't be checking his phone, she should just ask him about Amanda.

And what about Kiera? Ever since she'd learnt that she'd been at the conference and he'd stayed overnight at her flat when he'd lost his keys, she'd felt uneasy. She'd always been so close to Adam, but Lauren had never seen her as a threat before. Had she been a complete fool? An unwelcome thought crossed her mind. Kiera had a key to her flat… she wouldn't have had to break in to plant the doll.

Lauren shook the thoughts out of her mind and turned back to Adam's phone, checking his text messages. There were a lot from Kiera from before she moved in, back and forth between them. They were often arranging to go to the pub together or to chat on the phone. But then, that was what you did with friends, wasn't it? And there was no denying they were friends. Lauren frowned.

The roar of Adam's shower had quietened to just a drip and she quickly clicked back to the home screen, pressing the button on the side to lock the phone. She went to the other side of the room, her heart racing at the thought of being caught. Picking up her hairbrush, she ran it through her hair, trying to push down her guilty feelings.

She watched Adam get dressed, sliding his muscled arms into his pale yellow shirt.

'Alright?' he asked, coming up behind her and putting his hand on her shoulder. He pecked her on the cheek and she gazed at their reflection in the mirror. They looked like the perfect couple, she observed bitterly.

'I'm fine,' she said.

He squeezed her shoulders then whistled as he went to the other room, put on Radio 4 and made his breakfast. Once she was alone, she reached for his phone again and unlocked it.

Looking through his call log, she noticed there was a number who rang him regularly. Every day. They were all missed calls until yesterday, when he'd answered the phone and spoken to her for three minutes. The number was saved as 'A'. Amanda. It had to be. She grabbed an old envelope from Adam's bedside table and quickly scribbled down the number.

Her heart thumping in her chest, Lauren went through his Twitter DMs and Facebook Messenger too, but there was nothing.

She sighed, looking at his other apps. There was hardly anything else on his phone. She flicked into his PayPal app absent-mindedly. There wasn't much on it, except for an Uber receipt from two months ago. When she checked the Uber app, she didn't recognise the address. She quickly took a note of it, then returned the phone to the bedside table.

'Do you think A is Amanda?' Lauren asked Zoe. After Adam had left for work, she'd gone round to see her friend and told her everything. Harry was out at playgroup and they'd gone to Zoe's kitchen to talk.

'I don't know...' Zoe said carefully. 'I mean, I just don't think Adam would cheat on you.'

'There's an Uber receipt, too. A couple of months ago he took a taxi to an address I've never heard of. In the middle of the night. What if he slept with her?'

Lauren shook, feeling the weight of what she was suggesting. If Adam had been cheating, their relationship would be over; their future together impossible.

'Do you really think that?' Zoe replied.

Lauren paced up and down Zoe's kitchen. 'I don't know any more. I don't know what to do. Should I confront him?'

'Look, it's probably all innocent, but there is one way you could find out if A really is Amanda.'

'How?'

'Ring the number. See who answers.'

Lauren's heart pounded as she imagined listening to the ringtone, waiting to see if Amanda picked up.

'I can't ring her,' she finally replied. 'I'm a doctor. She's a patient. And even though she's not my patient... I don't know. It's just a bad idea.'

'*I'm* not a doctor,' Zoe said, with a glint in her eye.

'I'm not sure...' Lauren said, wondering if she really wanted Zoe to make the call, if she really wanted to find out what was going on, or if she wanted to stay in a state of blissful ignorance just a little while longer.

'How are you going to find out if we don't?'

'I should just ask Adam.' But Lauren already knew the flaws with that idea. He'd lied to her about Jimmy sending the card. How would she know that he wasn't lying to her again?

'Pass me the phone number.'

Reluctantly, Lauren handed over the envelope with the number scrawled on it.

Pressing a couple of digits to withhold her number first, Zoe typed the number into her phone and pressed 'call'.

She put the phone on speaker. Lauren's heart hammered as it rang and rang.

'Hello?' The voice sounded so normal, and Lauren felt a shiver of regret. Her whole world might be about to come crashing down around her. Suddenly she had an urge to run, to be anywhere but here. Her injured wrist started to throb and she realised she was pressing it too hard on the kitchen counter.

'Hello, am I speaking to Amanda?' Zoe said confidently.

'Yes, you are.'

Zoe raised her eyebrows at Lauren. Lauren felt sick, her stomach plummeting.

'Could you confirm your address for me, please?'

'Why? Who are you?' She sounded suspicious now, and Lauren thought Zoe would just hang up.

'Oh, I'm sorry,' replied Zoe, sounding surprisingly calm. 'I'm calling from the doctor's surgery. I... I have test results for you,' she said. Lauren squirmed, shaking her head violently at Zoe. She was taking this too far.

'Which doctor's surgery? How do I know this isn't a scam?'

Zoe hesitated for a moment, before evidently remembering the name of Adam's GP practice. 'Park View Surgery. Like I said, we have test results. You just need to confirm your address for me.'

Lauren widened her eyes at Zoe. 'Hang up,' she mouthed. She'd named Adam's workplace. What if Amanda told the surgery someone had called pretending to be from there?

'OK,' Amanda was saying, her voice calmer now, less suspicious. 'It's forty-nine Churchill Street.'

Lauren sank into Zoe's kitchen chair. She didn't listen as her friend said something about the tests being all clear. She was only thinking about the address. The street matched the address on Adam's Uber account. He'd been to Amanda's home. In the middle of the night.

CHAPTER THIRTY-FIVE

Adam

2001: Thailand

They lay on bean bags on top of sandy rattan mats, by the water's edge, drinking cocktails. She looked stunning, her face highlighted by the lights of the lanterns that graced every mat.

They saw a lone figure walking down the beach, back towards the beachside accommodation. 'Is that your sister?' he asked.

'I think so.'

'Shall we invite her over?'

'No,' she said. 'We've just escaped the family. I just want to be with you. Besides, you know she fancies you.'

He frowned. Did she? They'd always got on well, but he'd never thought there was anything more to it.

They watched her walk on, receding into the distance. Soon they were dancing on the sand to the beat of the bass from the speaker, arms flailing, stumbling and falling and getting back up again. The sound of their laughter and the booming music merged with the crashing waves.

A pair of fire breathers made their way up the beach, and put on a show, swallowing flames and jumping through blazing hoops. He put his arm round her and it felt like the performance was just for them.

Before they knew it they were lying on the beach together. Sand in their hair, in their mouths, dusting their skin. They found a place under the shelter of trees, away from the music, and they lay together under the stars that spotted the inky sky above them.

'I love you,' she said.

He paused for a moment, thinking of his mother, how she'd said he didn't know the first thing about love, how she'd regretted getting together with his father and having kids too young. 'I love you too,' he said, but his voice wavered.

'Do you think we'll have a family one day?' she asked.

He swallowed. 'I don't know,' he said. 'Maybe.'

She nodded. 'There's no rush,' she said. 'As long as I'm with you.'

CHAPTER THIRTY-SIX

Adam

Adam opened the door of the flat, clutching the bouquet of red carnations for Lauren. Kiera was going out tonight, meeting an old friend for some drinks, and he was coming home on his own for the first time in ages. In some ways it felt like a relief. The flat had felt more crowded with Kiera in it. He loved being with her, loved spending time with her, but on occasion he had longed for how it was before, just him and Lauren.

In his lunch break he'd finally plucked up the courage to ring the police. He knew that if he told them about Amanda, he would have to tell the partners at the GP surgery too, and in doing that he'd be risking his career. But he'd owed it to Lauren to tell the police his suspicions about Amanda. So he'd told them exactly what had happened; how he'd walked home with her and she'd tried to kiss him, how he thought she had stolen his key, how since then she hadn't stopped calling him. He was sure they'd take her in for questioning.

It had felt like a weight off his mind. He was finally facing what he'd done. He never should have walked home with Amanda, never should have hugged her or given her his personal number. It was all outside of the code of ethics. He didn't know what would happen to him. He could be investigated, maybe even struck off.

Still, the most important thing was that Lauren was out of danger. If Amanda was aware the police knew about her, surely she'd stop. Now he needed to focus on his wedding, his honeymoon and the rest of his life.

'Hello?' he called out, putting the flowers down on the kitchen counter. Misty slunk out of the bedroom and purred as she rubbed against his leg. He reached down to stroke her.

The flat was silent. All he could hear was the faint rumble of the traffic from the road outside.

He went into the bedroom, and could immediately tell that something was wrong. There was nothing on Lauren's bedside table. Not her hairbrush or moisturiser or make-up. Then he saw a scrap of paper on the bed. Leaning across, he picked it up, his eyes scanning the note.

Hi Adam. Everything that's happened lately has given me a lot to think about. I've been considering what you said about Amanda. I think I need a break from this flat to think things through. I'm going to stay with Zoe. Lauren

He stared at the message in shock. No kisses to sign it off. No 'lots of love'. His fiancée had left him.

CHAPTER THIRTY-SEVEN

Lauren

Lauren settled down on Zoe's sofa bed in her living room. Upstairs she could hear Harry screaming, Zoe's soothing voice trying to calm him. She'd offered to help earlier, but Zoe insisted that Harry just wanted his mother.

After the phone call to Amanda, Lauren had driven back to her flat, packed enough clothes for a few nights and scribbled a note for her fiancé. She needed time to think. She loved Adam, she always had and she always would, but could she trust him? He'd taken a taxi to another woman's house in the middle of the night and spoken to her on the phone just yesterday.

Lauren felt sick as she thought about the possibility of ending their relationship. Selling the flat that they'd worked so hard to buy, splitting years' worth of belongings in half. Being alone again, in a way she hadn't been since she was a teenager. Living without him by her side. It was the last thing she wanted.

She felt tears pricking her eyes. She couldn't marry him if she felt unsure, could she? What if she had to call the whole thing off? She imagined ringing round friends and family, telling them it was over between her and Adam, that there was no wedding. It would be humiliating. It would break her heart.

Lauren glanced at her phone. She had three missed calls from Adam and a new text. She knew she should speak to him, but she just didn't know what to say.

She had another message too. This one was from Tracey.

Just checking in to see how you are.

Lauren fiddled with her engagement ring, twisting it back and forth round her finger. It was early in the morning over in Thailand. Her sister must be really worried about her. Then she remembered her suggesting she check Adam's phone.

Lauren typed out a reply.

Not great to be honest. I found a suspicious number in his phone. Another woman. It's complicated. I'm staying with a friend.

Lauren's phone started ringing immediately.

'Oh, Lauren. I'm so sorry,' Tracey said, when Lauren answered the call. 'Are you OK?'

'Yeah…' Lauren tried to be stoic, but she felt the tears starting to fall. 'I don't know what to do.'

'You said you were staying with a friend. You've left Adam?'

'No, I haven't left him. I haven't decided yet. I'm just so confused.'

'This is so horrible of him, just before your wedding.'

'I know, I know,' Lauren said, the full horror of it hitting her.

'Are you… are you thinking of calling the wedding off?'

Lauren put her hands to her temples.

'I don't know. Maybe. I mean, if I find out for sure he's cheated I will.' Lauren swallowed down bile. She couldn't believe she was saying these words. He wouldn't have cheated on her, would he?

'You haven't got long…' Tracey said, and Lauren felt the pressure building inside her head, her temples throbbing.

Lauren let out a sob. She knew she'd have to decide what she was going to do quickly, but she felt like she couldn't face it. 'Look, Tracey, I need to go.' And before her sister could reply, she hung up.

*

Zoe knocked on the door of the living room the next morning and Lauren rubbed her eyes, feeling bleary and exhausted. Her back hurt from sleeping awkwardly and her injured wrist ached.

'I brought you a cup of tea,' Zoe said.

Lauren took it gratefully and Zoe sat down next to her on the sofa bed. 'Adam called me last night,' she said. 'He said you weren't picking up your phone.'

Lauren shook her head. 'I just can't face him.'

'Maybe you should try to talk to him. Maybe he can explain. He told you Amanda was a stalker, didn't he?'

'Yes.'

'So maybe that's all she is,' Zoe said reassuringly, resting her hand on Lauren's shoulder to comfort her.

'He went to her house,' Lauren replied, wanting to believe her friend but struggling.

'I know,' Zoe said, running her hand through her hair. 'But I just think you should hear him out. He might have an explanation. You guys have always been so good together. You can't just throw it all away. You can't let Amanda win.'

When Zoe left to take Harry to a toddler group, Lauren found herself using her day off to drive to the church where she was due to get married. She parked outside and looked up at the huge building, once the focal point for the area, now overshadowed by the tower blocks around it.

Inside it was peaceful and silent, her footsteps echoing on the wooden floor. She imagined being here with Adam in just over a week, walking down the aisle towards him. It felt like a mirage.

'Penny for them?' The vicar's voice that interrupted her thoughts was low and soothing and the bench creaked as he sat down beside her.

'I'm getting married here a week on Saturday,' she said quietly.

She glanced up at him, saw the kindness in his grey eyes and felt the tears start to slide down her face.

'I'm sorry,' she said, wiping her eyes.

'You wouldn't be the first to have doubts. What's bothering you?' he asked gently.

'I think I've found out… that my partner's cheating… but I don't know whether to believe it.'

The vicar didn't say anything for a moment. His eyes searched her face and Lauren flushed.

'I don't know what to do,' she said.

'Have you spoken to your partner?'

'Not yet.'

'OK.' He paused for a moment, and she fixed her eyes on the empty pews in front of her, trying to collect herself. 'And do you love him?' the vicar asked softly.

'I do,' Lauren said urgently. 'I can't bear the thought of being apart.'

'Well, that's already a good start. A better start than some people who walk down the aisle.'

'It's just… the wedding's so soon now. I don't feel… I don't know if I'll know for certain whether or not he's cheating by then.'

'I understand,' the vicar said. 'All marriages are about partnership. Give and take. It's not to be entered into lightly.'

'So you think I should cancel the wedding?'

'That's not what I said. But I do think that if you love him and he loves you then you can make it work. If that love is respected and nurtured, it can last a lifetime. But only the pair of you can decide if that's what you want. You need to work it out together.'

Lauren nodded.

'And what I would say is that you have the rest of your lives. If you love each other it doesn't matter if you get married next week or in two years' time. You will still have the rest of your lives together. So take your time and think about what you both want. If it's meant to be, your love will find a way through.'

CHAPTER THIRTY-EIGHT

Adam

The three steps Adam took across the corridor to Dr Andrew Jarrad's office felt like the longest walk he'd ever taken in his life. He usually thought nothing of his meetings with Andrew, who, as one of the senior partners, had looked out for him from the moment he'd joined the surgery. Andrew had said his door was always open and that if Adam ever had any issues, professional or personal, he could talk to him.

Adam had never taken him up on that. Now he wished he had. If he'd only told Andrew about Amanda's flirting, about her suspiciously regular appointments, then maybe the senior partner would have advised him to take her off his list. Stupidly, Adam had thought he could handle her. It had turned out he couldn't.

Since he had gone to the police, it was only a matter of time before what happened with Amanda got back to the partners at the surgery. If the police didn't come to see them themselves, then he was sure that Amanda wouldn't hesitate to make a formal complaint. She'd be angry that he'd reported her to the police. Who knew what she'd tell them, or how far she was prepared to go?

He paused for a moment outside Andrew's door, trying to slow his breathing. Then he knocked.

'Come on in,' Andrew called out.

Adam came through the door, his pulse racing.

'Take a seat.'

He sat down on one of the hard wooden chairs that were there for the patients, feeling small and insignificant.

'So,' Andrew said. 'What's up?'

'I've had an issue with a patient,' Adam replied, wanting to get straight to it. 'She seems very flirty and behaves inappropriately with me.'

'Amanda Jacobs?' Andrew asked, his eyebrows rising.

'How did you know?'

'You're not the first.'

'Yes,' Adam said. 'I've heard that.' He took a deep breath and launched into the speech he'd rehearsed at home. 'The thing is, I've made an error. I saw her out one evening at the pub and she came over to speak to me. She was very drunk and she asked me to walk her home. I was worried that she was vulnerable in the state she was in so I accompanied her for a bit and then paid for an Uber for her. I gave her my number to ensure she was home safely.'

Andrew's eyebrows were raised to the ceiling now. 'You must have known that was against the guidelines.'

'I do know. It was a mistake.'

'I'll have to take the details and file a report. I'll speak to other partners about how to approach it.'

'How serious do you think it is?'

'You're not in any kind of sexual relationship with her?'

Adam wondered if he should tell Andrew she tried to kiss him, but decided it was an unnecessary detail.

'No,' he said. 'There's never been anything at all between us. I was just trying to be kind, to walk her home when she was drunk.'

'Well, that's something in your favour. I'll need to talk to the other partners. There may need to be a formal investigation.'

CHAPTER THIRTY-NINE

Lauren

On the way back to Zoe's house from the church, Lauren made up her mind. She was simply going to ask Adam what was going on. Why he'd taken an Uber to Amanda's house. She'd been mentally preparing herself all day for his answers. Either he was cheating or he wasn't. Her life was at a junction, the two paths leading in completely opposite directions. In two weeks' time she might be enjoying her honeymoon with Adam. Or she might be single again. The thought of being without him was horrifying.

Yesterday, she'd phoned up the pub where they were having the reception, and, embarrassed, asked about the cancellation charge. If they called it off this late, they'd still have to pay for everything. But she could accept that they would lose all the money, if it was the right thing to do. If Adam wanted to be with someone else.

As she turned her car into Zoe's road, she thought about the possibility that Adam had cheated on her, but still wanted to be with her. The thought made her uncomfortable. Could she really stay with someone who'd done that to her? She'd need time to think about that, to work out what to do, how to decide whether she wanted to stay with him. And in that case, she'd have to postpone the wedding. She'd asked the pub about that, too, on the phone, and the woman had told her she could do that for a fee.

She just hoped that Adam would be able to explain everything. She'd go over and see him this evening, insist that he told her the truth. But as she neared Zoe's house, she saw Adam's car on the drive.

'Hello?' she called out tentatively, as she unlocked the door with Zoe's spare key.

'Lauren!' Adam called out, coming out of the kitchen.

Zoe appeared beside him. 'I let him in. I hope that's OK. He begged. And I think you both need to talk.'

Lauren could feel tears welling up in her eyes. Just seeing him again filled her with longing, to be together, to be close to him. But she held back when he reached out to hug her.

'You need to explain things,' she said firmly. And yet she dreaded his explanation.

'Let's sit down,' he replied, leading her to the kitchen.

'I'll get out of your way,' Zoe said. 'I'll be with Harry in the living room if you need me.'

Pulling a seat out from the kitchen table, Lauren sat down facing Adam. He had bags under his eyes and he looked exhausted. But he was still the man she'd fallen in love with.

'I'm so sorry for everything you've been through,' Adam said. 'I feel like it's all my fault. Because of Amanda. She's infatuated with me.'

Lauren thought about the Uber receipt. The phone call he'd had with her just yesterday.

'But how is that possible if you've never shown any interest?' she asked.

Adam got up from his seat and started pacing up and down the kitchen, making it feel small and claustrophobic. Suddenly Lauren wanted to be anywhere but here, about to listen to whatever he had to say.

'Look, Lauren,' he said. 'I made a mistake.'

'What mistake?' Lauren's breath caught in her throat. Her whole body tensed, like she was waiting for confirmation that her life with Adam was over. He had the power to say anything. Something that might bring them together or rip them apart.

'The night I walked her home I was drunk... and a tiny bit attracted to her, I admit it.' Lauren felt a tightness in her chest. She gripped the edge of the table, scared of what he might say next. 'And there was a moment when I hugged her and... we almost kissed. But we didn't. I pulled away. But I think that's what's spurred on her attraction.'

Lauren stayed silent, trying to make sense of it. It wasn't as bad as she'd thought. Not even a kiss. But he had been attracted to her. He'd been tempted. He'd got himself in a position where he nearly kissed another woman.

'You must have known,' she said finally. 'When you walked her home, you must have known she was attracted to you.'

She could imagine it. A cold night. An attractive woman, who needed walking home. And Adam offering, telling himself that it was because he was a nice guy, the kind of guy who wouldn't leave a woman asking for help. And he was a nice guy, that much was true. But that alone wouldn't have been enough to make him accompany her home. He was usually more sensible than that. She was a patient. He would have known that it was risky. And yet he must have gone ahead because he fancied her; because a part of him, no matter how tiny, had wanted something to happen between them.

Then Lauren remembered the receipt. He'd taken an Uber to Amanda's house. Was he still lying to her? Even now?

'That was the night you lost your keys, wasn't it? You took a taxi back to hers that night.'

'I didn't take a taxi to hers. I put her in a taxi home. She was drunk.'

'But then what happened to you? You didn't have your keys.'

'I walked to Kiera's. It's not far.'

Lauren's mind was spinning. Kiera had said he'd stayed at hers the night he'd lost his keys. It did make sense.

'So you're saying that you nearly kissed her, but you didn't. And that was all that happened between you?'

'Yeah. I'm so sorry, Lauren. I should never have put myself in that position.'

'You were attracted to her.'

'Yeah.'

'And you were tempted?'

'I know it's horrible to hear, but I was drunk and you were out at work and I'll admit I was tempted. But I didn't act on it. That's what counts, surely? I rejected her. I did the right thing.'

'Are you still attracted to her?'

'No! Not at all. It was only a split second of attraction. How could I possibly be attracted to her, after everything she's done?' Emotion choked Adam's voice.

Lauren felt relief searing through her. Despite everything, she believed him. Maybe, just maybe, she could forgive him.

'You spoke to her yesterday. What was that about?'

'She's called me several times a day since it happened. And the other day, I finally picked up. I picked up because I wanted to tell her to back off. She's dangerous. What she did to you – pushing you down the stairs, breaking into our home… I'll never forgive her. I wanted to give her a piece of my mind.'

'You didn't need to do that. You could just tell the police.'

'I've done that now. I didn't want to do it at first because if this gets out in the open, I risk being investigated, maybe even losing my job.'

Lauren swallowed. He was right. It was a big risk.

'But I wanted to do the right thing. The police need to look into her. She needs to be punished for what she's done. She's harassed you.'

'You're right.' Lauren looked down at her injured wrist, feeling a surge of anger at all the pain and fear Amanda had caused her.

'I regret it so much. It was such a crazy idea to walk her home, but I never knew it would lead to all of this.'

'At least we've changed the locks now,' Lauren said, shivering at the thought of that woman in her flat. 'She definitely can't get in any more. Can we promise that there'll be no more secrets?'

He hugged her. 'Of course.' But despite his words, she noticed he wasn't quite meeting her eyes. 'I've told you everything. Will you come home?'

Lauren looked at the man she loved. She wanted more than anything to marry him. And yet… She wanted to think through everything, check it completely added up. She wasn't going to let him fool her again.

'I need a bit more time,' she said, finally breaking the silence.

CHAPTER FORTY

Lauren

'How are you?' Zoe asked, coming into the kitchen after Adam had left.

Lauren cradled her cup of coffee. 'I'm OK, I think. It was a lot to take in.'

'So what had happened?'

'He hasn't cheated on me.'

'Thank goodness for that. I knew he wouldn't do that to you.' Zoe reached out and touched her arm.

'No, but… he fancied his patient. He walked her home, nearly kissed her.'

'But he didn't kiss her?'

'No, at least that's what he says.'

'Do you believe him?'

'Yes, but… he shouldn't have let it get that far, should he? He shouldn't have walked her home.' Lauren cringed at the thought of Amanda leaning in to kiss him.

'He made a mistake,' Zoe said.

'I know. And he's apologised.'

'Do you love him?'

Lauren felt that rush of emotion when she thought of Adam, the longing in her heart to be beside him. 'I love him so much,' she said. 'I just want to make sure I'm thinking things through.'

'Has he ever given you any reason not to trust him?'

'Not before Amanda. And he's doing everything he can to fix that now. He's told the police about her, and he's admitted what happened to the partners at work.'

'So he made a mistake and he's fixing it?'

'Yeah.' Lauren felt better now, her fears about marrying Adam starting to dissipate. She loved him. And she wanted to build a life with him, to have kids together, to grow old together. Perhaps this was just one of the hurdles they'd come up against in their marriage. There'd be more. No marriage was plain sailing.

'I'm going to go ahead with the wedding,' Lauren said. 'It's what I want and it's what Adam wants. No matter what Amanda does, she's not going to stop us.'

When Lauren arrived back at the flat, her travel case in her hand, Adam beamed at her. Then he ran across to her, wrapping her in a hug.

Kiera smiled from the sofa. 'You're back! Shall I leave you two to it?' She got up, poured herself a glass of wine and retreated to her bedroom. A second later, soul music seeped out from under her door.

'So you've had time to think?' Adam asked.

'Yes,' Lauren said. 'You crossed a line with Amanda. But I understand it was a mistake. And I think I can forgive you…'

Adam smiled gratefully. 'I'm so relieved. I thought I might have lost you.' She saw the tears in his eyes. 'I thought we might have to cancel the wedding.'

'We're not doing that,' Lauren said. 'We're not going to let her win.'

'I hope the police arrest her,' Adam replied. 'Before the wedding.'

'I'm sure they will. But even if they don't, we won't let her ruin it. We can get the ushers to stop her coming in at the door, give them her photo.'

'Yeah,' Adam said determinedly. 'We'll do that.'

'She'll never get past Jimmy.'

Adam laughed, and Lauren was starting to feel in control again, to look forward to their wedding. There would be no secrets between them any more. They could tackle Amanda as a team.

'I want my future with you,' Adam said to Lauren. 'Marriage, kids, all of it.' Lauren smiled. He was still committed to her, to their future as a family.

'Do you ever think about the baby?' she asked. 'It would be a few weeks old now, if it had been born.'

'Sometimes. But I try not to.'

'I was never a hundred per cent sure I wanted one until I was pregnant, but now I can't imagine a future without kids.'

Adam nodded. 'We'll start trying again after the wedding.'

'You know, since I was pregnant, I haven't been able to think of the spare room as anything other than the baby's room.'

Lauren glanced over at its closed door. Kiera would never be able to hear their conversation above the music.

'I know you'd prefer it if Kiera wasn't living with us.'

Lauren sighed. 'You're just trying to be a good friend, but I can't help feeling like she's invaded our space, just before our wedding. And it's not clear how long she's hoping to stay for.'

'I can speak to her,' Adam said, 'see what she's planning.'

'I want to keep the space free for us, for a baby.'

'I understand,' Adam said. 'I'll explain to Kiera, and we'll keep the room for us. Our wedding's the start of a new life. A new beginning.'

CHAPTER FORTY-ONE

Adam

One week until the wedding

Adam looked around the tiny box room, breathing in the tart smell of fresh paint. It looked so much better. Kiera had moved all her stuff out into the living room, so he could paint it. He'd covered the bed, chest of drawers and carpet in old sheets and then got to work, first filling in the scrapes and dents, and then painting the space a bright yellow.

After Lauren had told him how she still thought of this as the baby's room, he'd been determined to do something about it. He'd remembered when she was pregnant, how she'd talked excitedly about how she wanted the room to look. Last night when she'd gone to bed, he'd pulled up the Pinterest board she'd created at the time, and ordered the paint colours to collect from the local hardware store. She'd said she'd want yellow walls for a boy or a girl. It was a bright, cheerful colour. And with the sunlight streaming in now, it seemed perfect.

He heard footsteps outside the flat, the front door opening.

'Hello?' Lauren called out.

'In here,' Adam said.

'Oh wow,' she said as she came into the spare room, her face splitting into a huge smile. 'You've been painting. This colour's perfect.'

'I wanted it to be a room we could use. For us or for the baby.'

'But what about Kiera?' Lauren asked.

Adam smiled. The conversation with Kiera had been difficult, but ultimately she'd understood. 'I explained we wanted the room back – for us,' he said. 'She's going to move out when we're on our honeymoon.'

Lauren grinned, stretching up to kiss him. 'I love you,' she said. And at that moment he felt hopeful about their life together. No matter what had happened in the past, the future was theirs for the taking.

CHAPTER FORTY-TWO

Adam

2001: Thailand

He could feel the electricity flowing between them as they ate their dinner with their families. As the others talked, the tips of her fingers brushed his under the table. He swallowed the piece of bread in his mouth without chewing, every bit of his body alert to her touch. But then her fingers were gone. He reached out to find them again, not daring to look at her, imagining the playful look in her eyes.

Someone said something at the other end of the table that he didn't catch and everyone chuckled, including her. Her laugh was gleeful, the kind of laugh that some might say was too loud, a proper belly laugh. She completely let go, the joy taking over her whole body. He wanted to shift up closer to her, to hold her, to embrace her. Out of the corner of his eye he could see her hand on her water glass. That was why it wasn't under the table.

He was so acutely aware of her it hurt. Aware of every clink of her cutlery, the smell of her perfume combined with the slight salt tang of the sea. He could still taste the salt from her lips from when he'd kissed her earlier. He could see her wrist on the table, the charm bracelet he'd bought her dangling from it.

And then her hand came back under the table. Their fingers sought each other out, and entwined together. She gripped him so hard he could feel his circulation stopping. He blinked, a smile spreading across his face. He knew she was smiling beside him.

'This time tomorrow, we'll be recovering from our white-water rafting adventure,' Debs said, grinning.

'Not me,' Sam said, returning her smile. 'I'll leave that to you lot. I'm far too terrified of drowning.'

'Seriously, Mum. It's not scary at all,' Adam said. He couldn't wait. He'd been rafting once before and he loved the rush of adrenaline as the boat flew over the rapids. 'Maybe you should leave it to the younger generation,' he teased. 'We're much braver.'

'Is that right?' Debs challenged. 'Well, I'm doing it.'

'I think you're all mad,' Sam said, and everyone laughed.

CHAPTER FORTY-THREE

Lauren

Lauren was up early, the morning light filtering into the living room as she put the finishing touches on the bespoke bunting that would decorate the church. Its colours matched the blue and white of her bridal bouquet, and every third triangle had a space for a photo. Lauren had filled them with pictures of her and Adam at different stages of their relationship. Picking the photos out had brought back happy memories, from when they'd first felt that spark in Thailand, to their more recent meals out in restaurants and drinks in bars, to the photoshoot when they'd got engaged. She'd chosen a different image to the one on the wedding invitation, which now reminded her of Amanda's threatening card. Instead she'd chosen a picture of her and Adam sitting on a park bench, looking into each other's eyes, backed by the December frost.

She held up the bunting and surveyed her work, pleased with it. She imagined people looking at the photos as they waited for the bridal music to start, commenting on how happy they both looked. She had pictures of her parents, too, to include at the front of the church and at the reception, to make it feel like they were part of the day.

All the final arrangements for the wedding were in place now, and she was planning to go out tonight to relax and celebrate with Zoe, Kiera and some of her other friends.

She'd printed off all the paperwork she needed to look through before the day: the timings for the ceremony and then the reception, copies of the guest list to give to the groomsmen, the seating plan for the meal with a list of everyone's allergies and food intolerances. She'd even printed out the readings that the guests were doing, just in case they forgot their own papers.

Yesterday, she'd made herself search for Amanda on Facebook. She was easy enough to find, her smiling face beaming out from a sun-soaked beach, a cocktail in her hand. Looking at her picture, Lauren had felt faint. Amanda looked perfectly ordinary, like thousands of others on Facebook. But this was the woman who'd caused her so much harm. Lauren had downloaded the picture and printed it out to hand to the groomsmen so that they could watch out for her in case she came to the church. She hadn't heard anything further from the police, and when Adam had phoned them to ask for an update it had sounded like the investigation had stalled. There had been no arrests.

Once again, she looked at the running order for the day. Adam was going to get to the church before her, at the same time as the guests. Zoe had asked if she could arrive a bit early, so she'd have time to give Harry his morning snack in the church and try to get him to settle before the ceremony started, so he wouldn't interrupt. Lauren just needed to ring the church and check what time its doors would be open. She looked up the number and dialled, but there was no answer. She made a mental note to try again later.

Just then Adam came in, ready to go to the GP surgery. She greeted him with a kiss. He'd been so wonderful since she'd moved back in, attentive and thoughtful. They were both trying to put everything behind them and get on with planning their future. But Lauren couldn't help feeling shaky. Amanda had pushed her down the stairs and she was walking the streets freely. Lauren had no idea what she might be planning next.

'How was work yesterday?' she asked Adam. She'd stayed at the hospital late last night, so they hadn't had time to catch up. She knew he was worried about what would happen now he'd told the partners about Amanda.

'It was OK,' he said. 'I haven't heard any more about an investigation. I thought Amanda might have reported me, but I don't think she has, which is good news.'

'Do you think it's because she's going to do something else?' Lauren asked nervously, thinking of the perfect wedding day that she'd prepared so carefully, the day that would mark the first day of the rest of their lives.

'I don't think so. Actually I had some good news today on that front.'

'Oh?' Lauren said, putting the paperwork back in her folder. 'Did the police call?'

Adam smiled. 'No, I'm afraid not. But Amanda came into the surgery yesterday to see the nurse. She needed injections. Travel injections. She's going away on holiday in a few days. She's not going to be in the country when we get married.'

Lauren grinned. She needn't have worried about Amanda coming to the church. Finally, she could start to relax.

'Have a good day at work,' she said to Adam, as he leaned over to kiss her, before he went out the door.

She smiled to herself as she stroked Misty, and decided to try and call the church again.

'Hello? Mary speaking,' Lauren jumped, startled. She hadn't got through the last three times she'd tried to call, and she wasn't expecting to now.

'Is that St Peter's?'

'Yes, it is.'

'I'm getting married on Saturday, and I just wanted to check what time the guests would be allowed into the church. A friend of mine wants to get there early to settle her toddler before the ceremony.'

'Well, the doors are open all morning. Usually the florist comes in first to decorate the aisles, and then the guests afterwards. But your guests are welcome to come in any time.'

'Brilliant. Thank you.'

'Before you go – can I just check the date of your wedding? I'm looking at the wall calendar now. I think I must have misheard you earlier, but I thought you said this Saturday.'

'Yes, that's right.'

'Well, I'm afraid that can't be right. We have another wedding on Saturday. All morning. It's the wedding of an old friend of mine, a regular churchgoer. We had a last-minute cancellation and we were able to slot her in.'

Lauren shook her head. 'You must have the date wrong. Saturday the nineteenth of August – that's when my wedding is.' She swallowed, panic searing through her. The woman must be confused.

'What's your name?'

'Lauren Haywood.'

'Lauren Haywood? You're the woman who cancelled.'

'What? No – that's wrong, I haven't cancelled.' Lauren took a deep breath, trying to steady herself.

'I can see your name on the calendar. It's been crossed out.'

Lauren tried to keep her voice calm, tried to reign in her feelings. She was shaking. 'It can't be. I'm getting married on Saturday. At your church. There must be a mistake.'

'I'm sorry, but there's no mistake. Your wedding here has been cancelled.'

'But how could that happen? I didn't cancel it. Can I reinstate it, please?' Lauren felt like she might be sick. She thought of all her guests, the florist, the photographer, the reception afterwards. The church couldn't do this to her. They couldn't just cancel her wedding.

'I'm afraid that won't be possible. Like I said, we have another wedding booked in now…'

'That can't be…' Lauren's heart was beating so fast, she thought it might fly out of her chest.

'Hang on a minute – I'll get the vicar.'

She knew the vicar would sort it out. It must be some kind of misunderstanding. She'd only spoken to him the other week. But Lauren felt her heart drop through her chest as she remembered. She'd spoken to him about her doubts about Adam… and he'd said that if they loved each other it didn't matter when they got married, their love would endure regardless. And she had agreed. Had he taken that agreement as her wanting to cancel the wedding?

'Hello, David speaking.'

'Hi, David. It's Lauren Haywood here.'

'Ah, Lauren. How are you feeling? Any better now?'

'Well, a bit worried, actually. I've just spoken to Mary and she's told me my wedding has been cancelled.'

There was a pause. David cleared his throat. 'Lauren, yes, that's right. Are you saying you want to go ahead with the wedding now? I'm afraid we can't do that. We have another couple who've taken your slot.'

'What?' The room was spinning.

'Look, after our chat I think it's probably best that you don't rush into anything.'

'But… but I didn't say I wanted to cancel the wedding. I was confused, just thinking things through. It's not up to you to decide whether my wedding should be cancelled.'

'I appreciate that you're having a hard time and I know you're upset, but you can't keep changing your mind like this. You rang a few days ago in tears, asking to cancel. I told you I'd hold the slot for you if you wanted to have more time to think. But you were adamant. You said you'd had enough, that you'd made up your mind and you didn't want to go ahead.'

CHAPTER FORTY-FOUR

Lauren

'That wasn't me,' Lauren said breathlessly. 'I didn't cancel the wedding. I wouldn't. I haven't ever called you.'

'Well, in that case, I'm so sorry, but there seems to have been a mistake.' The vicar sounded flustered now. 'I'll see what I can do for you. There may be another day we can suggest, although we do get very booked up.'

Lauren felt sick. 'Who was it who called you? What did she sound like?'

It must have been Amanda. They'd worried she would turn up to the wedding to ruin it, but all the time she'd had something worse planned: to cancel it entirely and jet off on holiday.

'She said she was you. She was crying down the phone. Said she couldn't trust Adam, said he'd cheated, that he loved someone else. It was hard to make out the words, any particular accent. Everything was muffled. I was just trying to calm her down, to get sense out of her. But it was clear that she wanted to cancel the wedding. That was the one thing I checked over and over again.'

'Do you know what number she rang from?'

'We don't keep records, I'm afraid. Quite old-fashioned here. It's just a landline, not even a digital phone.'

'So there's no way of knowing who called you?'

'I don't think so, Lauren. Perhaps I can ask Heather from the congregation. She works in IT, I think. But I doubt there's a way.'

'Please could you try and find out?'

'Of course. Hang on a minute – Mary's just told me there's an email, too, from your email address.'

'From my address? It can't be. It must have been a fake account.'

'It's the same one you emailed from before.'

'What?'

'You sent an email about where we were planning to place your parents' pictures in the church. That was you, wasn't it?'

'Yes.' Lauren was biting her nails, a habit she hadn't had since she was at school.

'Well, the email confirming the cancellation was from the same address.'

Lauren's mind spun. She remembered when she'd lost her phone. Adam thought that Amanda had stolen it. Lauren always left her emails open on her phone. Had Amanda managed to get into her email account? It was the only explanation.

'That wasn't me,' Lauren said, her voice almost a whisper. She wiped a tear from the corner of her eye with the back of her hand.

'Well, it appears there's been a mix-up. I can look and see if we've got any other dates you could move it to.' She wondered if he believed her, or if he thought she'd cancelled the wedding and then changed her mind. She felt sick. Everything was booked for Saturday. All the guests had made arrangements to be there.

'Oh, hang on a minute,' he said, before Lauren had had time to gather her thoughts. 'Mary's shaking her head at me. I'm afraid I don't think we have any more dates for this year.'

'Well, can you move anything? Move the couple who've taken our slot?'

'I can't move them, no. I'll see if there's anything else I can do. But I'm sorry, Lauren, your wedding won't be happening on Saturday.'

*

Lauren burst into angry sobs the instant she hung up the phone. She threw her shoes on, grabbed her bag and went to the surgery to see Adam.

'Lauren!' Kiera said when she saw her. 'Can't wait for our drinks tonight!'

Lauren turned her head away to hide her face, but Kiera had already seen she was crying.

'What's wrong?' she asked, pulling her behind the reception desk and taking her to a little room at the side.

'I need to speak to Adam.'

'Has something happened?'

'The wedding's cancelled, Kiera. Someone rang up and cancelled it.'

'Oh, no! Can you uncancel it?'

'No, I don't think so. The church has already given the slot to another couple.'

'Oh, Lauren, I'm so sorry. Right, I'll get you some water. You just stay there. I'll pop in and see Adam and tell him to hold off calling his next patient in. Then you can talk to him.'

'OK,' Lauren said, grabbing a tissue and blowing her nose.

As Kiera went back into the busy reception area, Lauren could hear the phones ringing, and the sound of the team of receptionists taking calls and speaking to patients. Everything seemed so normal. She could hardly believe her wedding ceremony had been cancelled.

Biting back tears, she picked up her phone and messaged her friends. *Sorry, drinks tonight are off. I'm feeling under the weather. I'm going to have to go to bed and rest.* She couldn't bear to tell them the truth. Maybe the wedding was still salvageable. There must be something she could do. She couldn't go out and celebrate tonight, not without trying to fix things.

*

Five minutes later she was in Adam's consulting room. Aside from the picture of their engagement on his desk and a dying pot plant in the corner, the room was sparse and clinical, with no signs of personality.

'Lauren, what's going on? Kiera said our wedding ceremony has been cancelled.' Adam's eyes were wide and his brow crinkled in concern.

'That's right. I spoke to the vicar. He said someone rang up pretending to be me and cancelled it a few days ago. And now they have another booking.'

'What?' He put his hand over his mouth in shock.

'Do you think it was Amanda?'

'I don't know… What are we going to do?'

'The vicar is looking at other dates, although it doesn't look likely there'll be anything this year. And we'll have to rearrange the photographer, the florist. Not to mention the entire reception. And what if our guests can't make the new date?'

'This is a disaster…' Adam said. He paused. 'Maybe we could try and find another church.'

'But that church has so much history for us. My parents got married there.'

'I know… it's awful, what's happened. But if we want the wedding to go ahead and we already have the reception in place, then maybe there's another church that could accommodate us in the morning.'

'I doubt it. They usually get booked up ages in advance.'

'It's worth a try though, isn't it?'

He was right, Lauren realised. They didn't have many other options. 'I'll ring round. Explain the situation,' Lauren said. It felt better to have a plan, to be taking action.

'OK,' Adam said, standing up and starting to pace his consulting room.

'Or we could try and move the date. But it will be a real hassle. And we'd need to check the pub can still do the reception afterwards.'

'So we need to ring the pub, too. See what other dates they might be able to do. Just in case we don't find a new church. I can call them now.' Adam picked up the phone.

Lauren hardly heard Adam's call; she was too focused on frantically googling different local churches. But then she heard his voice get louder, his tone change, and she stopped what she was doing.

'What do you mean?' he was saying.

'No, that definitely wasn't us.'

'I mean seriously, what kind of business are you if you don't check who's calling?'

Lauren looked up at him in alarm.

'Well, that's just not good enough.' Adam was red in the face, his hands gripping the desk, his knuckles white.

'No, I want to speak to the manager.'

Lauren couldn't make out what the woman on the other end of the phone was saying but she could guess, her stomach plummeting.

'Well, I'll call back later then. Tell her it's urgent.'

He hung up, throwing the phone down on the table, his face ashen. 'Our booking's been cancelled there too. Whoever rang the church, rang up the pub too. Our whole wedding has been cancelled.'

CHAPTER FORTY-FIVE

Adam

'I'm so sorry,' Adam said, folding Lauren into a hug. 'I'm speaking to the manager later. I hope she'll be able to help.'

Lauren's eyes brimmed with tears. 'But even if we can get the reception sorted, we still won't have a church to get married in.'

'I know.' He didn't know what to do, how he could fix this. He squeezed her tighter. 'I'm so sorry,' he said again.

'It's not your fault.'

But it was, wasn't it? If he had never let Amanda walk home with him, had never done anything to encourage her, then none of this would have happened. Lauren was paying the price for his foolishness.

'We can get through this together,' he said. 'I know we can. There'll be another way to get married, I'm sure of it. The only thing that matters is that we're together.' But as he said the words, they felt flippant, as if he was ignoring all the work that Lauren had put into the wedding, all the hours she'd spent planning it.

'There must be something we can do,' replied Lauren, desperation in her voice.

Adam looked at his watch, aware that he needed to start seeing patients again. Mrs Martin was next. He could picture her sitting in the waiting room, looking anxiously at the clock on the wall. 'I'm so sorry,' he said. 'I'm going to have to see my next patient.

But I'll be thinking all day about how to handle this. There must be another way we can get married.'

Lauren nodded, wiping a tear from her eye. He moved towards her and kissed her, drawing her towards him, holding her close.

'I'd better go,' she said, and he hugged her tighter for a moment before loosening his grip.

As he watched her walk out the door, Adam realised he was still shaking. He took a deep breath, pulled himself together and went into the waiting room.

'Mrs Martin?' he said with a smile. But his face fell when he saw who else was in the waiting room.

'Hi Adam,' Amanda said, smiling.

He glanced nervously towards the reception area. Kiera wasn't there, but the other receptionists were watching with interest.

'Hi,' he said. 'Not here to see me, are you?' All the receptionists had been told not to offer her appointments with him.

'No,' she said loudly. 'I wasn't allowed.' He felt a trickle of sweat running down the back of his neck. How dare she come and sit there in the waiting room as if she was entirely innocent? But he couldn't do or say anything.

He nodded brusquely at her and turned away. Mrs Martin was shuffling towards him, and he waited patiently, then walked towards his consulting room.

'Hope you're all ready for your wedding,' Amanda called out behind him. It was all he could do to stop himself turning round and screaming at her.

CHAPTER FORTY-SIX

Lauren

After Lauren left Adam, she went behind the reception desk to see Kiera, who escorted her back into the side room. 'Thanks for helping out,' Lauren said.

'No problem. I got your message that our night out tonight is cancelled. Are you sure?'

'I can hardly go out and celebrate a wedding that's not happening, can I?'

'I don't see why not. It's not that you won't get married, is it? It's just that you might not get married on Saturday. And I think you need to let your hair down after today.'

'Thanks, but I don't think so… I need to try and sort out the wedding, see what alternatives there are.'

'OK, then,' Kiera said. 'How about you spend the afternoon doing that, and then we go out in the evening?'

Lauren thought about how nice it would be to see Zoe and her friends. Maybe they'd even have some ideas about how to fix this mess.

'OK, then,' she replied.

'I promise it will make you feel better,' Kiera said with a smile.

That evening, Lauren sat on a long table with her friends at the back of an Italian restaurant, surrounded by the scents of roasted garlic and freshly baked bread. None of them could believe what had happened. Kiera had ordered a bottle of red and a bottle of white, and they were already finished before the starters had even arrived. As the waiter brought more wine, Lauren let him top up her glass of Sauvignon. She was starting to feel better.

'But what I don't get,' Zoe said, sloshing her wine around her glass, 'is how the church just believed it was you, without even checking, asking for ID or something.'

'I don't know. I guess it's not something that happens every day. Apparently I rang up in tears. Both the church and the pub. They didn't consider that it might not be me. And Amanda sent a follow-up email from my email address. She must have got into my emails when she took my phone at the club. I've looked up how she did it, and it's not that difficult to hack into a stolen phone.'

Zoe touched her hand across the table. 'I'm so sorry she's done all this to you. It's completely shocking.'

'I think the church and the pub need to sort you out with another wedding. They should never have believed her,' Kiera said, banging her fist lightly on the table and making the cutlery rattle. 'It was their mistake.'

'The church has already said they'll look into it. But no chance for this year.'

'Right,' Zoe said. 'Enough is enough. I'm publicising this. I'm letting everyone know.'

'What do you mean?'

'I'll just put a call out on Twitter. I have a lot of followers, from when I was producing music videos. Who knows who they all are – maybe there'll be someone who can help.'

'I'm not sure.' Lauren felt uncertain. She hadn't even let the rest of her guests know what had happened yet.

'You should totally do that,' Kiera said, knocking back more wine.

'OK.' Zoe got out her phone. 'Gosh, the screen's a bit blurry.'

'I think you might be a bit drunk,' Kiera said, grinning. Around them the starters were beginning to arrive. Plates of garlic bread, bruschetta and prawns. The waiter moved the candles around to make space for all the food they'd ordered.

Lauren watched over Zoe's shoulder as she typed.

My friend has been totally BETRAYED by The Black Horse pub and St Peter's Church. They have CANCELLED her wedding. Without telling her. With less than a week to go. #helpLauren

'I think that's a bit much,' Lauren said, worried. After all, the church and the reception venue had received an email they'd thought was from her. 'Are you sure you should name them?'

But Zoe had already pressed send, publishing the tweet to her 10,000 followers.

As they worked their way through the generous starters, Zoe provided them with updates on the tweet. A hundred retweets. Then 500. And now 2,000. Lauren felt nauseous. At least it didn't give her full name, she told herself as she saw the numbers multiplying.

'People are so sympathetic,' Zoe said. 'So many people are replying, wishing you luck. A couple have offered up venues, but they don't sound that great. Do you want to get married in someone's garden in Cambridge?' Zoe asked, her eyebrows raised. 'Apparently they have a scenic pond.'

They all burst into laughter and Zoe read out more of the messages. Some suggested they should just turn up at the church anyway and insist on getting married there. Others suggested just waiting until next year. As the evening wore on, they worked through the menu at the restaurant, sharing all the specialities between them, from the veal in breadcrumbs to the Neapolitan sausages. And they kept ordering more wine.

'Come on,' Kiera said, when the food was finished. Lauren and Zoe were still poring over Twitter, absorbing other people's

anger about what had happened, and reading through their sug-
gestions about what to do next. Kiera looked pointedly at them.
'You can't stay buried in your phone all evening. Let's go to a bar.
The night's still young.'

CHAPTER FORTY-SEVEN

Adam

2001: Thailand

He lay in bed beside her. He'd waited all evening for her to arrive, sneaking into his room at 2 a.m. He hated sleeping alone these days, longed for her to be beside him. Every waking moment he wasn't with her felt wasted.

He smiled at her, lying tangled in the lightweight sheet next to her.

'We'll be like this forever,' he said.

'I really hope so.'

He opened the window so they could hear the sea, the waves breaking against the shore. She turned in the bed and smiled back at him, stroking his arm.

'You know I'm planning to stay out in Thailand, to continue travelling,' she said. 'I'm not going back home.'

He nodded. He'd been thinking about this, about her. He wasn't sure he wanted his life in England either; wasn't sure if he was really suited to medical school. His mother was wrong about their relationship. They were meant to be together.

'You know,' he said, as he stroked her hair, 'I could come with you, travelling round Thailand. We could make our lives here together.'

He expected her to laugh, but she didn't. Instead she just nodded. 'Yeah, we could do that.'

'Tracey,' he said, his voice wobbling. 'I want to spend the rest of my life with you. In Thailand or in England. It doesn't matter to me. As long as I'm with you.' Her face split into a smile and her eyes sparkled.

He held her in his arms and they spent the rest of the night fantasising about a life together in Thailand. They'd live simply, not waste money on things they didn't need. They'd go to the beach every day and spend every evening together. Adam would find work, perhaps train to be a diving instructor.

The world seemed vast, an empire of opportunity. They could do anything they wanted. Be anyone they wanted. As long as they were together. Adam and Tracey.

CHAPTER FORTY-EIGHT

Lauren

Lauren's head was pounding when she woke up the next morning to the sound of her mobile ringing. She sat up slowly and saw a cup of tea that Adam must have put on her bedside table. It was stone cold. She'd overslept.

Glancing at her phone, she saw it was Zoe calling.

'Lauren, hi. How are you feeling?' said Zoe, when she answered.

Lauren groaned. 'Pretty awful.' She could hardly hold her head up. She wanted nothing more than to lie back down under the warm duvet and go to sleep.

'I have good news,' Zoe said excitedly. 'That tweet went viral. And I've already had a reply from the pub offering you a full refund. Or, if you do decide to go ahead on Saturday, they can reinstate the booking.'

Lauren felt her heart flutter and she sat up a bit more in bed. 'Really? Wow, that's great, Zoe. Thanks so much.'

'And better than that… lots more offers of wedding venues have come in. Most aren't licensed and it's hard to book an officiant. But there was one really interesting offer…' Lauren smiled into the phone, feeling a surge of love for her friend. She could always rely on Zoe to come through for her. She must have been working on this while Lauren was fast asleep.

'What was the offer?'

'There's a hotel in the Orkney Islands. They say they can host the wedding and the reception, as well as provide an officiant. On Saturday.'

'Wow. This Saturday? That's brilliant.'

'It is in Orkney, though,' Zoe said. 'It's hard to get to. You'd need to fly to mainland Scotland and then on.'

Lauren's mind started to spin. How would she get all her friends and relatives up to Scotland and then to the Orkney Islands? And would Tracey be able to get a connecting flight from London to arrive there in time?

'Thanks so much,' she replied. 'It's brilliant you've managed to sort something out for us. I just need a bit of time to think how we can make it work.'

'They'll want an answer pretty soon. There's not much time.'

'OK, I'll speak to Adam about it.'

When she got off the phone she went to find Adam in the living room. He looked tired and dejected. She remembered that his stag do was supposed to be tonight, which was why he had the day off.

'Are you OK?' he asked her.

'Yeah,' she smiled. 'Pounding head, but otherwise fine.'

'I've cancelled the stag do,' he said, sadly. 'It didn't feel right without a wedding.'

'Well,' Lauren said, smiling. 'We might still be able to have a wedding.'

Adam sat up straighter. 'Has the church managed to fit us in?'

'No, not that. We've had an offer of another venue.'

After she'd explained that the wedding would be all the way up in Orkney, Adam told her he didn't mind where the wedding was, as long as he got to marry her. 'At least Amanda won't be in Orkney,' he said, grinning. 'But seriously, Zoe has done a great job finding another venue.'

'I'll miss the church, though,' Lauren said wistfully. She didn't even know what the hotel in Orkney looked like yet.

'Of course you will.' Adam put his arms around her. 'You spent so long on every detail.'

Lauren nodded. She wasn't getting married at St Peter's Church any more. She had to let that idea go. 'I'll get in touch with our guests, explain what's happened and see how many can still make it,' Lauren said. She really hoped a lot of them could still come. 'And I'll ring Tracey. See what she thinks. She has to be there, whatever happens. She's my only family.'

Lauren looked at the time. It was 11 a.m., which meant it would be 5 p.m. in Thailand. She sat down at the dining table, the same table where she'd written the wedding invitations just a few months before, with no idea what was going to unfold. She rang Tracey from her laptop, but there was no answer.

Misty jumped onto Lauren's lap and she stroked her as she looked out the window. Rows of terraced houses stretched out below her, and beyond them was the grey haze of central London. In the other room, she could hear Adam speaking to his mother and telling her their plans. She picked up her phone and crafted a message to her friends explaining what had happened and asking who would be able to make a wedding in Orkney.

Replies started to trickle in immediately. Some of her friends were excited and said they'd do anything they could to make it, but her friends from work didn't think they'd be able to get any time off. She understood. It would have to be a smaller wedding. She shivered with excitement at the thought that there was a chance she'd still be getting married on Saturday. They could always throw a party in London to celebrate the marriage when they got back from their honeymoon for those who couldn't make it.

She tried to ring Tracey again, but there was no answer. She sent her an email to explain the situation. She just hoped Tracey would be able to find a connecting flight and make it to Orkney. She wouldn't go ahead without her.

*

In the evening, Sam rang her, interrupting her search for a new photographer. Adam was in the bedroom, on the phone to a florist based in Orkney.

'Hello?' Lauren said, surprised to hear from her.

'I've been trying to get hold of Adam,' she said. 'But his phone's engaged.'

'He's been sorting out the wedding.'

'Look,' Sam said. 'About Orkney. Can you really have your wedding there on Saturday?'

Lauren frowned, wondering what this was about. Adam had told her earlier that Sam was happy to travel to Orkney. 'I don't see why not.'

'Did you give notice to the local council for your marriage?'

'Of course.' Going to the marriage registrations office had just been a formality that they'd gone through months ago.

Sam sighed. 'I've been looking into everything. And it seems that you can't just change the venue at short notice. The marriage wouldn't be legal.'

Lauren swallowed. 'I don't remember that.'

'OK, well, hopefully I'm wrong. Maybe you should look into it.'

As soon as Lauren hung up, she scoured the internet for ways to get round the rule. But Sam was right. She couldn't legally get married on Saturday unless it was at St Peter's.

Just then she saw an email come through from Tracey. It was the middle of the night in Thailand, and Lauren imagined Tracey desperately searching for flights to Orkney deep into the night. But it was too late. Lauren put her head in her hands. It didn't matter what Tracey's email said now. Whether or not her sister could get to Orkney, there wouldn't be a wedding there.

It took ten minutes and one glass of wine before Lauren made herself open Tracey's email.

She read the first few lines, blinking back tears.

> *I'm sorry, Lauren, but the flight times just don't work. I won't be able to make it to Orkney.*

She felt a strange mix of disappointment and relief. Disappointment that Tracey couldn't come and relief that it no longer mattered. There wasn't going to be a wedding.

But then she read the next few lines.

> *I've been thinking… this might sound crazy, but why don't you have the wedding here? In Thailand, at my hotel. We've been running weddings for the last few years and we have space a week on Thursday. It would all be free of charge, of course. The accommodation and the wedding. I can sort out all the paperwork. You'd have to sort flights, but you're already coming on your honeymoon here – you could just change the dates. And as the wedding will be free, you might be able to afford to fly some guests out too. I've been thinking it over and over and it seems to make sense to me. That way the family can all be together. And it's much hotter than Orkney! Let me know what you think. We'd love to have you here.*
>
> *Lots of love,*
> *Tracey xxxxxx*

Lauren read the email three times, hardly able to believe what it said. Her face broke into a huge smile. Everything was going to be alright. She could marry Adam. And her sister would be able to come. As long as Adam agreed, the wedding would be in Thailand.

CHAPTER FORTY-NINE

Lauren

Five days later: Thailand

Lauren stepped off the plane onto the metal staircase, the wall of heat hitting her. She felt the glow of the hot sun on her face as a film of sweat formed on her back. She'd been cold on the flight even with a jumper on, but once she got down the steps, she started to strip off her layers. Moving her head from side to side, she stretched out her neck muscles. She'd slept on and off throughout the flight, leaning into Adam's warm body, and she had a crooked neck.

She thought briefly of London, how if everything had gone to plan they would have been married yesterday. Instead they'd been boarding a flight to Thailand to have the wedding ceremony here.

The excited chatter of holidaymakers made her smile, as they got on the bus to the terminal. But then she stopped for a second, her breath taken from her body, remembering how excited they'd been on their first trip here with her parents. It was supposed to be an adventure. But it was the last one her parents would ever have. As the memories engulfed her, she reached for Adam's hand and gripped it tightly.

They entered the terminal together. Behind them, Lauren could hear Sam and her ex-husband making strained conversation. They'd sat apart on the flight, but now, for the first time, they had to face each other. Luckily, Tony's latest much younger girlfriend wasn't coming to Thailand. To their great relief, she had work commitments, so she wouldn't be there to antagonise Sam.

Lauren thought how lucky they were that so many people had been willing to make the last-minute trip for the ceremony. Zoe had managed to wrangle refunds from the pub, the photographer and the florist, which had paid for flights for some of her closest friends and family. Fifteen of their friends had been able to attend, including Zoe, Kiera and Jimmy. It was the first time Zoe had been apart from her son for longer than a few hours, and Lauren was full of gratitude that she'd been willing to travel so far for the wedding.

Lauren thought of Tracey, how kind she'd been to them, how much she'd wanted to help. She had organised everything in Thailand and was sorting out the paperwork with the Thai authorities. Maybe in the future they would grow even closer, more like the sisters they used to be. She vowed that she would try to put more money aside so she could visit more often. And maybe Tracey could come and stay with her in the UK too.

She felt a sense of longing for her sister, a yearning for the close-knit family of four they used to be. But she reminded herself that she had Adam now. Soon they would have a family of their own.

They stopped in the passport queue and she looked up at him. 'I love you,' she said, placing her hand on the warm skin of his cheek and kissing him lightly.

'I love you too,' he replied. She saw the same swirl of emotions in his eyes and realised he felt it too, the sense of loss at the memories, the bittersweet thoughts of the holiday they'd had before the accident. Things would never be the same, but one thing was certain – they would be together.

*

They shared a taxi to the hotel with Kiera and Zoe, Adam offering to take the middle seat, even though he was the biggest. 'That way you can have seat belts,' he said.

'Don't be silly,' Kiera had said, 'I'm the shortest.' So she'd wedged herself into the middle seat between Lauren and Adam. Lauren bit her tongue.

Adam gazed out the window. 'It's beautiful here, isn't it?' he said. Everyone agreed. They could see the bright blue ocean, the boats bobbing on its surface. A row of huts lined the beach, mounted on stilts set deep into the sand, colourful beach towels hanging from their railings. The huts looked weathered, the wood darkened with salt and water from the sea breeze.

Lauren remembered that they'd had a tsunami here, the one that had killed Jasmine's biological parents. She'd watched the footage on the news in shock, unable to comprehend how the islands would ever recover. It both comforted and saddened her that everything was back to normal now, as if nothing had ever happened. Everything could recover and heal. Just like the world kept moving on without her parents in it.

A tear formed in the corner of her eye and she wiped it away quickly before the others noticed. The taxi rounded a corner a bit too fast and Kiera squealed. Lauren saw her hand grip Adam's knee as she tried to stop herself falling into him.

The air conditioning in the cab started to circulate, and Lauren leaned back into the seat, relieved at the cool air. She'd forgotten how hot the air was here, how thick and oppressive. The sun shone through the window, a blur of heat.

'It's boiling here,' Kiera said. 'I can't wait to jump in the pool.'
'Me too,' Zoe said.

'No pool at my budget hostel, though, so I think I'll be using yours.' Kiera punched Adam playfully and Lauren clenched her teeth. She reminded herself that after their honeymoon Kiera would be moving out of their flat and they'd have more space and time alone.

'Better make the most of the weather while it lasts, though. It's the rainy season here,' Kiera continued.

'Is it?' Lauren asked. There'd been so much to organise that she hadn't thought to look up the weather on the island. She'd assumed it was sunny all year round, and Tracey hadn't mentioned otherwise.

'Yeah, the rain can be torrential at this time of year,' Kiera confirmed.

'I'm sure it won't be on your wedding day,' Zoe said. 'I bet they just get the occasional storm in the summer.'

'The wedding will be wonderful, whatever the weather,' Kiera said breezily. 'And besides, it's not like you're guaranteed good weather for an August wedding in England. It could have rained there, too.'

The taxi turned onto the main street of the resort, lined with restaurants, bars and massage parlours. They dropped Kiera off at her hostel first, in front of a group of backpackers sitting on plastic chairs and drinking from buckets of alcohol through straws. Tracey had offered all the wedding guests rooms at a discounted rate, but only Jimmy, Zoe, and Adam's parents had taken her up on it.

They continued on to Tracey's hotel, turning off the main road and weaving round the coast to a small bay. Luxury wooden cabins were spread out along the mountainside, and there was a six-storey main building. Lauren had visited once before, but the beauty of the place still took her breath away. The taxi pulled up in front of a grand white marble entrance, a row of colourful flags fluttering in the gentle breeze.

As they stepped out of the car, a roll of thunder rumbled and a porter rushed out to take the bags from the boot of the taxi. They were paying the driver when it started to rain, huge drops pummelling them from the sky.

CHAPTER FIFTY

Adam

Adam's eyes roamed around the expansive hotel lobby, taking in its opulence. Chandeliers hung from the ceiling and trees rose from the back of the room, their branches overhanging a vast indoor fountain. In the corner, by a bar, a pianist played classical music, barely audible above the rain that pounded on the central glass dome of the ceiling. A receptionist came and greeted them with a little bow, presenting them with glasses of chilled champagne and a platter of exotic fruit.

Adam felt uncomfortable and underdressed, his feet hot and sweaty in his trainers. He shifted his weight from side to side nervously. He was going to see Tracey again. For the first time in nearly eighteen years. He hadn't wanted to have the wedding here, it held far too many memories, but Lauren had been so excited about it, he'd been unable to say no. To her it had seemed to be the perfect solution. But he'd spent the last few days with a building sense of dread.

He didn't know what Tracey had been thinking, offering to host the wedding. For so many years she'd been estranged from Lauren. Lauren had thought it had been to do with the argument they'd had over selling their parents' flat, but he had always wondered if it might be something to do with him. He and Tracey had planned their lives together, but then he'd treated her abysmally. He felt a rush of shame as he remembered how he'd behaved. But maybe now she'd forgiven him, put it all behind her. She'd married and had her own family. He told himself she must have forgotten about him, moved on.

It will all be fine, he reassured himself for what felt like the millionth time. Tracey hadn't mentioned their fling to Lauren in all these years. She was hardly going to do that now.

But still, he felt flushed and sweaty, his heart pumping frantically, as if he was waiting for something awful to happen. At least they were away from Amanda. They could have their dream wedding here, and the worst thing that could happen was some awkwardness between him and Tracey.

'Hello,' an English voice said, and Adam jumped, nearly spilling his champagne. But it wasn't Tracey. It was just his mother, his father appearing behind her.

'Great hotel, this,' his father said appreciatively. 'Tracey's really done well for herself, hasn't she?'

'Yeah.' Adam nodded. Lauren had visited the hotel before but he'd never been here. He hadn't realised just how luxurious it was. Tracey had really landed on her feet.

'And to think that when she said she wanted to settle in Thailand, we all thought she'd be back within a year.' Tony laughed. Adam was surprised his father had ever paid any attention to what Tracey was doing. He'd been so distant after the divorce, cutting himself off from his former friends. The last time he'd seen Tracey would have been at her parents' funeral.

A uniformed member of staff appeared and handed champagne to his parents, before escorting them to a sofa in the corner of the lobby to take them through their registration details. Adam and Lauren sat down on the sofa where they were as the receptionist processed their passports. Lauren grinned at him as she sipped her champagne. 'That was quite a welcome, wasn't it?' she said.

'Glad we impressed,' a voice said from behind them.

'Tracey!' Lauren squealed as she stood up and turned to hug her. Adam's heart stopped when he saw her. She looked the same as he remembered; standing as straight as an arrow, her dark hair flowing down her back. Her carefree energy had been replaced with a kind of serene authority. Even now, so many years later, she took his breath away. He stood stock-still waiting for her to greet him.

'And Jasmine!' Lauren said, hugging the girl that stood behind her wearing the hotel's uniform, a name badge pinned to her shirt. Jasmine smiled at them all and Adam held out his shaking hand to introduce himself. Tracey still hadn't said hello.

'Adam,' he said to Jasmine. 'Nice to meet you.' Her hand was cold and clammy in his, and he was suddenly aware that his palms were sweating. He turned back to look at Tracey.

'Thank you so much for hosting the wedding here,' Lauren said. 'We're so grateful.' She squeezed her sister's arm and Tracey shifted awkwardly, meeting Adam's eyes behind her back. He couldn't read her expression.

'Yes,' Adam said, aware of the quiver in his voice. 'Thank you. You have a lovely hotel.'

'Just wait until you see the honeymoon suite,' she said with a grin. 'It's on the beach. Very secluded. You'll love it.'

He tried to smile, but he couldn't help thinking back to the time he and Tracey had made love in the beach hut all those years ago. Was she thinking about that too?

'It's ages since we've all been together,' she said. 'I'm so glad the two of you have come back to Thailand. I've been waiting so long for this moment.' Adam shifted uncomfortably, feeling the intensity of her gaze. She was speaking to both of them, but she was only looking at him.

CHAPTER FIFTY-ONE

Lauren

'This is our wedding planner, Noi,' Tracey said, and Lauren smiled at the Thai woman who had appeared beside her. 'I'll leave you in her capable hands.'

'Will we see you later?' Lauren said quickly. She was desperate to catch up with her sister, and disappointed she was rushing off.

'Let's meet for dinner. Noi's planned a tasting for you so you can try all the delicious food on our wedding menu and decide what you want to eat on your big day. I'll join you then.' Tracey leaned over and gave Lauren a peck on the cheek, before nodding to Noi and moving away with Jasmine, who waved as she walked off.

'Would you like some more champagne?' the wedding planner asked, indicating their empty glasses.

Adam and Lauren shook their heads.

'In that case, we're ready for our tour,' she smiled. 'Let's do it now, while the rain has stopped. I'm sure you'll be amazed by the facilities we have here.' Noi led them through the hotel, down to the beach. Even though Lauren had visited before, she hadn't remembered so many swimming pools. So far she'd counted eight, including an infinity pool where you could swim right up into the sunset. There were restaurants specialising in every type of cuisine and people who delivered the food of your choice to your sunlounger as you lay by the pool.

'Does it rain a lot this time of year?' Adam asked, stepping over a puddle. Above them the sun was shining again, the water already starting to evaporate.

'It's the rainy season,' Noi said with a shrug. 'But I've checked the forecast for your wedding on Thursday. It's sunny.'

'Phew,' Lauren said, reaching for Adam's hand. He squeezed hers tightly.

On the beach, there were rows of tiny huts a few metres from the crashing waves.

'These are beautiful,' Lauren said, clutching Adam's hand.

'You haven't seen the best bit yet. I'll take you to where you'll be getting married.'

She led them away from the grounds of the hotel, down a path to a private beach lined with palm trees. Noi pointed out a picturesque wooden restaurant perched on stilts above the sea, at the end of a meandering wooden pier. 'You'll say your vows at the end of the pier. Then you and your guests will walk over the water to the restaurant for the reception. We'll do the food tasting there this evening.'

Lauren drank in the scene around her, the sparkling water below a bright blue sky and a burning sun. 'It's so beautiful.'

Noi nodded, clearly used to receiving this kind of compliment. 'For weddings, we put tea lights along the pier. It's looks wonderful. You say your vows at the end of the pier and they're broadcast through tiny speakers on the beach. After the vows, the wedding party will come up the pier and throw confetti on you, before you all go to the restaurant for the reception.'

Lauren nodded, tears in her eyes.

'Are you OK?' Adam asked, his arm around her.

'I think I'm in heaven,' she replied. He leaned towards her and kissed her gently on the lips.

'Would you like me to show you to your residence now?' Noi said, after she'd given them a moment.

'Our residence?' Lauren asked. That sounded so extravagant.

Noi nodded. 'I think you'll like it. The honeymoon residence.' She took them down a winding path to yet another beach. It was completely deserted, not a single person in the sea, just the sound of the waves crashing against the pristine white sand.

There were two rocking chairs on the huge terrace that ran all the way round the expanse of the hut, dotted by cushioned sunloungers and a love seat.

Noi unlocked the door with the key card and they stepped into a lounge area with a long corner sofa and a chaise longue. Their cases had already arrived and had been placed in the bedroom, where there was a luxurious four-poster bed, covered in cushions and pillows.

Next to the terrace there was a glass-covered jacuzzi, with a small stone ornament of two kissing doves at the entrance. 'You can take the roof off if you want some sunshine, or keep it covered if you don't,' Noi said, pressing a button that retracted the glass roof and opened the jacuzzi to the beating sun.

'Wow,' Lauren said.

Once Noi had left them, Lauren went over to the hamper in the middle of the sitting room. It was full of expensive chocolates, fruit and champagne, plus vouchers for the spa.

She passed Adam a chocolate. 'Just one,' he said with a grin.

Opening hers, Lauren held it in her mouth until it melted, absorbing the dark, rich flavour. Then Adam popped the cork of the champagne, pouring them each a glass.

'More fizz,' she said, with a laugh.

'Well, we need to raise a toast,' he said. 'To us, and to the many happy years ahead of us.'

'To us,' Lauren echoed, feeling herself start to relax as the bubbles danced on her tongue.

They went outside and drank the champagne standing on the terrace, looking out over the ocean, the breeze gently blowing through Lauren's hair. Adam finished his drink quickly and went back inside to get changed and refresh himself after the long journey.

Lauren wandered in after him and placed her glass by the hamper. It was then that she noticed a piece of paper sticking out of the side. A message from the hotel, congratulating them on their wedding. She smiled. It was really happening. At last.

There was another note underneath it, this time in a little envelope. 'To Lauren' it said, in neat handwriting, a tiny heart drawn next to her name.

She opened it, smiling.

The message inside was written in pale blue ink, and she let the paper fall from her hands as if it burned.

You haven't got away from me, Lauren.

CHAPTER FIFTY-TWO

Lauren

Lauren froze, her hand trembling.

She stared at the piece of paper. The writing was neat and tidy, each letter clear. Entirely different from the typed congratulations note from the hotel, but slotted in underneath. The envelope had been placed in the basket with the champagne and chocolates, which meant someone had deliberately put it there. Someone at the hotel. Or someone who had broken into their room.

She'd come to the other side of the world, and she'd thought they were far away from Amanda and any threat to their wedding. She looked down at the yellowing bruises on her bad wrist and remembered her fall down the stairs at the club. Adam had reported Amanda to the police, but they hadn't arrested her. She'd been getting injections for a holiday. Could the holiday have been in Thailand? Lauren's blood ran cold. Could Amanda have cancelled their wedding in the UK and then come all the way here to ruin it, when she found out it had moved? But no, that didn't make any sense. Amanda had had the injections at the surgery before the wedding had even been moved to Thailand. She wouldn't have known, she couldn't have.

It must be someone else, someone in Thailand right now. She and Adam had had a long tour of the hotel and wedding venue. There'd been plenty of time for someone to slip into her room and plant the note. Her mind flashed to Kiera. She thought of the way she'd gripped Adam's leg in the taxi as they'd rounded the corner. But she quickly dismissed the thought. They were just friends.

But who else could it be? It had to be someone on the island. Someone in the wedding party. One of the twenty people she trusted most in the world.

'Are you going to join me?' Naked, Adam popped his head round the door of the bedroom and grinned. 'I'm just about to try out the rainforest shower.'

'No, sorry,' she said distractedly.

'Your loss.'

Lauren would have loved to join Adam, to relax under the cascading water, to feel his skin on hers. But she couldn't. Not now. She needed to deal with the note. Work out who'd sent it. And then get them away from her wedding.

Her heart thumping in her chest, Lauren went round checking all the doors and windows, to see how someone might have got in. But they were all locked, and Noi had used the key card to open the front door when they'd arrived. It hadn't been left open. Which meant that maybe the person hadn't come into the room to put the note there at all. Maybe it had already been in the hamper.

She called to Adam that she was just popping out, scribbling a quick message in case he hadn't heard over the shower, and then hurried back to the hotel reception. It was a long walk over the beach. Her mind spun as the waves crashed against the shore and the sun beat down on her. She was supposed to be in paradise, but it felt like anything but. She thought of her parents, of the picturesque Thai river shaded by trees where their lives had ended. Pulling a tissue from her pocket, she dabbed her eyes as the sea wind swept through her hair. Paradise could be deceiving.

She saw a figure walking along the beach towards her and swallowed back her tears. It was Tony. Adam's father. She'd hardly spoken to him over the years, and Adam rarely saw him. He'd been such an absent father, always working at the hospital, never there to go to Adam's school parents' evenings or to take him to football at the weekends. Her own father had been the opposite, diligently taking her to every extra-curricular activity she fancied and saving up for her to have piano lessons. It seemed so unfair that Tony was here, getting to share their special day with them, when her father couldn't.

'Hi,' she said politely, swallowing her resentment.

'Hello!' he said. 'All ready for the big day?'

'Just about.' She never could think of anything to say to Adam's dad. It should have been easy, they were both hospital doctors, but she still found it hard.

He seemed to be struggling too. 'I hear you're breaking with tradition and having a best woman rather than a best man – Kiera.'

Lauren frowned. How did he know Kiera? He'd never taken any interest in Adam's friends.

'Yes,' she said. 'It was what Adam wanted.'

'They're close, those two. I saw them at the conference together. Best buddies.' He said the words slowly as if they meant something else. Did he think they were more than friends? Or was he just trying to wind her up? Adam had always said he had a cruel sense of humour.

Lauren smiled at him politely. 'Well, have a good day,' she said. 'Enjoy the beach.'

'See you later,' he said, with a casual wave, and continued on his way.

When she reached the hotel reception, she saw Jasmine behind the desk in a neatly ironed uniform. Her heart sank. There was no way she could tell her niece that she'd got the vicious note. Jasmine had such an idealised view of her relationship with Adam. Lauren didn't want to admit there were any cracks.

'Jasmine!' Lauren said to her niece, forcing a smile. 'You look great. Very smart. It's so good to see you here. I didn't get the chance to ask you earlier – how was your revision course?'

'It was fine. It finished yesterday.' One of the benefits of moving the wedding date back a few days later and holding it in Thailand was that now Jasmine could attend.

'That's great,' Lauren said. She wondered if she should just leave reception and come back later when Jasmine wasn't there.

'I'm so excited you're having the wedding here. A perfect family reunion.' She smiled bashfully at her aunt. 'So, what brings you over to reception then? Is your room OK?'

Lauren swallowed. 'It's wonderful. It's just that…' She paused, her mind scrambling as she thought of a lie. 'It's just that I had a lovely congratulations note put in my room, in my hamper. It was in a little envelope, handwritten. It must have been one of my guests, I suppose. I wanted to say thank you, but I don't know who to thank. Is there any way you can find out who put it in there?'

Jasmine smiled. 'Do you have it with you?'

Lauren had brought it with her specially, in her handbag. But she couldn't show it to Jasmine. 'No, I don't, I'm afraid.'

'OK, so you say it was handwritten, in English and in your hamper. I'll see if any of the other staff know anything about it. Excuse me one moment.'

She went to a little back room behind reception and Lauren heard her speaking to the other receptionists in Thai.

She came back smiling. 'So, the note didn't come from the hotel,' she said. 'Or anyone in it. It arrived in the post, with instructions to take it out of the postal envelope and put the smaller envelope in your room. The maids must have thought it should go in your hamper.'

'It came in the post?'

'Yes, a few days ago. Before you arrived. The reception staff waited for you to come and then put it in your room.'

'Did it come from abroad or from Thailand?' Lauren asked, even though she already knew the answer.

'It came via airmail. It was from the UK.'

CHAPTER FIFTY-THREE

Adam

Adam stood on the terrace of the restaurant at the end of the pier, looking down at the waves crashing against the supporting wooden stilts. They were meeting Tracey for dinner, trying the tasting menu, and he was more nervous than he'd been for years. Aside from earlier in the lobby, they hadn't been in the same room at the same time since they'd been at her parents' funeral.

Lauren came and stood behind him, and he slid his arm round her. 'We're so lucky that Tracey's arranged all this for us,' she said.

'I know,' he replied, staring down at the ocean. 'Are you feeling better now?'

Lauren had shown him the note from the hamper earlier. Although Jasmine had told her it had been sent from abroad, she'd still seemed worried.

'Yeah, a bit. The note was just a shock.'

'It's only Amanda. It must be. It was sent from the UK. She's just... trying to hurt us still. But she can't. She's not here. You can't let her ruin everything.'

Lauren squeezed his hand. 'You're right,' she said. 'Of course you're right. It just reminded me of everything that happened back home. I'm still a bit on edge.'

'Look out at the view,' he said reassuringly. 'We've escaped all the way to paradise. There's nothing to worry about here.' He leaned in to kiss her and she returned the kiss hungrily, her body pressed into his.

'Hello!' a voice called out, and he jumped, pulling away from Lauren. Tracey came over, hugging them each in turn. Was it Adam's imagination, or did she hold him for just a moment too long?

'Come and sit down,' Tracey said, leading them to their table on the terrace. A white linen cloth was crowded with glasses and cutlery. Three glasses each: one for fizz, one for white and one for red. And three sets of cutlery for the starter, main course and dessert.

They sat down, Lauren exclaiming delightedly over every little detail – the elegant candles, the soft moonlight, how you could see the sea through the gaps between the planks that made up the floor.

Noi appeared with a bottle of champagne and poured. 'Let's raise a toast,' she said. 'To the happy couple. I hope you have a wonderful wedding day.'

Tracey held up her glass and clinked Lauren's. Then she pushed her glass towards Adam. 'To the happy couple,' she said, loudly, but she couldn't even look at him.

Memories flooded his mind of the time they'd had together, scuba-diving among shoals of tropical fish; riding a motorbike to a beachside restaurant; his hands wrapped round her body, in bed together. Back then he had imagined it would be Tracey he'd be marrying. They'd promised they'd spend the rest of their lives together, and he'd meant it at that moment in time. But things between them had been over as fast as they'd begun.

He felt full of guilt and regret when he thought of how he'd treated Tracey, ignoring her at her parents' funeral because he couldn't face her, ashamed that even though he was at medical school, he hadn't been able to save her parents.

Tracey had escaped to Thailand, leaving Lauren behind. Lauren had been a wreck when she'd moved in with him and Sam, hardly able to function with her grief. He'd been her shoulder to cry on, and in supporting her he'd started to feel worthwhile again himself. They'd needed each other. He'd been the first person to make her smile again, and then later, they'd slept together. He hadn't been able to tell her about his relationship with Tracey. She'd been too fragile.

Tracey took a gulp of champagne, and Noi started talking to Lauren and Adam about the choice of starters. They could try everything on the menu if they wished, and then choose what they wanted to be served at the wedding. After much discussion, they chose the scallops and oysters to try.

'Locally farmed,' Tracey said, and Adam nodded. She met his eye and he flushed.

He thought of the letter she'd sent him from Thailand, six months after her parents had died and his relationship with her had finished. She'd told him how much she loved him, invited him out to live with her, like they once promised they would. He hadn't known why she'd sent the letter so many months later. He'd been with Lauren by then. But for a moment, as he read her words, he'd thought of the carefree life they'd imagined together and was tempted. But then he'd come to his senses, and replied to say no.

Tracey couldn't have known he'd got together with Lauren – the two sisters had hardly been speaking, even back then. But a couple of weeks later Lauren had decided to tell her sister about their relationship. Without telling Adam what she was planning, she'd emailed over a smiling photo of the two of them, accompanying it with a gushing note about how happy they both were. He'd felt ill when he'd read it. He still remembered Tracey's reply, even now. It had just been one line. *You look like the perfect couple.* After that, Lauren hadn't seen Tracey for fifteen years.

CHAPTER FIFTY-FOUR

Lauren

Lauren waited for her sister under a palm tree in the gardens of the hotel. Tracey had seemed very tense from the moment they'd arrived, her hug slightly awkward, her conversation over dinner overly cheerful and superficial. Lauren had been worried about her, sure it was something to do with the divorce. It must be playing on her mind, particularly with Lauren and Adam getting married in her hotel. Lauren was grateful they were meeting, just the two of them, to have a proper catch-up.

As Lauren walked through the gardens, she thought about the note she'd received in the hamper. Jasmine had told her it had been posted from abroad, but whoever had sent it had known which hotel they were at. That wasn't public information. Adam was convinced that it must be from Amanda, but how would she have known where they were staying?

A little boy bounded up to Lauren, stopping suddenly and staring up at her. His brother appeared beside him. They were dressed identically in bright red shorts and Manchester United shirts.

'Ken's favourite team,' Tracey explained, when she saw Lauren looking. 'I picked the boys up from his house this morning.'

'How's it going?' Lauren asked carefully. 'With Ken?' She hadn't wanted to ask last night in front of Noi. It hadn't seemed appropriate.

'Oh OK, he's still being funny with Jasmine. But then I kind of understand. She can be difficult.'

Lauren thought of Jasmine working in the hotel reception yesterday, how polite and professional she was. Tracey seemed so critical of her. 'I saw her at reception yesterday. She works hard.'

'Yes, she's saving up to go travelling.'

'Like you.'

'Yes.'

The boys were running in and out of the bushes now, playing hide and seek.

'One, two, three... coming, ready or not!'

'They're so cute, Tracey.'

'A bit of a handful, too,' she grinned. 'Four-year-olds have a lot of energy.'

'I'll bet.'

'Boys – come and say hello to Auntie Lauren.'

They ran over and Lauren crouched down on the ground, sweeping them both into her arms. They laughed joyfully and Lauren hoped that one day she'd have this kind of happiness with her own children.

'I'm so thrilled they're going to be at my wedding,' Lauren said, beaming. 'And Jasmine, too. The whole family together at last.'

'It's been a long time, hasn't it?'

'I was going to ask you,' Lauren said. 'Could Jasmine be a flower girl for the wedding? I know it's usually a role for a child, but I love the idea of someone spreading petals across the beach as I walk down the aisle. And I really want Jasmine to be involved. A kind of junior-bridesmaid-slash-flower girl, I suppose.' Lauren wrung her hands together nervously, unsure what her sister was going to say. They'd been estranged for so many years before they reunited, and she still wasn't completely sure the past was behind them.

'Of course,' Tracey said quickly. 'If that's what you both want. I'll help her pick out something to wear.' She took Lauren's arm and Lauren felt a warmth spreading over her. They felt like a real family again. The boys ran ahead and they walked on until they came to a small square with a statue where Tracey stopped. 'I wanted to show this to you.'

The statue was of two granite hearts curved into each other and entwined. Lauren read the inscription at its base. *In loving memory of Debbie and James Haywood.*

'It's beautiful,' she said, tears in her eyes.

'You always thought that I'd just moved on, didn't you?' Tracey said. 'Run away to Thailand and forgotten them.'

'No…' Lauren said. But a part of her had felt that. At seventeen she'd felt abandoned, her parents dead, her sister in Thailand. Only Sam had been there for her in the beginning, looking after her in London. And then Adam.

'I needed time on my own, space to get over what happened. And then I met Ken and adopted Jasmine. My life was here.'

Lauren nodded. 'All those years we didn't speak. I just wish we had been closer. They're gone now. We can't get them back.' Her voice broke with emotion.

'I—'

'Was it about the inheritance?'

That was when Tracey had stopped speaking to her. When she and Sam had been clearing out her parents' flat to sell. It had been horrible, bagging up their lives and taking everything to charity shops. Her dad's suits, her mum's dresses, a lifetime of mementos from their holidays. Tracey had wanted the whole process speeded up so she could get the inheritance quicker. But she hadn't wanted to come home and help. Luckily Lauren had had Adam to support her.

Tracey looked surprised. 'Not only that,' she said. 'But I needed my share quickly. I was running out of money in Thailand.'

'You could have come home.' Lauren thought of how much she'd longed for her sister's support back then, how alone she felt.

'I couldn't…' she said. 'I just couldn't face you then. Not after what happened with Mum and Dad. The accident…'

Lauren's head was suddenly full of that day. The raft bouncing over the rapids. The shouts of the instructor. Her parents in the water, being carried over the rocks. Then being dragged out of the river, their bodies battered and broken. They'd all tried their best to revive them. Mouth-to-mouth by the side of the river. Adam had done chest compressions. But there was no response. They couldn't save them. *She* couldn't save them. The guilt overwhelmed her.

'I know,' Lauren said, touching Tracey's arm lightly.

'Yoga has helped me to come to terms with everything. And meditation. I've… let's just say I've accepted what happened. Everyone's role in it.'

Lauren felt sick with relief. Tracey had accepted what had happened. She still worried that her sister blamed her for her parents' deaths, the way she blamed herself. It would be understandable, but Lauren had never plucked up the courage to ask her, to talk to her, to try and explain what had happened, why she'd done what she did. She'd been too scared, in case Tracey had told her the one thing she didn't want to hear: that it was all her fault.

Just then, Lauren felt a big drop of water fall on her shoulder.

A storm broke above them, lightning splitting the sky. The heavens opened.

Rivers of water ran down the path, and the boys splashed gleefully as Tracey rushed them to the hotel reception. Lauren ran, holding her hands over her head to protect herself, but by the time they were inside the hotel reception, they were drenched from head to toe. The rain pounded on the glass roof of the lobby, the air inside still hot and humid. Lauren watched lightning cut across the darkened sky, and thought of her wedding.

'Tropical island,' Tracey shrugged. 'It will pass.'

'By Thursday?' she asked. Her wedding day.

'The forecast says so,' said Tracey. 'Although these things aren't entirely predictable.'

Lauren's brow creased.

'Don't worry,' Tracey said, reaching out to touch Lauren's arm, 'we're always prepared for rain. We've got a marquee for the guests and a canopy that can stretch the whole length of the pier. Just in case.'

'Thank you,' Lauren said, relieved. 'Hopefully the forecast is right and we won't need them.'

'I'm sure it will be,' Tracey said reassuringly. 'Look, I need to get the boys changed, they're soaked.' She wiped her wet hands on her dress. 'Can I get one of our drivers to take you over to your hut? They have jeeps that go over the sand, right to your door.'

'Yes, please,' Lauren replied.

'He'll just be a few minutes,' she said, after she called over a driver and explained where Lauren needed to go.

The jeep took her down a deserted back alleyway and then bounced over the sand dunes to the honeymoon hut on the beach. As she approached it, she realised how isolated it was, sitting alone among the vast dunes that stretched for miles. The beach hut had looked like a paradise in the sunlight, the perfect place to get away from it all. But under the rolling storm clouds, it looked tiny and vulnerable.

Lauren stepped out of the jeep into the pouring rain. All she could hear was the sound of the waves crashing, loud and angry. She jumped as a rumble of thunder added to the din. The man driving the jeep had sprung out of the car, and held a huge umbrella over her as he walked her to the door. He wasn't wearing any rain protection either and the rain lashed against his hotel uniform.

'It's OK,' Lauren said, indicating the umbrella, as she tried to get her footing in the wet sand dunes. But her voice was barely audible against the storm.

She fumbled with her key card to open the door, until the driver took it from her hand and swiped it over the sensor.

The door opened, and the driver bowed and left.

'Adam?' she called out, finally out of the rain.

'Over here.' She could hear the muffled sound of the TV. Inside the storm wasn't quite as loud and she started to relax, seeing the home comforts of the hut: the little kettle, the minibar, the huge sofa.

'You're soaked,' Adam said, standing up from the sofa and switching the television off.

'I got caught in the storm. I hope it's not like this on our wedding day,' Lauren said anxiously.

'It won't be,' Adam replied. 'It's been very humid up until now. It felt like it needed to rain. This storm will get the rain out of its system.' He came closer and put his arms round her, his hands resting at the bottom of her back.

Lauren shivered, her body goose-pimpling in her wet dress.

'You look stunning,' he said. 'Even soaked through.' He stepped away from her and looked her up and down appreciatively. 'That dress is clinging in all the right places.'

Pulling her towards him, he kissed her passionately.

'There's only one thing we can do in a storm,' he grinned. 'Let's get you out of those wet clothes and into the bedroom.'

CHAPTER FIFTY-FIVE

Adam

2001: Thailand

Adam adjusted the strap on his helmet while he listened to the safety briefing for the white-water rafting. The guide was speaking in heavily accented English, and Adam had to concentrate to understand what he was saying.

'At end, we pull over and tie boat to rock,' the guide said. 'End of the river is dangerous. Very dangerous. So no one in water at end. During rafting lots of people fall in. Fun, fun, fun. But at end, when I shout 'paddle to side' no more fun. We pull in. OK?'

Adam nodded, although it couldn't be that dangerous, could it? Otherwise they wouldn't let them raft on the river in the first place. Besides, he'd done this before on holiday in Europe; the rougher the river, the better. He couldn't wait.

They all cheered when they got into the boat and Adam grinned at Tracey, sitting opposite him. He thought of their conversation last night. About living together in Thailand. Would they really do it, or had it just been a fantasy? For the moment, he didn't care. He just knew she wanted to be with him, and the thought made him buzz with excitement.

Soon they were paddling as hard as they could beneath the lush Thai forest, the trees hanging over the sides of the valley, shading the river. Below their raft the water ran angrily over the rocks. In front of them, another boat careered over a small drop and half the tourists tumbled out into the water. They swam back to the boat and the others pulled them in.

'Your turn next,' their guide shouted, a wild grin on his face.

They paddled furiously towards the drop, and the boat started to spin round. They were approaching the rapid at an angle, sideways on. Adam's heart raced with the thrill of it all. Now they were facing backward. Adam felt a rush of adrenaline as the boat started to tip, the back of it heading down the rapid, while those of them at the front were lifted out of their seats. He gripped the rope round the edge of the boat and crouched down, trying to maintain the boat's equilibrium.

The tail of the boat slammed into the shallow water, and they all screamed with excitement. Adam met Tracey's eyes and saw the huge smile on her face. Then the boat righted itself, before spinning into the next rapid. This time they couldn't keep the boat steady and they all catapulted into the air and then into the river. Adam wiped the water from his face and climbed back into the raft, helping Tracey up behind him. Then with a grin, he pushed her back in.

'You idiot,' she shouted as she splashed in the shallow water. As soon as she got back in the boat, she returned the favour, pushing him into the water.

'Come on, you two, stop flirting,' Tracey's dad shouted, with a grin. Adam caught Lauren's troubled expression. She didn't seem to be enjoying the trip.

'Onto the serious stuff now,' the guide shouted. 'Tougher rapids. Scarier. Can you do it?' He punched his fist in the air.

'Yes!' Adam and Tracey shouted together.

And they all started paddling again, the boat turning back and forth in the fast-flowing water. 'I haven't forgiven you,' Tracey shouted, laughing as they careered over the next rapid.

CHAPTER FIFTY-SIX

Lauren

Two days until the wedding

Lauren lay by the spa pool with Sam. They'd been there all day, relaxing in the heated indoor pool and indulging in massages, manicures and pedicures. Finally, Lauren was starting to feel calmer about the wedding. Adam was right; she shouldn't let a malicious note ruin it for her. She rubbed her wrist. The swelling had gone down now, but the bruising was still visible. She thought of the person who'd pushed her down the stairs, and how the police hadn't caught them yet.

'I'm so glad things have improved now between you and Tracey,' Sam said, pulling her out of her thoughts.

'Me too.' Lauren gazed at the palm trees in the garden beyond the swimming pool. 'I think she's forgiven me now.'

Sam paused for a moment as if considering what to say, and Lauren wondered if she realised Lauren was referring to her parents' accident. 'It's been hard for her,' Sam said finally. 'But she's invited you and Adam to have your wedding here. That must have been a huge deal for her.'

'Yes, I'm grateful.'

'You know marriage isn't easy,' Sam said. She smiled ruefully. 'Well, at least mine wasn't.' Lauren nodded, even though she knew Adam was nothing like his father.

'I don't expect it to be all plain sailing,' she replied, thinking of everything that had happened recently, all the threats to their relationship. They'd come through it together, as a team.

'Good. You know, Adam's always been a private person. He doesn't always reveal everything.'

'I trust him,' she said firmly, as if to convince herself.

Just then her phone beeped, a message from Adam popping up on its screen. *Me and Kiera are going to the happy hour at her hostel. Fancy joining us? Meet at her room. 24 Thai Heights Hostel.*

Lauren frowned. She'd hoped that she and Adam would get the chance to spend some time alone before the wedding.

'Something wrong?' Sam asked.

'No,' Lauren said quickly. 'It was just Adam suggesting drinks with him and Kiera.'

Sam gave a knowing smile. 'Oh, I see. He's always been close to Kiera, hasn't he? She's his best woman for the wedding.' Lauren thought of how Tony had said the same thing to her on the beach.

'What do you mean?' Lauren couldn't stop herself asking.

'Oh, nothing. Just that she's his closest friend. She looks out for him.' Sam patted Lauren's arm. 'I'll see you later,' she said. And before Lauren could question her more, Sam got up from her lounger and disappeared into the locker room.

Twenty minutes later, Lauren knocked on Kiera's door at her backpacker hostel, still feeling relaxed from the spa.

'Come in,' Kiera said, with a smile. 'I just need to find my shoes.'

Lauren stepped over the threshold. 'Wow, this place is…' She looked at the mattress on the floor, the thin sheets of material in place of curtains.

'Basic? Isn't it?'

'I was going to say authentic.'

'It doesn't even have a flushing toilet. You pour water from a bucket down to flush it.'

Lauren peered into the bathroom, a tiny electric shower shoved into the same small space as the toilet.

'It seems like a really relaxed place,' Lauren said.

'Yeah, it reminds me of backpacking. I've missed it. I spent six months in Thailand not that long ago. Mainly in cheap and cheerful places like this. That is until I met Carmelle and she introduced me to a more luxurious lifestyle. But I feel more at home at the backpacker bars.'

'It looks fun at the bar.' Lauren had walked past it earlier. 'It's rammed.'

'Yeah,' Kiera replied. 'The people here are a laugh. Let me just change my top. This one's a bit sandy.'

Kiera pulled off her T-shirt, opened the tiny wooden cupboard and pulled out a couple of tops.

'What do you think, red or blue?' she said, holding them up. The red one had a V-neck of sequins and the blue was a midnight shade with lace sleeves.

'I like the red…' Lauren said, but then she trailed off.

From the bottom of the cupboard, a pair of glass eyes stared out at her.

She looked closer and saw the carefully crafted features of a lifelike doll. It had blue eyes and dark hair with a small button nose. It was strikingly familiar.

Without being able to stop herself, Lauren reached into the cupboard and pulled it out. She felt the hair under her hands, as real as her own. The blue dress the doll wore was perfectly tailored, the colour matching its eyes.

It was the same kind of doll she'd found in her flat in London. Not the exact same one – the hair was different, the nose too. But it was close enough.

She looked at Kiera now, thinking how she'd been the last one to leave the flat before the hen night, how she had a key to the flat, how close she was to Adam.

Fury surged through her veins. 'It was you,' she said.

CHAPTER FIFTY-SEVEN

Lauren

Kiera hadn't heard her. She was too busy admiring herself in the mirror in the red top, turning back and forth to check how it fell over her figure.

'It was you,' Lauren repeated, staring down at the doll in her hands, feeling its hair between her fingers.

There was a light knock on the door and Adam let himself in just as Kiera said, 'What was me?'

'Look!' Lauren thrust the doll into Adam's hands. 'Look at this.'

Adam studied it, realisation dawning. 'Where did you get this from?'

'It's mine,' Kiera replied.

'She must have done it,' Lauren said. 'Put the doll in the bath. Sent the card. All of it. It must be her.' Her voice broke, on the verge of tears. She felt nauseous at the thought of how she had let Kiera move in with them. She had trusted her.

Adam looked from Kiera to Lauren and back again.

'What?' Kiera asked, her eyes wide. 'I bought this doll at the market. It's a present for my god-daughter.'

'I don't believe you,' Lauren said. 'You don't want me to marry Adam. You're planning something to ruin the wedding. It was you who put that note in our hamper.' Lauren felt her heart hammering in her chest. Everything was starting to make sense. How Kiera had moved into her home just before the wedding. How she'd split up with her girlfriend. She'd been after Adam all along.

Kiera laughed. 'Why wouldn't I want you to marry Adam?'

Lauren lunged at Kiera, but she felt Adam's hands grabbing her shoulders, holding her back.

'Lauren – calm down. You're not making any sense. We know who sent the card and who planted the doll. It was Amanda. She stole my keys. And the note you received in Thailand was sent from the UK. That must be her, too. It's nothing to do with Kiera.'

'But how do you explain the doll then?'

'I told you,' said Kiera, her eyes flashing. 'I got it from the market. I was looking for a present for my god-daughter. And Tracey recommended the stall. She said she'd bought her daughter a doll from there every year until she was twelve.'

'I don't believe you,' Lauren spat out.

'Lauren, don't do this,' Adam said.

'Do you like her? Do you like Kiera?' she asked, the words tumbling out of her.

'We're just friends, we always have been.'

'Nothing ever happened between you?'

Adam sighed. He looked weary. 'It's ancient history.'

'What?' Lauren's mind raced. Something *had* happened between them?

'We slept together once. At university. It meant nothing.'

'You slept together?' Lauren glared at Adam. She remembered back when she'd first met Kiera, how she'd thought there was something between them. Until Kiera had introduced her to her girlfriend. Then she'd relaxed, assuming Kiera would never be interested.

'Don't you think you should have told me?'

'You always said you didn't want to know about my previous relationships.' Lauren clenched her teeth, angry. He was right. She had said that. But it didn't apply to his closest friend. She'd have wanted to know that.

Lauren's stomach churned as she muttered the words. 'Has anything happened between you since we've been together?' She could hardly look at them, not wanting to hear the answer.

'Honestly, Lauren,' Kiera reached out towards her and Lauren flinched away. 'I'm not interested in Adam. Not in that way. I'm here to see you get married. You know that.'

'But what about the doll? I don't understand. It's just too similar to the other one for it to be a coincidence.'

'Let me show you where I bought it,' Kiera said. 'I'll take you to the market.'

The three of them got a taxi together, Kiera in the front, Lauren and Adam sitting silently in the back. Lauren couldn't help thinking of the cocktails they were supposed to be sipping together by the sea. But how could they do that now? It was like she'd always suspected; the instinct she had chosen to ignore was right – Adam and Kiera had a connection that was deeper than friendship. The fact that they'd slept together proved that once they'd wanted more.

When they got to the market, Kiera led them past the tiny stalls that showcased everything from silver jewellery to plate sets, the vendors shouting out to them, competing to sell their wares. As the sun warmed Lauren's back, sweat pooled on her skin. Adam fanned himself with a leaflet about boat trips he'd picked up as he'd passed a travel agent.

They reached the back of the market where it was less crowded. The craft stalls were here, the paintings and ornaments shielded from the sunlight by a vast grey canopy. Then there were the toymakers. The first stall sold wooden xylophones and tiny trucks.

'It's around here somewhere,' Kiera said, turning from stall to stall, as Lauren held her breath. Surely Kiera wouldn't have taken them all the way out here if she was lying.

'Here it is,' Kiera said suddenly, pointing to a stall with rows of plastic dolls at the front.

The ones at the front were boxed, all identical. They weren't like the personalised one Lauren had received, that had looked so like her. Or the one in Kiera's cupboard. This wasn't right. Kiera was lying.

'There you go,' said Adam. 'We can go now.'

'These aren't the same,' Lauren said.

'No,' Kiera said. 'The ones they put together themselves are round the back.' She pointed to a curtain. 'Can we see?' she asked the slim Thai man standing by the stall.

He pulled back the curtain to reveal a little workshop, a table in the middle. A row of plastic dolls' heads lined the work surface behind him, beneath a shelf of plastic bodies. The head of a doll sat on one side of a wooden desk, and he was halfway through stitching in the hair. Lauren stood and stared, her brain starting to compute what she was seeing. The style of doll. The thick, dark hair. The glassy eyes.

He nodded. 'All handmade. We have many more. I show you. All different sizes. There are many more.' He pointed up to the makeshift shelves at the back of the stall. Lined up were lifelike dolls, exactly like the one that had appeared in her bath at home. Kiera was right: she had bought her doll here. But Lauren was also sure of something else. Whoever had planted the doll in her bath had also bought it here, in Thailand.

CHAPTER FIFTY-EIGHT

Adam

Adam looked at Lauren, who was still staring at the plastic dolls suspiciously. 'Are you alright?' he asked, breaking the silence.

'Fine,' she nodded. 'Just shocked the dolls are available here.' She turned to Kiera. 'I didn't know.'

'It's OK,' Kiera said. 'You told me about the doll in the bath, but I had no idea it looked like these. If I had realised, I'd never have bought one. I feel a bit freaked out by the whole thing now, to be honest.'

'At least we have an explanation now,' Adam said, although he could tell from the tense expression on Lauren's face that she still felt on edge.

'Let's go back to happy hour,' Kiera said. 'I think we all need a drink after that.' She reached out to guide Lauren away from the stall. At least Kiera had forgiven his fiancée for her outburst. She didn't seem to be holding it against her.

'I'd prefer to go back to our suite and have a rest. I'm exhausted,' Lauren said, her face pale.

Adam smiled apologetically at Kiera. 'Maybe another time.'

In the taxi back, they were all silent. Kiera seemed irritated that she was going to happy hour alone, and Lauren was lost in her thoughts. Adam wondered if she was angry about him and Kiera. He promised himself that he would speak to her about it later, check she was alright.

His phone vibrated in his pocket and he took it out. There was a text from an unknown foreign number.

We need to talk before your wedding. Can we meet? Tracey x

He gulped and closed the message. His stomach knotted when he thought of the possibility of Lauren finding out about him and Tracey. If she felt angry that he hadn't told her about Kiera, she would feel a million times worse about her own sister. He knew she'd feel betrayed. He should have told her about it years ago.

When they got back to the honeymoon suite, Lauren collapsed onto the sofa. 'Don't you think it's weird?' she said. 'That the doll I got was exactly the same as the ones they sell here? Whoever sent it must have bought it in Thailand.'

'It is odd,' he said, rubbing his temples. 'But I don't think it means anything. I'm sure there are other places you can get dolls like that. Amanda could easily have picked one up on a holiday and brought it back.' He said it as much to convince himself as her. But even he was no longer completely convinced that Amanda would have gone to all these lengths to hurt Lauren. She'd never even met her.

'What about the note?'

'That was sent from abroad,' he said, trying to remain calm. 'Most likely Amanda too.' He stroked her back, wanting to put her at ease, to stop her worrying. But she was right, it was strange that they sold that type of doll here. Kiera had said Tracey had told her where to get it. He thought of the way Tracey had squeezed him just a bit too tightly when she'd hugged him at the restaurant. Why did she want to meet him?

'Why don't we make the most of the honeymoon suite?' he said, trying to distract Lauren from her worries. 'I'll go and turn on the jacuzzi.' While Lauren showered, he poured them two glasses of champagne and placed them on the side of the jacuzzi. He opened up the bifold doors to feel the fresh sea breeze. When he pressed a button the glass roof whirred open, revealing the hot sun.

He was about to start the bubbles when his phone vibrated in his pocket.

It was the number of the front desk of their flat in London. Why would they be calling? He felt a shiver of worry. Had there been another break-in?

'Hello?' he said, answering.

'Hi. It's William. From security. We've found your keys.'

'What keys?'

'The keys to your flat. We got some cleaners in to sort the paving slabs outside. Your keys had fallen into one of the small drains. I've got them now. They're behind the security desk.'

Adam thought back to when Amanda had had her panic attack, when he'd stood outside the flats with her, rubbing her back, trying to calm her down. His keys must have dropped out of his pocket and fallen down the drain.

'Thanks,' Adam said, putting his hand to his temple. 'We don't actually need them any more. We've changed the locks.'

'OK. No worries. Do you want me to dispose of them then?'

'Yes, please.'

Adam hung up the phone and stared at his handset. They'd never needed to change the locks. No one had taken the keys. Which meant it couldn't have been Amanda who'd broken into his flat. It wasn't her who'd planted the doll and stolen the bracelet. It was someone else. Someone who already had a key.

CHAPTER FIFTY-NINE

Lauren

One day until the wedding

Lauren and Jasmine walked through the hotel grounds, down the shady paths under the palm trees and past the bright displays of flowers. They paused at the statue dedicated to Lauren's parents and Jasmine gave a little bow towards it. 'I always pay my respects when I go by,' she said quietly.

Lauren reached out and touched her niece's arm. 'It's so lovely to have a memorial to them here,' she said, her eyes smarting with tears. They stood in silence for a moment, each lost in their own thoughts. Then they walked on, past the many swimming pools and restaurants, until they came to reception, where their taxi was waiting to take them to the market to choose Jasmine's flowers for the wedding tomorrow. Jasmine would scatter fresh flower petals as she walked in front of Lauren and Tracey.

'It must be wonderful to grow up here,' Lauren said.

Jasmine laughed. 'That's what everyone says. But it's not easy living with Mum.'

'What do you mean?' Lauren remembered her conversation with her sister. It must be difficult for Jasmine dealing with Tracey's divorce.

'I don't know. She has a set idea about my future. It's all about school, a career. Not rushing into marriage like she did. As if I would. I just want to travel, to see the world.' Lauren stifled a smile. She sounded just like Tracey had at the same age.

'What about your father?' Lauren asked tentatively, aware that things were strained between them.

Jasmine narrowed her eyes at Lauren. 'He's not my father. But then you knew that, didn't you?'

Lauren flushed, unsure what to say.

'He's the one who brought you up,' she said, her mind reeling. Did Jasmine know she was adopted?

'I suppose I have to give him that,' she said grudgingly. 'But these days, he's only interested in my brothers, not me.'

'I doubt that's true,' Lauren said, trying to reassure her, even though Tracey had said the same thing.

'I overheard him and Mum talking. He said he didn't need to be as big a part of my life as he was for the boys, because he wasn't my real father.'

'I'm so sorry, Jasmine.' Lauren processed what she had said, reaching out and stroking her niece's arm. She didn't seem to realise that Tracey wasn't her biological mother either. If she ever found out, it would devastate her.

'Oh, it's OK,' Jasmine said. 'I'm almost over it now. I found out months ago. I'm just angry with Mum for not telling me, for lying to me all these years. I just want to find my real father now.'

Lauren swallowed. Jasmine's father had died in the tsunami. Both her biological parents had. But it wasn't Lauren's place to tell Jasmine that. Lauren would have to talk to Tracey, ask her to tell Jasmine the truth. She couldn't keep her in the dark like this.

'Did you know my father?' Jasmine asked, clearly desperate for any morsel of information on him.

'No,' Lauren said quickly, 'I didn't.'

'Oh,' Jasmine said. Lauren could hear the disappointment in her voice.

'You need to talk to your mum about this.'

'I can't talk to her. She's hidden it from me for all these years. Tried to make me accept Ken.'

'I'm sure she only wants what's best for you.' Lauren tried to imagine having her own children. She was sure she'd just want to act in their best interests, but sometimes it would be impossible to tell what their best interests were.

'Do you think you'll have children?' Jasmine asked, reading her mind.

'I hope so,' Lauren said.

'It would be so exciting if you did. Then when I move to England I could be your babysitter.'

'I'd like that,' Lauren smiled. 'I'd love us all to be closer, to get to know you better.'

When they got to the market it was hot and bustling. Jasmine started weaving through the maze of traders, leading Lauren to the stall where Noi bought all the wedding flowers. They chose a woven basket and picked out some white and blue flowers, whose petals Jasmine would scatter from the basket.

'I love these colours,' Jasmine said. 'They'll match Mum's dress. She's wearing blue, isn't she, for her bridesmaid's dress?'

'Yes, she is.' She'd bought the dress without Tracey, a few months ago. 'Does it fit OK?' she asked.

'I don't know,' Jasmine said. 'I'm sure it will be fine. What would you like me to wear?'

'Oh!' Lauren suddenly realised what Jasmine was getting at. She wanted to match the wedding party. 'Do you want to wear a dress the same colour as your mum's? We could look in the market.'

'Yes,' Jasmine said. 'Actually, I know a tailor at the market. If you have a picture of Mum's dress, he'll be able to copy the design exactly.'

'Will he be able to turn it round quickly enough?'

'Twenty-four hours,' Jasmine said with a smile, looking at her watch. 'Just in time for the wedding tomorrow.' Lauren wondered briefly how much it might cost, and then dismissed the thought. It was important to make Jasmine feel like a proper part of the day.

'Let's go there now.'

They found the tailor easily and Jasmine spoke quickly to him in Thai, while Lauren browsed his market stall. His dresses were lovely, high-quality and well stitched.

'Do you have a photo of the bridesmaid's dress?' Jasmine asked.

'Sure.' Lauren pulled up the picture of the dress on her phone and showed it to the tailor. He nodded, then said something to Jasmine in Thai.

'He can make one for me for tomorrow,' she said excitedly. 'Three thousand baht. I've negotiated him down to local prices.'

Lauren quickly calculated in her head. About £80. She could afford that. Paying for Jasmine's dress would be a way of thanking Tracey for holding the wedding here. She checked that it would be ready by the next morning, and the tailor told Jasmine he would personally deliver it to the hotel.

After they'd confirmed the order for the dress, they had a break in a small café, sipping sugary tea and watching the world go by.

'I'm so pleased I'm coming to your wedding,' Jasmine said. 'I've watched so many weddings at the hotel, and I've always been jealous of the guests, always wanted to be part of it.'

'Oh?'

'I think it's the families I'm most jealous of,' Jasmine said wistfully. 'They always seem so together. A proper unit.'

Lauren pushed her hair back behind her ear. 'I'm sorry I haven't been around to see you grow up,' she said. 'You've just been so far away.'

Jasmine gazed into her tea. 'I know it's not just about distance. Mum didn't want to see you.'

Lauren nodded. 'We've put the past behind us now. We can be a proper family.' She squeezed Jasmine's wrist across the table.

'Really?' Jasmine asked. 'Mum didn't even want me to go to your wedding.'

The comment felt like a punch to the chest. But then Lauren remembered what Tracey had said about Jasmine, how she hadn't been studying at school, how she needed to go on a summer revision course to catch up and it had clashed with the wedding.

'I thought you needed to go on your revision course.'

'Yeah. But I don't see how Mum could have thought it was more important than your wedding.'

'I don't know…' Lauren said. She didn't know the ins and outs of Tracey and Jasmine's relationship. 'I'm sure she was just trying to do what's best for you.'

'Yeah, right.' Jasmine sighed. 'She didn't want me to go to the wedding. She booked me onto the course after she knew the date. I'm not sure if she even wanted to go to your wedding herself.'

Lauren's heart ached, and she put her hand to her head. Surely Tracey wouldn't have felt like that? But then she was getting divorced. Maybe attending her sister's wedding had felt too painful for her. 'Really?' she asked.

Jasmine sighed. 'I was so pleased when you two reconnected. I'd always wanted to get to know you, despite everything that Mum said about you.'

'What do you mean? What did she say about me?' Lauren asked. A part of her didn't want to know. But she had never completely understood why she and Tracey had been estranged for so many years. She'd told herself that her sister just needed a break from England, that she was angry about their parents' flat. But deep down she'd always worried it was more than that.

Jasmine hesitated for a moment, swirling the dregs of tea around the bottom of her cup. 'She told me the things that happened before I was born. How my grandparents died. She's always been sketchy on the details. But she never really forgave you.'

Lauren felt suddenly dizzy, as if she might faint. *It was an accident*, she told herself. *Just an accident.* But Tracey must have thought it was her fault, too. She thought back to the days after her parents' funeral, when her sister had left, returning as quickly as she could to travelling the world. She'd worried that Tracey had blamed her for what had happened to her parents. Uninvited images flashed through her mind. Their limbs flailing as they bounced over the rocks. Their wet bodies lying out on the muddy riverbank, still and lifeless.

'For what happened to our parents?' Lauren asked, hardly daring to breathe.

'Yes,' Jasmine said softly, finally meeting her eyes. 'She said you as good as killed them.'

CHAPTER SIXTY

Adam

Adam was reading on the terrace when he heard Lauren get back, the door slamming shut behind her. A moment later she appeared behind him.

'How was the market? All sorted with the flowers?' he asked, turning round.

She didn't reply, sobs racking her body.

'What's wrong?' he asked, jumping off the sunlounger.

Lauren could hardly get the words out through tears. 'It's Tracey—'

'Tracey – has something happened to her?'

'No, not that. I've just about managed to hold it together in front of Jasmine. But… Tracey thinks I killed Mum and Dad.'

'What? That can't be right. It was an accident.' Adam stroked her hair away from her face, then wiped her tears gently with the back of his hand.

'I— You know how I felt after the accident. If I hadn't stood up on the raft in the first place, Mum and Dad would still be here.'

He squeezed her tightly, holding her as she let the sobs out. 'It wasn't your fault. The company were negligent sending us down those rapids.' He remembered when they'd first got together, how they'd gone over the accident again and again, him always reassuring her that it wasn't her fault. It was the first time he'd felt useful in a long time. He'd felt ashamed of how he'd treated

Tracey, and guilty that he hadn't been able to save their parents. Listening to Lauren had made him feel like he had value, like he was righting his wrongs.

'I know,' Lauren said. 'But Tracey thinks I'm responsible.'

'What did Jasmine say exactly?'

'That Tracey had told her I'd as good as killed our parents. That that was why she didn't speak to me for years.'

'That seems like a cruel thing to say.'

'She's only seventeen. She just wasn't thinking.'

'You were only seventeen when the accident happened,' Adam said softly. 'You have to forgive yourself. I thought you already had.' He wished he could make things better for her. He knew how much she had beaten herself up over her parents' deaths.

Lauren shook in his arms. 'I... I've done so much to try and make things better. I've always reached out to Tracey. And I became a doctor so I could help others. So I could save lives.'

'Lauren,' he said firmly. 'It wasn't your fault.'

'But I didn't listen. In the briefing... I didn't realise how dangerous it was.'

She clung to him. 'She's forgiven you though, hasn't she?' he said. 'She invited us to have the wedding here.'

'I suppose so. But it's weird. Jasmine said Tracey wasn't even sure whether she'd come to the wedding. So why would she invite us to Thailand?' Adam ran his hand through his hair. He'd assumed that everything was fine between Lauren and Tracey now, and that Tracey had invited them here out of kindness. But what if she hadn't? What if she had other motives?

'I don't know,' he said.

'Do you think I should talk to her?'

Adam frowned, thinking about what was best for Lauren. He didn't want Tracey to upset her just before the wedding. And he didn't know how Lauren would cope if she found out about the relationship the two of them had had.

'I think you should wait until after the wedding. There's no point dredging up the past just before the big day.'

'OK,' Lauren said. 'I'm sure it isn't as bad as Jasmine said, anyway. It can't be. Maybe Jasmine just misunderstood what her mum was saying. Jasmine did say she was sketchy on the details.'

'That's probably it,' Adam said, but his mind was whirring. He thought of Tracey's message asking to meet. He'd been a coward, worried that she wanted to talk to him about the past. He hadn't wanted to discuss it, to face up to how he had treated her. Now he realised that he was going to have to meet her. If she'd blamed Lauren for their parents' accident all these years, then who knew why she'd invited them here.

When Lauren went back inside, he took out his phone and messaged Tracey.

I can meet up. Just let me know where and when.

CHAPTER SIXTY-ONE

Adam

2001: Thailand

Adam laughed as they went over the rapids, paddling as fast as he could and then letting the boat career over the rocks. He was having the time of his life. He looked at Tracey, sitting opposite him in the raft, and grinned. They hit the next rapid straight on and all of them flew into the air, crashing into the water.

Tracey climbed back into the boat beside him, where Lauren had been sitting, forcing Lauren to the other side.

'OK,' the guide shouted. 'That was the last rapid. Finish now. Paddle to the side.' He pointed to a small platform on the riverbank a little further up where they could tie the raft. Adam sighed with disappointment as they began to slow down. 'Paddle in,' the guide was shouting. 'Paddle in.' The raft rocked from side to side as the water got rougher.

Tracey turned to him. 'We should do that again some time.'

'Sure,' he said, grinning as he thought of them living out here. Her hand fell onto the leg of his wetsuit and he didn't move it away.

The boat suddenly tilted to the side and he looked up to see that Lauren had got to her feet and was taking a wobbly step towards them, glaring at Tracey.

'Sit down,' the guide shouted.

Screams echoed round the valley as they hit the edge of a rapid and Lauren tumbled down into the centre of the boat, as her parents were thrown backward into the water. Adam saw Lauren reach out towards her mother's hand to help her back in, but their fingers slid over each other, unable to grip.

He stood up, the boat rocking below him, ready to jump in. 'No!' the guide shouted at him, grabbing him roughly and forcing him back down into the boat. 'You must paddle now. Get to side first. Dangerous here.'

In the water, Debs's foot had got caught between the rocks and she was struggling to stay above the surface. Lauren's father was just a few metres away, trying to swim back towards them.

'We have to get them!' Tracey screamed, tears running down her face.

'No!' the guide shouted. 'Stay in the boat!'

At the riverside a Thai man reached for the rope on their raft and pulled them in. Adam turned back towards the river. Debs was nearly free of the rocks, but he couldn't see Lauren's father. He saw Debs twist her body round, releasing the foot that had been caught. But his gasp of relief became one of fear, as the current took her, throwing her body over the rapids like a rag doll, her limbs flailing at awkward angles as she hit rock after rock.

CHAPTER SIXTY-TWO

Lauren

Lauren came down the steps onto the beach where she'd be getting married tomorrow. She'd gone there to clear her head, to think about everything Jasmine had said. But as she approached the beach, she saw that Tracey and Noi were already there, deep in conversation.

'Hi,' Tracey said, smiling. 'We've just getting ready for your wedding tomorrow. We're putting down markers on the sand to let the team know where to put all the seats.'

Lauren hesitated, relieved and flustered by the fact that Tracey was behaving perfectly normally. 'Great,' she said, finally. 'Thank you.' She knew that Adam was right – it would be foolish to bring up what Jasmine had said to her just before the wedding. After all, Tracey had kept her feelings from her for the last eighteen years.

'Do you want to see how we've set the restaurant up?' Noi asked.

'Sure.'

'Noi's been working on it all morning,' Tracey said with a smile.

Lauren walked with Noi along the pier. It shook slightly as they moved across it and Lauren looked through the gaps between the planks at the churning water beneath her. 'The current is very strong here,' Tracey said, following her gaze. 'That's why the hotel's main beach is the other side of the bay. It's too dangerous to swim here.'

Lauren nodded. As the pier narrowed, Noi walked in front with Tracey behind them. Lauren imagined herself walking down it tomorrow, the train of her dress flowing behind her, lifting in the sea breeze. She felt a shiver of excitement, alongside something else. Fear. No matter how much she tried to tell herself there was nothing to worry about, she couldn't seem to shake off the feeling that something still wasn't right.

'It's supposed to be beautiful weather tomorrow,' Noi said. 'We got the storm out of the way.'

'That's a relief.' Lauren smiled. The sky was cloudless, bright blue. With the sun streaming down it was hard to even imagine the storm a couple of days before.

The wind lifted Lauren's hair and she felt the breeze on her face. She imagined Adam beside her here, just the two of them. *It will be perfect*, she told herself. Noi led her down the platform into the restaurant. White streamers ran down the walls, and three long tables were decorated with purple Thai orchids in bowls of water. Fairy lights and paper lanterns lined the walls. It looked stunning.

Tracey disappeared into the kitchen, while Noi went through the details with Lauren.

'You mentioned you wanted bunting?' Noi said.

Lauren had brought the bunting she'd prepared in London to Thailand.

'Yes, it's in my room. It has photos of me and Adam in the triangles. I can get it for you.'

'You can bring it down later. Do you want it put up in here? It could go behind the top table.'

Lauren looked at the spot Noi was referring to. She'd imagined people looking at the photos, talking about them. 'I think I'd prefer it on the beach, so people can see the photos as they're waiting for me to arrive.'

'Oh, that's a lovely idea. We have white poles that we can hang the bunting between. It can be around the sides of the seats. A focal point.'

'I have photos of my parents, too. I want them on display, to feel like they're included in the day.'

'That sounds like a perfect plan,' Noi said, placing a comforting hand on her arm. 'I could put a little table up near the beginning of the aisle. Just in front of the archway. It can have all the photos on it. Are they framed, or do you want me to sort that out?'

'I've already framed them.' Lauren had spent hours finding the best pictures of her parents, and then the frames that complimented them. She'd imagined them in a church in England, but they'd work just as well in Thailand.

Tracey came out of the kitchen, carrying some empty boxes.

'Do you like the decorations?' she asked with a smile.

'I love them! Thanks so much for doing this for me,' Lauren said to her sister, folding her into a hug. 'You don't know how much I appreciate it.' If Tracey blamed Lauren for her parents' deaths, then it must have been a huge deal for her to hold the wedding here.

As they walked back along the pier to the shore, it occurred to her that Tracey might want to honour her parents too.

'Do you have any photos of Mum and Dad?' she asked. 'I'm planning on including a few at the wedding, to remember them.'

'Oh,' said Tracey. She hesitated for a moment, then continued. 'I do have a few. Do you want to see them?'

Tracey led her back to her home on the hillside overlooking the bay. It was set back a little from the hotel, on a small winding road. A maid opened the electronic gates for them, and Lauren stared up in awe at the wooden lodge. On her last visit here, Tracey had only shown her the hotel. She'd never seen her home. The lodge was three storeys tall, surrounded by palm trees. Multiple balconies stretched out into the trees. The views over the bay and the hills must be spectacular.

In the living room, a maid brought them cold glasses of orange juice while Tracey pulled out a box of photos from a drawer.

'These are all the old ones, all I have left of Mum and Dad. I don't have as many as you, of course, because you took the ones from their flat.'

Lauren nodded. Was Tracey annoyed that she had more pictures? She'd never expressed an interest in taking any herself.

'I can make copies of any of my photos you'd like,' Lauren said.

Tracey didn't reply, and Lauren started flicking through the pictures in the box. They were family photos – some of her parents, some of the two sisters. The ones of her parents she'd never seen before. They were mainly taken here, in Thailand, on their final holiday. Her mother reading a book on a sunlounger. Her father having a beer by the pool. The pair of them smiling over a platter of seafood.

'These are great,' Lauren said. 'Can I use some for the display?'

'Of course.'

She picked up another set of photos from the box and flicked through them. They were mainly of scenery. Lush mountains and beautiful sandy beaches, tourists in the background. The clothes were typical of the early noughties, vest tops and denim shorts and oversized T-shirts.

Lauren suddenly stopped still. There was a photo of Tracey. Pregnant.

It was an old photo, clearly over ten years ago, long before she had the boys.

Tracey snatched it out of her hand.

'What?' Lauren asked. 'What happened?'

'What do you mean, what happened?'

Lauren bit her lip. Tracey had a pronounced belly in the picture. She'd looked heavily pregnant. 'Did you lose the baby?' Lauren whispered.

Tracey shook her head, staring down at the floor. 'No,' she said.

'What do you mean?' Lauren's mind was racing, calculating the time when Tracey would have been pregnant, putting everything together. The baby would be a teenager by now.

'Jasmine isn't adopted, is she?' Lauren said. 'That baby's Jasmine. You gave birth to her.'

CHAPTER SIXTY-THREE

Adam

Adam sipped his beer, sitting on a small plastic stool in the bar on the main road, watching tourists amble by on the pavement. Kiera had organised an impromptu stag do tonight to replace the one that had been postponed when his wedding in the UK had been cancelled.

'Have another, mate!' Jimmy said, thwacking him on the back and indicating Adam's nearly empty pint. 'And stop looking so miserable. It's your last night of freedom.' Even though there were only five of them and it was the night before the wedding, Jimmy was clearly looking for a huge night out.

'Go on then,' Adam said, as Jimmy called the waitress over. Adam's leg shook under the table and his palms sweated. He couldn't focus on relaxing and enjoying himself when he knew he was meeting Tracey after the drinks. He didn't want to leave his own stag do early, but he had no choice. He needed to speak to Tracey before the wedding, to clear the air and to work out exactly what she was playing at, telling Jasmine that Lauren was responsible for their parents' deaths. He felt sick to his stomach at the thought of seeing her, but he had to do it. For Lauren's sake.

'All ready for tomorrow?' Kiera asked.

'As ready as I'll ever be.'

'I can't wait to be best woman. The rings are in the safe in my room.'

'I hope you're looking after them,' he teased.

'Of course. You could trust me with your life.'

He smiled at her. He was glad she was here, keeping things normal, when everything else seemed so out of control.

'A bit tame, this,' Jimmy said, interrupting his thoughts. 'We need to liven it up a bit. Time for shots.'

'No thanks, mate,' Adam said, looking at the full pint Jimmy had just got him. But his friend was already striding over to the bar, returning minutes later with a tray of shots.

Adam downed his quickly and then snuck a look at his phone. He was due to meet Tracey soon, and after that he had to go back to the honeymoon suite to pick up his suit for tomorrow. Then he'd go and sleep in Jimmy's room. It was bad luck for him and Lauren to stay together the night before the wedding, and they both felt they'd had enough of that already. He took another gulp of his pint and pretended to stifle a yawn, even though his heart was pumping so loudly in his chest he thought that everyone must be able to hear it.

'I'm knackered,' he said. 'And I've got a big day tomorrow. I think I'm going to call it a night.'

Jimmy scoffed. 'You lightweight! Have another.'

Adam shook his head. 'No, mate, I can't be a mess for the wedding tomorrow. Lauren would kill me.'

'Under the thumb already – and you're not even married!'

Adam stood up to go and Jimmy hugged him good-naturedly. As he walked away, he heard him turning to the others and suggesting another drink.

His stomach churned as he walked back to the hotel. He chose a seat in the corner of the reception bar out of view of the check-in desk. The bar was empty except for a middle-aged couple, who stared sullenly at each other as they shared a bottle of wine. He felt a stab of guilt. He should be with Lauren. Not here on his own, meeting Tracey.

He went to the bar to order a drink to steady himself. The girl behind the bar was cleaning a glass and she turned to him and smiled. Jasmine.

'You're working late,' he said before he could stop himself.

'You're up late, too, night before your wedding,' she replied, her eyebrows slightly raised.

'Just had a drink with my stags,' he said.

'But you're in here now. On your own?' Adam felt a prickle of worry. She wouldn't tell Lauren, would she?

'Yeah,' he blushed. 'A last drink to calm my nerves.'

'No need to be nervous. If you love her.'

He nodded. Of course he did, but he didn't want to talk about it with Jasmine.

'A rum and Coke, please,' he said. He felt the need to explain why he was here. After all, she'd know soon enough. 'I'm meeting your mother here.'

'My mum? Why?'

'She wants to talk.'

Jasmine laughed lightly. 'Is that a good idea? You know how she feels about the wedding.'

Adam shook his head, thinking of what Jasmine had said to Lauren. 'How does she feel about it?'

'Not too happy. But I guess you two can discuss that. Strange you're meeting the night before your wedding. She must mean a lot to you.'

'It's not like that,' he said quickly.

'Like what?'

He frowned and took the drink. 'I'm sorry. I thought you meant... Never mind.'

He went back to his table, sat down and sipped his rum and Coke, waiting.

He kept checking his watch as the minutes ticked away. He felt exhausted and slightly drunk. All he wanted was to go to bed, and wake up in the morning to marry Lauren. He wanted his wedding day to be perfect. But first he needed to see Tracey.

CHAPTER SIXTY-FOUR

Lauren

Lauren walked past the infinity pool, the twinkling lights of the hotel reflected in the water. She'd just finished having a cocktail with Zoe at the overpriced pool bar and she was feeling calmer. Lauren had been thinking about the doll in Kiera's room all day, playing over in her mind how close Adam and Kiera were, how they'd slept together at university, how quickly Kiera had moved into their flat when she'd split up with her girlfriend. She'd confided in Zoe about her suspicions and Zoe had calmed her down, convinced her there was nothing to worry about. Despite that, Lauren had made Zoe promise to keep an eye on Kiera at the wedding. Just in case.

The area by the pool was vast and deserted, with all the loungers piled into stacks out of the way. Lauren slipped off her shoes in the warm night and dipped her foot into the water. She pulled it out quickly, shocked by how cold it was without the sun to heat it.

Heading slowly out of the hotel grounds, she walked over the little bridge to the private bay where she was getting married tomorrow. There was no event on tonight, and no lights on at the restaurant. She could hardly make out the pier over the dark water. All she could hear was the waves gently lapping against the shore. There was no sign of the vicious current that Tracey had told her about, but she knew it lurked underneath, just out of sight. She thought of her sister, how she hadn't felt able to tell Lauren that she was pregnant with Jasmine. A tear pricked her eye. They had lost so many years, because Tracey had thought that she couldn't trust Lauren, because she blamed Lauren for the accident. She needed to tell Tracey how guilty she'd felt over the years, and ask for her forgiveness. She wished she could go back in time and apologise, and tell Tracey that everything would be OK with the baby, that nobody would judge her for having Jasmine so young.

Carrying her shoes, she went down to the beach, feeling the soft sand beneath her toes. Tomorrow this beach would be full of friends and family celebrating her marriage to Adam. Moving to the water's edge, she looked out at the sea. She heard the sound of a motor cutting through the night silence and watched a little fishing boat go by. The hotel offered night-time fishing trips, but that was on a bigger boat. This one was tiny, with only two people on it, moving slowly along the shoreline.

Suddenly aware she was on her own on a deserted beach in the middle of the night, Lauren walked away up the bank and to the path that led to her honeymoon suite and put her shoes back on. She could hear crickets chirping in the long grass on either side of the path. She was relieved when her beach hut came into view. A light was on in the porch, the only light on that entire beach, except for the tiny ones dotting the path. Lauren felt exposed and she wrapped her arms around herself. She couldn't see anything for miles.

When she got to the hut, she quickly took her key card from her pocket and unlocked the door, looking behind her as she did, checking there was no one around.

Once she was inside, she felt a bit better. The bed was neatly made, the rooms had been cleaned. Then she was plunged into darkness. It took her a second to remember that the lights had switched on automatically when she came in and she needed to put the key card into the slot by the door in order to keep them on. She fumbled around trying to insert it in the dark. She thought she saw a shadow of a figure behind her and her heart raced.

Then the key card found the slot and the lights burst back on.

There was no one there. The shadow was only her wedding dress hanging up against the cupboard.

Adam had said he'd be back by 11 p.m. to collect his suit, and there was only an hour to kill. Lauren set out her things for the morning. Her wedding shoes, her underwear. The new make-up she'd brought specially. A bag of essentials for the day that Zoe had said she'd look after during the ceremony.

At half eleven, when Adam still wasn't back, Lauren started to get irritated. She wanted to wake up feeling refreshed on her wedding day and she didn't want to miss out on sleep because she was waiting for him.

She rang his number and texted him, but heard nothing back.

The clock ticked on and she tried to distract herself with a book, but she couldn't concentrate. She felt alone and isolated in the luxurious suite. And worried. What if Adam wasn't just delayed drinking with his friends? What if something had happened to him? She thought of her pre-wedding nerves earlier, how she'd become suspicious of him and Kiera. He was drinking with her tonight – she'd organised the stag do. What if he'd chosen to be with Kiera over her?

Lauren shook her head, dispelling the crazy thoughts. She was just nervous about tomorrow. She was sure Adam was just drinking with his stags and had lost track of time. She tried to call Kiera and Jimmy, but neither of them answered.

When it got to midnight, she rang Zoe, who came straight over. She bustled into the room and then stopped for a moment, admiring the suite. 'Wow, this place is amazing.' She gave Lauren a hug. 'Have you heard from him?'

'No,' Lauren said. 'I don't know where he is. How could he go missing the night before our wedding?'

'He might not be missing,' Zoe said reassuringly. 'Maybe he's still drinking with Kiera and his mates. Let's go and look for him.'

'Do you think he's had too much to drink?' Lauren said, cross with him, but at the same time hopeful that that was the answer. It seemed like the best of the possible scenarios, she reasoned, as a shiver ran down her spine.

CHAPTER SIXTY-FIVE

Adam

Tracey still hadn't arrived at the bar. It was late now, after midnight, and Adam knew he should leave.

'Another rum and Coke?' Jasmine's smooth voice interrupted him and made him jump. She sounded so like her mother, and as he looked at her he realised there was something in her mannerisms and gestures that was so familiar. She put the drink down in front of him, already made without him asking. 'I thought you'd want one for the road.'

'Your mother works you hard,' he said. 'I didn't think you were allowed to serve in the bar. You're only seventeen.'

Jasmine shrugged. 'The rules are different here. We grow up faster. Besides, we were short-staffed.'

He nodded, and took a sip of his drink. He felt woozy and exhausted, and he knew he needed to be on good form for his wedding tomorrow.

'I don't think Mum's coming,' Jasmine said.

'Right,' Adam replied wearily. He needed to talk to her. It couldn't wait.

'She's not always that reliable,' Jasmine said, with a sigh.

Adam frowned. 'She's stood me up?' He shifted in his seat, unsure whether he should just get up and go, give up and hope that he was wrong about Tracey.

'I think she finds it hard to be around you.'

Adam swallowed. The way Jasmine was talking, it sounded like she knew about the two of them.

'Really?' he said. He managed an awkward laugh. 'I'm really not that bad, you know. I'll be a great brother-in-law.'

'I'm not sure a brother-in-law is what she wants.' Jasmine paused and then took the seat opposite him. 'You know she was in love with you.'

Adam felt a flush rising up his body to his cheeks. 'You know about us?'

'Of course I do. She talked about you all the time when I was growing up. She was obsessed.'

Adam felt the blood drain from his body. 'Why didn't she ever say anything?'

Jasmine shrugged. 'You got together with her sister. She could never forgive you for that.'

Adam felt like he'd been punched. He'd felt guilty about how he'd treated Tracey when they'd split up, but it seemed insane for her to still hold it against him today. Years ago, she'd asked him to move to Thailand, but since then she hadn't even contacted him.

'I never realised…'

'She was devastated when she saw the wedding invitation. It was like it was designed to taunt her – with that picture of the two of you on the front, gazing into each other's eyes. It was like you'd shattered all her dreams. She'd always imagined her future was with you.'

Adam took a gulp of his drink. 'But… she was happy here. She got married.'

'Yeah, just for the money,' Jasmine said dismissively, wrinkling her nose. 'I don't think she ever really loved Ken.'

Adam's mind was spinning. 'If she hasn't forgiven me, then why did she offer to hold the wedding here?'

Jasmine laughed. 'Oh, she didn't offer that. I did. I was upset when I found out your wedding was cancelled, and I wanted to help. It seemed crazy not to when we have a brilliant wedding service here and you were already coming out for your honeymoon. I hacked into Mum's account and suggested it. By the time Mum realised what had happened, you'd already agreed.'

She looked delighted with herself. But Adam was worried. Tracey had never wanted them to come here, never wanted them to get married. He was starting to feel a bit queasy. He remembered Lauren being pushed down the stairs, remembered the disfigured doll being planted in the bath, the bracelet being stolen. Their mother's bracelet.

He looked at Jasmine. 'Do you think – do you think your mum would ever do anything to hurt Lauren?' he asked.

'I – I don't know.' Jasmine threw Adam a confused look. 'She does get angry sometimes. Why are you asking?'

'I think she's been trying to stop the wedding going ahead.' Adam's head hurt, trying to put all the pieces together.

Jasmine frowned. 'Really? I suppose it's possible. She'd not happy about the wedding. It must be so hard for her to see you marrying Lauren. She's never forgiven you for leaving us.'

'Leaving you?' What did she mean? He hadn't left anyone. It had been Tracey who'd continued travelling, while he stayed behind in England. His mother had invited Tracey to stay in their house in the UK, but she hadn't wanted that. She'd wanted to go travelling. She was the one who left.

'Me and her. You abandoned us. At least, that's how she sees it.'

'I didn't abandon anyone.'

'You did. I was just a baby. You left her as a single mother.' Adam's head hurt. He hadn't been responsible for Jasmine. Her father had died in the tsunami. She hadn't even been born when Tracey and Adam's fling ended.

'But you… you're nothing to do with me.'

A frown played out on Jasmine's face. 'I'm everything to do with you. I'm your daughter.'

CHAPTER SIXTY-SIX

Lauren

Lauren walked through the hotel gardens, shouting out Adam's name. Jimmy had eventually answered her calls, and told her that Adam had already left the stag do, alone. Zoe thought that maybe he'd forgotten about his suit and gone straight to Jimmy's room, where he was staying. But when they knocked, he wasn't there.

Lauren's heart raced as she walked by an empty restaurant. Above her the palm trees cast huge shadows and beside her the vegetation was thick, the buzz of insects the only sound in an otherwise silent night. Searching for Adam seemed futile. The hotel was so large, and he might not even be here. She tried to reassure herself, talk herself out of her worry, but she couldn't think of a good reason for Adam to go missing.

Lauren wished she'd spoken to him before he left for the stag do, but by the time she'd got back to their suite after seeing Tracey's photos, he'd already gone. Her mind had been all over the place, and she hadn't given a second thought to Adam's stag night. She'd been so upset that Tracey hadn't trusted her enough to tell her about the pregnancy, that she'd lied to her all these years about Jasmine being adopted.

Lauren picked up her phone and tried his number again. It went straight to voicemail. Worry clenched her heart and her shoulders hunched. What if he'd run away, left her? She shouldn't be searching for him the night before her wedding.

'Lauren! Lauren!' Zoe's voice echoed out from near the swimming pool. 'I've found him. He's here.'

Lauren ran over to the other side of the pool, her sandals slapping against the paving stones.

'Adam!' she said, her heart lifting with relief at the sight of him. But her relief quickly turned to anger. What was he doing, worrying her like this? And why hadn't he answered his phone?

He was just the other side of the infinity pool, sitting on a bench at the top of the cliff, looking out at the dark expanse of sea.

'Lauren? Why aren't you in bed?' he asked, slurring his words.

She glared at him, furious at his lack of awareness. 'I was worried about you. I couldn't get hold of you.'

'Oh, I turned my phone off. I thought it was best not to be disturbed until the morning.'

'What are you doing out here?'

'I was looking for your sister.'

'My sister?' Lauren said, her eyes widening. 'Is she OK?'

'She's fine. I just need to talk to her… it's… about the wedding.'

Lauren exchanged a look with Zoe. 'Why would you need to talk to her about the wedding?'

'I just need to confirm something with her. A detail. You don't need to worry about it.'

He wasn't making sense. Zoe took his arm, helping him up from the bench. He wobbled on his feet, clearly drunk. Lauren sighed, seeing the state of him. He was just confused and anxious about tomorrow. The best thing he could do was get some sleep and try and be fresh for the morning.

'Really, you don't need to worry about the details,' Lauren reassured him. 'Tracey has everything under control.'

'I know. I just need—'

'You're drunk,' Lauren said firmly. All you need is to get to bed.'

'No, I—'

Zoe intervened, pulling him up to his feet. 'Adam – get a grip. It's your wedding tomorrow, and you've gone out and got blind drunk. Just listen to your fiancée while she still wants to marry you.'

'But—'

Lauren's face flushed. What if he'd been drinking to quiet his nerves about the wedding? She swallowed back tears, and forced herself to ask the question. 'Are you having doubts? Do you still want to go ahead with the wedding?'

'Of course I do! There's just something I need to do first.'

Lauren's jaw clenched. She was completely frustrated with him. There was nothing so important that it couldn't wait until after the wedding.

Zoe smiled sympathetically at Lauren. 'He's too drunk to listen. Do you want me to go back and pick his suit up for him?' she asked.

Lauren nodded. When they looked over at Adam, he'd sunk back onto the bench, his head lolling to the side. He was already half asleep.

Zoe brought the suit to Adam and escorted him home, leaving Lauren to walk back to the honeymoon suite alone. She looked out at the choppy sea, her stomach swirling with emotion. It would all be OK, she reassured herself. Adam hadn't gone missing; he had just had too much to drink. She still loved him. He still loved her. And they were going to go through with the wedding.

When she got to the honeymoon suite, she felt calmer. Everything was under control. Zoe had messaged her to say that she'd put Adam to bed in Jimmy's room. He would be there for the wedding tomorrow. And Lauren knew that Zoe would watch out for Kiera in case she was planning anything. All Lauren had to do was get a good night's sleep and be fresh for the wedding. The beginning of her married life.

Lauren went straight into the bedroom and stopped stone still. Instantly she could tell that something was wrong. Her stomach knotted as she glanced around the space. The things she'd prepared for the next day had been moved. Her wedding shoes weren't by the cupboard any more, and the underwear she'd put out for the morning had been moved from the chair and left in an untidy heap on the floor.

Lauren swallowed her fear, aware of how far away she was from her family and friends in the isolated beach accommodation. She crept through the suite, worried she wasn't alone, that whoever had moved her things was still there. She switched the light on in the bedroom, but it only revealed the expensive teak furnishings and the four-poster bed. The heel of a shoe stuck out from under the bed. Someone had pushed her wedding shoes under there. Trembling, she checked the bathroom. Nothing. Whoever had been here had left.

She went back into the living room, double-checked the front door was locked and then placed the shoes below her dress, which hung from the cupboard. As she stood up, she looked at the dress. There was something wrong. Her pulse quickened as she stared at it in shock.

The dress had been slashed with a knife, right down the middle.

CHAPTER SIXTY-SEVEN

Lauren

2001: Thailand

Lauren saw her mum break free of the rocks and then get dragged away by the current, bouncing over the rapids. Bile rose in her throat.

She jumped out of the boat onto the shore and started running along the path by the riverside, trying to keep pace with her mum's orange life jacket. The man who had helped pull the boat in shot past her, a coiled rope in his hand. It wasn't too late, Lauren told herself. It wasn't too late.

Her heart raced as her feet pounded on the muddy path. The river beside her had widened, her parents out of sight. Then she saw the drop. A waterfall. A crushing weight bore down on her and she couldn't breathe. Her mind flashed back to Tracey putting her hand on Adam's leg, how angry she'd been, how she'd stood up in the boat, making it rock, throwing her parents overboard. It was all her fault.

In front of her, the man and the guide from the raft were shouting to each other in Thai, scrambling down the stone steps on the bank alongside the waterfall. Lauren rushed after them, slipping and hitting her knee. She got to her feet quickly, ignoring the sting.

At the bottom of the steps she saw the pool at the base of the waterfall, the two floating bodies, their orange life jackets shining out from the deep blue water.

The Thai man was wading in now, then swimming towards her parents. Adam jumped in behind him. The man grabbed her mother by the back of her life jacket and pulled her towards the shore. Adam took her father, bringing him in and laying him on the muddy riverbank.

The waterfall pummelled the rocks, and birds chattered in the forest above them as Adam sat her father up, pumped on his back so the water came out, then started giving him mouth-to-mouth. The Thai man checked her mother's pulse, then shook his head and put her back down gently.

'No!' Tracey screamed, rushing to the body. Lauren crouched down beside her mother, and tried to copy what Adam was doing, pumping her back to get rid of the water, then giving mouth-to-mouth on her mum's cut and bloody face. She couldn't stop the sobs coming, could hardly catch her breath to give mouth-to-mouth. She let Tracey take over, but it was no good. Beside her, she saw Adam starting chest compressions on her father.

CHAPTER SIXTY-EIGHT

Adam

The wedding day

Adam woke up feeling woozy, his head pounding. Sunlight was streaming through the gap in the blinds. He checked the time – 11.45 a.m. He bolted up from the bed. It was today. His wedding. In two hours' time. He'd overslept, and Jimmy was snoring in the twin bed beside him. They must have both slept through the alarm.

Adam felt an iron fist of dread clamping round his heart as he recalled everything that had happened last night, and what Jasmine had told him. Tracey had been obsessed with him. And Jasmine was his daughter. At first he hadn't believed her, but then it had started to sink in. She'd told him that as soon as she'd realised Ken wasn't her father, she'd searched through her mother's papers. Before Tracey had met Ken, Adam had been named as her father on Jasmine's hospital records.

It wasn't until he'd left Jasmine last night that it had hit him. Tracey had denied him his daughter. He'd missed out on her childhood. When she wrote that letter all those years ago it must have been because she was pregnant, and she wanted him to live with her and her daughter. And when he'd refused, she'd decided not to tell him about Jasmine.

Everything had started to make sense. Tracey hated Lauren, blamed her for their parents' deaths and for stealing Adam from her. He was certain it was Tracey who'd been trying to ruin the wedding, Tracey who'd pushed Lauren down the stairs, sent the card and planted the doll. Tracey who was hosting their wedding in Thailand, who was in a perfect position to punish both him and Lauren.

He had to stop her.

But first he had to tell Lauren the truth about their relationship. He should have done it years ago. Now, on the day of their wedding, he could avoid it no longer. He needed to confess, to ask her to forgive him for not telling her. He needed to ask her to accept Jasmine as his daughter and he needed to warn her about Tracey. His head hurt with it all.

He picked up his phone and dialled Lauren's number.

It went straight to voicemail. Of course. It was her wedding day. Her phone would be switched off.

He swallowed and then rang Tracey. It was time to confront her, to face the past.

But she didn't pick up.

He sent her a text. *We need to speak. Where are you?*

She replied instantly. *Are you having doubts?*

He hadn't meant it like that. *No. No doubts whatsoever. I need to speak to you about Jasmine.*

We're already on our way to Lauren's to get ready. It will have to wait.

I need to speak to you first.

No. Lauren's expecting us. I can't let her down.

Adam grimaced and threw the phone angrily on the bed. It bounced off and landed with a clatter on the floor.

Jimmy stirred in bed and opened his eyes. 'Mate…' he said, his words mumbled, his breath stinking of alcohol. 'What's going on?'

'Nothing,' Adam replied.

Jimmy rolled over and looked at the time. 'We need to get you ready.'

Adam was sweating as he walked with Jimmy to his wedding. He hadn't eaten since last night, unable to face breakfast. His wedding suit had been chosen for a mild British summer and his dark striped trousers clung to him uncomfortably. He'd already ditched the suit jacket, but even the collar of the pressed off-white shirt felt far too tight.

He hadn't been able to get hold of Lauren, and now he was going down to the beach where he would get married. His heart lurched as he thought of Tracey meticulously planning every detail, Tracey helping Lauren get dressed and posing for photos with a fake smile. What did she have in store for them?

All he had managed to do this morning was get in touch with Jasmine. He'd tried not to sound too panicked as he told her to watch out for her mother. She'd got the message, promising she wouldn't leave her mother's side. But would that be enough?

They passed the bench where Adam had been last night when Lauren had found him. He should have told her then what was going on, but his mind had been jumbled, trying to make sense of it all. He hadn't believed that Tracey could still harbour feelings for him after all these years. He hadn't believed that Jasmine could be his daughter.

At the top of the wooden steps that led down into the bay, Adam hesitated. 'Ready for this, mate?' asked Jimmy.

'As ready as I'll ever be.' Adam wiped his sweaty palms on his trousers. He wished Jimmy or Kiera could accompany him all the way to the end of the pier and wait beside him, but it wasn't wide enough. He'd be alone with the officiant.

At the bottom of the stairs, Kiera bounded up to him in an aquamarine dress and gave him a hug. 'Looking handsome,' she said with a grin. 'Good luck.'

He smiled at her. 'Thanks.'

She reached out and gripped his hand. 'You're shaking. Are you nervous?'

'Why would I be?' He managed a small laugh, but inside he was terrified. He scanned the beach for signs of Tracey. She wasn't there. She'd be with Lauren.

His parents appeared behind him. 'Good luck, son,' Tony said, giving him a hearty slap on the back. 'I'm proud of you.'

'Me too,' said Sam, wrapping him in a hug. 'You're lucky to have Lauren.'

Her words stung. Would he still have her after she found out about Tracey, about Jasmine?

He saw his father taking a glass of champagne from a waiter and reached over to grab one himself.

'Dutch courage?' Jimmy asked.

'Something like that.'

He walked through the guests, greeting everyone and thanking them for coming. His expensive leather shoes filled with sand as he made his way across the spotless white beach. The entrance for the bride was lined with red carpet, and he imagined Lauren appearing at the top of the steps, looking beautiful. If Tracey didn't stop her.

It was too late to do anything about it. Noi was approaching, indicating that he should go down to the end of the pier and wait for Lauren. He hesitated. It felt like he'd be too far away down there, unable to protect her.

'Go on then,' said Kiera. 'It's time.' She gave his arm a squeeze. 'No need to feel nervous. You'll be brilliant.'

Adam glanced around, wondering if there was a chance that the wedding would go to plan, that everything would be alright.

'You seem on edge. Is something wrong?' Kiera asked. He looked at her, tempted to tell her everything. But then he saw Noi waving him over, and he knew that he couldn't delay it any longer.

'I'm just a bit hung-over, I think.'

Kiera laughed and gave him a peck on the cheek. 'Good luck,' she whispered in his ear. 'It's going to be spectacular.' She stepped back and held out the two ring boxes to him. 'Take the rings, you can't forget those.'

Adam took the boxes, his hands shaking.

Then he made his way to the end of the pier.

CHAPTER SIXTY-NINE

Lauren

The make-up artist's brow furrowed in concentration as she disguised the huge bags under Lauren's hooded eyes, rubbing the foundation carefully into her skin, and then applying highlighter to bring out her cheekbones. Tracey and Jasmine would be here soon, and then Lauren would feel better, no longer alone. She hadn't been able to sleep last night, afraid of the person who had broken into the honeymoon suite to rip her dress, aware of how isolated she was, how far from the main hotel building.

She'd thought about phoning Adam after she'd seen the ripped dress, but he was in no state to help her, and Zoe was too busy escorting him home. So she'd phoned the one person who she thought might be able to help fix it. Noi. She'd come over immediately, despite the time, and arranged for it to be mended overnight. Lauren shifted in her seat and looked at her watch. There were only a couple of hours until the wedding. She hoped Noi would return with the dress soon.

Lauren had hardly slept, her mind spinning with thoughts of Kiera and Adam. She was sure it was Kiera who'd ripped the dress and planted the doll. But she couldn't quite believe she would go as far as to push her down the stairs. She just didn't seem capable of it.

Eventually, Lauren had gone outside and sat on one of the sunloungers on the terrace, listening to the waves breaking against the shore, until the sun had started to rise, its light spreading out around her, illuminating the sandy beach and making the world feel safe again. Later she'd eaten her room service breakfast on the terrace, and thought of the day ahead. A day she'd remember for the rest of her life.

'How does that look?' the make-up artist asked, stepping back to admire her work.

'Perfect,' Lauren said. She thought of her parents, how proud they'd have been if they'd been here to see this day. Her eyes started to well up and she blinked back the tears, not wanting to smudge her mascara. If her mother had been around, she could have confided in her about what was going on, her fears about Kiera. She would have known what to do. Her father would have hugged her and told her everything would be alright.

A knock at the door interrupted her thoughts. She got up, hoping it would be Noi with the dress.

It was Sam, with Tracey and Jasmine behind her in their royal-blue bridesmaids' dresses. The resemblance between them was so clear now, from their straight noses to their green eyes. How had Lauren managed to miss it before? She felt guilty that she hadn't paid enough attention, hadn't realised that Jasmine was Tracey's biological daughter.

'Your make-up looks perfect,' Sam gushed. 'You look like a film star.'

'You look wonderful, Lauren,' Tracey agreed.

Lauren sat back down and the hairdresser began spraying her hair, then braiding it into a plait.

'Very boho,' Sam said, as the hairdresser weaved in flowers. 'It looks great. Your parents would be so proud of you today. You've always been like a daughter to me. I can't wait for you to become my official daughter-in-law.' Lauren could see the tears in her eyes and she felt her eyes getting watery again too. Sam had always been there for her.

Tracey coughed, and Sam turned to her and squeezed her arm. 'You've both done so well for yourselves,' she said quickly. 'They'd be proud of both of you.'

Lauren swallowed back her emotions. She wished so much that they could be here to see this.

'Are you nervous?' Tracey asked.

'A little,' Lauren said, unable to admit to the ball of fear that sat in her stomach, weighing her down. 'I didn't sleep well last night.'

'Neither did Jasmine,' Tracey said bitterly. 'She was out half the night. The privilege of the young.'

Jasmine glared at her mother, but before she could say anything, the photographer arrived and Tracey and Jasmine managed to hide their anger and smile for the camera.

Lauren looked at her watch again. Half an hour until the wedding. She felt sick. Where was the dress? Was this Kiera's final revenge, somehow intercepting Noi and stopping her getting her dress in time?

Lauren put her earrings on, and then her necklace. The photographer snapped away, then looked at his own watch. 'I'd like some photos of the three of you,' he said.

Tracey glanced at Lauren. 'Shall we get you in your dress?'

Lauren shook her head slowly. 'It's having some alterations. I noticed a small tear in it last night. Noi's getting it fixed.'

'Oh no!' Jasmine's eyes widened in alarm. 'Your beautiful dress. How did that happen?'

'I don't know. It—' But Lauren didn't have to explain because Noi burst in, full of smiles. 'Here it is,' she said, holding the dress up with a flourish. 'It's as good as new.'

She pointed at the new stitching. 'You can hardly see the lines,' Lauren said, running her finger over the faint repair.

Lauren stepped into the dress, feeling the silk slide over her body. Tracey laced up the back for her, her hands gentle on Lauren's skin. She attached the train, letting it drift out behind her, its sequins sparkling as she picked up her bouquet.

'You look stunning,' Tracey said.

Lauren caught a glimpse of herself in the mirror, the purple, blue and white orchids the hairdresser had woven into her plait complementing her bridal bouquet. The dress fitted perfectly, a tight bodice turning into a flowing skirt. It was sleeveless, and showed off her tanned arms. The bruises on her wrist were fading to yellow now and were much less noticeable.

Sam stayed for a couple of photos with Lauren and then hurried away to get down to the beach. The photographer took photos of Lauren, Tracey and Jasmine together on the terrace next to the stone ornament of two kissing doves. The sea lapped against the shore behind them and the sun warmed their faces. Lauren felt too hot, encased in the tight silk bodice of her dress. But she didn't care. She grinned into the camera, delighted to have her sister and niece beside her, a family at last.

Noi bustled in. 'Are you ready to go? We've got ten more minutes and then we need to be out. Adam is making his way to the beach as we speak.'

Lauren nodded and gently touched her hair, pulling a stray strand away from her face. She checked her make-up in the mirror, then slipped her key card into the small pocket in the dress's skirt. Her stomach twisted with nerves and excitement. This was it. She was getting married. 'Yes,' she said. 'I'm ready.'

They walked out of the beach hut together, the photographer's camera following their every step. Lauren held her head high and her back straight as they made their way along the wooden path over the sand. The wind picked up and rustled her dress around her ankles. Behind her, her train lifted and floated on the breeze.

They stopped at the bottom of the steps that led over the rocks and then down the other side into the bay. There were just a few more steps up and then they would be visible to the guests.

Lauren took a deep breath.

'You should go first, Jasmine, as the flower girl. Then me. Then Tracey.'

They both nodded, and then Tracey embraced her, before releasing her with a smile. 'Good luck,' she said. The photographer caught the moment and Lauren thought of how the pictures would look. The three of them together, their likeness evident. Her family.

'Right,' she said. 'Let's do it.'

As Jasmine reached the top step, the bridal march started to play. Although Lauren had imagined the march echoing round a huge church, it was perfect here, too, echoing out of the speakers on the beach.

When Lauren appeared behind Jasmine at the top of the steps, she heard the small crowd below whooping and cheering. She was relieved to see Zoe standing beside Kiera. Tracey's little boys were standing next to them, dressed in bright white shirts with tiny bow ties, a member of the hotel staff watching over them. The other guests had flutes of champagne in their hands and were facing towards her, standing in front of the white chairs set out on the beach. The bunting she'd prepared fluttered in the wind.

The archway stood out in white against the bright blue sea, reflecting the azure sky. And at the end of the pier, she could see Adam. He was faced towards her, and even from here she could see he was beaming.

She grinned as she followed Jasmine, stepping carefully down the steps and then onto the carpeted aisle that led across the beach to the rows of chairs. She smiled at each guest as she passed. Lauren couldn't help marvelling at the details of the wedding: the blue sashes on the chairs which matched the shade of Tracey and Jasmine's dresses; the pictures of her parents at the end of the aisle; the white archway; the bunting. It was exactly as she had imagined. Perfect.

She looked at the nearest photo on the bunting. It looked unfamiliar, with a palm tree in the foreground and a bright blue sea in the background. But then she recognised the shack in the corner of the picture. It was in Thailand. Adam smiling out of it, his arm round her. She was wearing a red halterneck bikini she didn't remember having. Confused, she stepped closer to it to get a better look.

She paused, staring, the realisation dawning. It wasn't a picture of her.

A young Adam smiled out at her, but the face beside him wasn't hers. It was Tracey.

She took one more step forward. The next photo featured the same red bikini. Tracey again. And this time she and Adam were kissing.

Lauren felt the bile rise in her throat. Then she turned and ran, throwing off her slip-on shoes so she could run faster over the sand, away from them all.

CHAPTER SEVENTY

Adam

It was a moment before Adam realised what was happening.

He'd gasped when he'd seen Lauren walking gracefully towards him, the sun shining down on her, bright flowers adorning her dark plaited hair. He'd been mesmerised as he'd watched her descend the steps onto the red carpet, her tanned arms clutching her blue and white bouquet, her silky white dress reflecting the sunlight. His daughter had led the way across the beach, scattering blue and white petals over the red carpet. A huge wave of relief had rushed through him when he'd seen Tracey bringing up the rear. She hadn't done anything to hurt Lauren. She hadn't managed to wreck his wedding. He was marrying Lauren, and they would be happy.

He watched as Lauren walked among the guests, coming slowly towards him as the bridal music played, her train floating behind her. She paused to look at a photo on the bunting. He remembered her lovingly preparing it, filling it with the pictures of them.

But she was pausing a bit too long, leaning closer now. The music was halfway through. It would finish before she got to the end of pier, before she reached Adam. Lauren was stopping to look at the next photo now.

Something was wrong. Adam's breath caught in his throat.

And then he saw her turn, slipping out of her shoes and running into the grassland behind the bay.

There was a silence and then a collective gasp from the crowd, before Tracey set off after her. Adam started running, his feet thudding down on the wooden pier, the planks shaking beneath him. He needed to reach Lauren. He couldn't let Tracey get there first. Sweat soaked through his white shirt, his heart pumping loudly in his chest.

He saw Jasmine pulling Tracey back, making her pause, an argument breaking out between them.

Adam was level with them now, panting and out of breath. 'Where did she go?' he shouted to Jasmine.

'That way,' Jasmine said. 'Into the scrubland.'

Adam waded through the long grass, shouting her name, his feet sinking into the sand, as the vegetation brushed against his legs. It was desolate here, endless grass and sand in every direction, the slight smell of sewage permeating the air, the grass teeming with buzzing insects. He couldn't tell which direction she'd gone in, if he was going the right way.

'Adam!' Zoe was running towards him, clutching Lauren's bunting. When she reached him she was panting, trying to catch her breath.

'Look,' she said. 'This is what Lauren saw, what made her run away.'

He looked closer at the bunting, at the nearest photograph.

'This isn't Lauren, is it?' Zoe said.

Adam swallowed the bile that rose in his throat. It wasn't Lauren. It was Tracey.

He turned round the threw up his champagne into the long grass.

CHAPTER SEVENTY-ONE

Lauren

Lauren sat out of sight, hidden behind the sand dunes in the vast scrubland behind the beach. She'd remembered the secluded spot from when the jeep had dropped her off in the rain, had known no one would find her here.

She needed to be alone, to think. Tracey and Adam. She couldn't get her head around it. All these years she'd been with him, all the times they'd spoken about her sister, and he'd never mentioned that they'd been together. She thought of that last holiday. How she'd seen Tracey climb back into the raft and sit down next to Adam. How she'd stood up to force her along and sit next to him herself. That split-second decision had led to their parents' deaths.

Lauren's head ached from lack of sleep and the thoughts that pounded round her head, dragging her in endless circles. Adam could have told her about Tracey any time. But he hadn't. Someone had wanted her to know now. On her wedding day. Someone had wanted to ruin it.

She stumbled over the sand, back towards the honeymoon suite. She could hear voices on the beach, although she couldn't hear the words over the crashing waves. She crept round the back of the suite, onto the porch, placed her key card in the slot by the back door and let herself in.

Inside, she paced back and forth in her wedding dress. Then she heard Adam's voice. 'Lauren! Lauren!' He sounded desperate. She rushed to the door and put the chain across. She didn't want to see him. She couldn't bear to look at him any more. Not after this.

She heard his key card slotting into the lock, watched the door open, until it jarred and bounced back as the chain reached its limit.

She hid, stepping behind the sofa, out of sight of the door.

'Lauren! Let me in!' He was so close it was like he was in the room. He banged his fist on the door. 'Lauren!'

She clutched her head in her hands. She couldn't deal with this now, couldn't deal with him. All his lies. Amanda. Kiera. Tracey. This was the final straw. Her sister. Her own sister.

'Lauren! I'm sorry. I don't know what to say. Please let me in. We can talk. I love you. I want to marry you.'

Tears started running down her face and she wiped them away angrily. She couldn't marry him. He had kept this from her all these years. Just like he hadn't told her about Kiera.

'Lauren!' His voice was more desperate now, almost a whimper. She heard him fiddling with the chain, trying to reach in and take it off.

She found her own voice then. 'No!' she said, marching over, the sandy train of her wedding dress trailing behind her. 'Just leave me alone.' She reached the door, saw Adam's face through the gap and slammed it shut with all her might. Then she collapsed against it and cried, her body shaking with sobs.

CHAPTER SEVENTY-TWO

Adam

Adam stared at the closed door. He could hear Lauren crying behind it and his heart broke. All he wanted to do was hold her in his arms and tell her everything was going to be alright. But how could it be? He sat down in front of the door, leaned against it and let his own tears fall. It was the only way he could feel close to her.

Eventually he heard her move away from the door. He tried knocking again. 'Lauren?' he called out hopefully.

'Just go away!' came the muffled reply. Shoulders slumped, he did as she said, following the path round the back through the sand dunes.

'Adam?' Jasmine approached him on the path. 'Are you OK?' The concern in her eyes only made him feel greater despair. She was his daughter; he should have been looking out for her, not the other way round.

'I'm fine,' he said, reaching out to her. 'Lauren's just angry with me. For good reason.'

'Did she find out about me? Is this my fault? I'm so sorry.' Jasmine's brow creased and she squeezed her hands together.

'No, no, it's not your fault… she… she doesn't know about that.' His heart sank further when he thought of how Lauren might react to the fact that Jasmine was his daughter. He wasn't sure if she could take any further shocks.

'Oh, that's a relief… I'd hate for our new relationship to wreck yours.'

'Really, it's not that. Lauren and I… I'm not sure we're as strong as I thought we were.' It was his fault. He'd built the relationship with the woman he loved on a foundation of lies.

'Maybe she isn't right for you after all,' Jasmine said gently.

Adam sighed. 'I don't think it's that way round. I think it's me that's not good enough for her.' He thought of how he'd treated Jasmine last night, how when she'd first told him he was her father, he'd been in complete denial, saying it couldn't possibly be the case.

'I wasn't very nice to you either, last night,' he said. 'I'm sorry – it was just such a shock, the night before my wedding.'

'Maybe not the best timing,' she said. 'But I'd tried to find you before. In England. I went to the GP surgery and then followed you and Kiera to the pub. I was going to introduce myself, explain that you were my father. But I chickened out. Do you remember?'

'Oh,' Adam said, realisation dawning. 'You were the girl I spoke to in the pub. I thought I recognised you from somewhere. I'd assumed it was from one of Lauren's photos.'

They were at the end of the sandy path now, and they'd come out by a quiet bar by one of the hotel's many pools.

'I've wanted to tell you I was your daughter ever since I found out,' Jasmine said. 'But I thought you'd just ignore a letter, that you might not believe me.'

Adam nodded.

'That's why I came to the UK. It was to see you. Mum didn't want me to go to your wedding. She said it was because of the revision course, but I think she was worried about you meeting me, and putting two and two together.'

'I'm glad we've met now,' Adam said. He thought of Lauren. He needed to speak to her. To tell her about Jasmine. To try and win her back. Maybe, just maybe she'd be able to accept Jasmine as his daughter. Lauren liked her niece. She'd asked her to be her flower girl, after all.

Jasmine sat down in one of the chairs at the bar and pulled out her phone. 'After you questioned me last night about whether I really was your daughter, I went back home to find the documents I mentioned. With your name on.'

Jasmine held up a photo to show him on her phone. It was a picture of some kind of nursery school application. And where the father's name was listed, there was Adam's name, as clear as day. *Dr A. Glenister.*

'Don't worry,' he said to Jasmine. 'I believed you.'

She smiled and nodded. 'I don't want you to leave Thailand,' she said. 'I want to get to know you better.'

Adam swallowed, thinking of the days ahead. Would Lauren forgive him? They were supposed to be on their honeymoon after the wedding, travelling round Thailand, but he couldn't see that going ahead. Perhaps she'd want to go straight back home. He blinked back his emotion.

'Could I come to England?' Jasmine said. 'Stay with you for a bit while I search for a job?'

Adam hesitated, unsure what his life would be like in England after this. But he couldn't turn her down. 'Of course,' he said.

'Adam!' a voice called out, interrupting them. It was his mother. 'I've been looking everywhere for you,' she said. 'I wanted to check you were alright. What do you want everyone to do? Is the wedding going ahead? Everyone's still drinking the champagne at the moment.'

Adam shook his head. 'I don't know. Lauren's not speaking to me.'

'Do you want me to leave you to talk to your mum?' Jasmine asked.

'You need to find Lauren,' his mother said firmly. 'I know she loves you.'

He saw a look of irritation cross Jasmine's face and remembered how Lauren had told him that Jasmine wished she'd met her grandparents. Adam owed her that much.

'Mum,' he said softly. 'I've got something to tell you. Jasmine is my daughter. She's your granddaughter.'

CHAPTER SEVENTY-THREE

Lauren

Lauren lay on the sofa in her wedding dress. It was sandy and dirty from when she'd run through the scrubland, but she couldn't take it off. It was over two hours since she'd been due to get married, but to take it off would be to admit defeat, to admit that her wedding wasn't happening, that her relationship with Adam was over. She wasn't ready for that.

Now she didn't know what to do with herself. Zoe had come round earlier, but she'd sent her away, wanting to be alone. She was thirsty. She walked across the room towards the fridge, the image of the bride in the mirror shocking her as she passed. It didn't feel like her any more.

She heard a whirring sound, like an engine or distant building work. She frowned, following the noise through the living room and towards the terrace. It was coming from the jacuzzi. Was someone in there?

'Hello?' she called out tentatively.

There was no answer to her call. Fear clamped her heart and quickened her breathing. She pushed the door open to the room that housed the jacuzzi and blinked. It was completely dark, the blinds pulled down and the glass ceiling covered by shades. She couldn't see anything.

'Hello?' she said again. She took a step back and then reached for the light switch.

Light filled the room. The jacuzzi was empty, bubbling invitingly.

She stood rooted to the spot, scanning back and forth. Whoever had turned the jacuzzi on seemed to have gone. Unless they were hiding, crouched down behind the raised pool.

Walking over to the jacuzzi, she switched the bubbles off. Daylight streamed in as she pulled the blinds up. She couldn't see anyone there, but she still felt the danger, the heavy sense of threat.

The bubbles had subsided now. Instead there was something else. Stepping closer, she saw dark hair floating up towards the surface of the water.

Lauren gripped the edge of the jacuzzi, stifling her scream. Another doll. It was just a doll. She reached into the water to pull it out. A doll with long dark hair, in a wedding dress.

Its matted hair wrapped round her arm. Its white dress was torn, its body cut open.

She heard footsteps behind her and she screamed. A hand clamped over her mouth, small and strong. And then her head was pulled up, as if it was her who was the doll, and forced down into the water.

She couldn't lift her head back out. Strong hands held it under the water, keeping it down. She wanted desperately to take a breath, but she couldn't. All around her was swirling water. She pushed upwards against the hand that held her down, but it was no use. She was going to die here. To drown. On her wedding day.

CHAPTER SEVENTY-FOUR

Adam

After Adam had left his mother with Jasmine, he'd walked around the hotel grounds, trying to work out what he should say to Lauren, how he could make things better. His mother had been shocked by the news that she was a grandmother. She'd insisted that Adam went to talk to Lauren, to try and put things right, while she spoke to Jasmine. But he'd been walking for nearly an hour now, and he still hadn't worked out what to say.

He'd apologise first, ask for her forgiveness for keeping his fling with Tracey from her. He squeezed his hands together, thinking how that one omission might have destroyed them. He didn't want any more secrets between them. He needed to tell her that Jasmine was his daughter and that Tracey had tried to wreck their wedding out of jealousy. Then he and Lauren could try and rebuild their relationship.

As Adam approached the honeymoon suite, he realised he hadn't seen Tracey since the ceremony. He felt a shiver of unease. Would she be happy, now the wedding was ruined? Would that be enough for her? He got to the door of the beach hut and knocked, shouting out Lauren's name. No answer.

He paused for a moment, unsure what to do. The whirring sound of a motor came from inside. The jacuzzi. He went round the side of the building to the terrace, to see if he could spot Lauren. But he could only see shadows through the tinted glass.

If you were in the jacuzzi you could see out to the spectacular views, but no one could see in.

He thought he saw a shadow of a figure standing there, hunched over and still. It struck him as odd. It didn't make sense.

'Lauren!' he shouted, his voice shaking. Something wasn't right. But she couldn't hear him through the soundproof glass.

The figure moved slightly to the right and he thought she was about to climb into the jacuzzi. But then he noticed something. The colours were dim through the tinted glass, but the person there wasn't in a swimming costume. They were in a royal-blue dress. The colour of the bridesmaid's dress. Tracey's dress.

A flash of white appeared in front of the blue. A wedding dress.

'Lauren!' he shouted. But neither of them moved.

Before he could even think what he was doing, Adam grabbed the solid stone ornament of two kissing doves from the terrace and threw it with all his might through the window.

CHAPTER SEVENTY-FIVE

Lauren

Lauren kept pushing against the hand that held her under the water, but she was losing strength. Her vision was fading and her lungs burned. She didn't think she could do it any more, didn't think she could keep fighting.

The sound of shattering glass echoed through the water and for a second Lauren thought she must be imagining it. But then the hand was gone and she was free and up above the surface, gasping for air and throwing up the jacuzzi water.

'Lauren, Lauren!' Adam was beside her, holding her in his arms, lifting her away. She looked around the room in a daze. The glass panelling had shattered and the water of the jacuzzi was swimming with the tiny shards of glass that covered everything from the floor to the white towels that hung around the edges of the room.

He carried her into the living room, and they heard the door slam shut.

'She tried to kill me,' Lauren said, shaking.

'I'll call the police,' Adam said. 'Pass me your phone.'

She watched him take charge, finding the number for the police and then calling it and trying to explain.

Lauren's stomach churned with fear. Whoever had tried to drown her must still be out there. It must be Kiera. It couldn't be anyone else at the wedding. Her brain was foggy, trying to make sense of it. She hadn't realised that Kiera hated her so much. Enough to try and kill her.

'They don't speak English,' Adam said, frustrated. 'I can't get them to understand.'

'I'll call Tracey, get her to call them,' Lauren said. She thought of her sister, of her fling with Adam. She needed her help now.

'No—' Adam said quickly, alarm on his face. 'Not Tracey. Don't call her. You shouldn't be doing anything except resting. I'll call Jasmine. She speaks Thai. She can call the police.'

Lauren sighed, sinking back into the sofa, while Adam took the phone into the bedroom. She'd let Adam take care of it. She felt light-headed, hardly able to believe that just five minutes ago, she was being held under the water, convinced she was going to die.

Adam came back into the room and sat down beside her on the sofa. 'It's OK,' he said, putting his arms around her. The straps of her wedding dress were still wet, her hair had come apart and was spread chaotically over her shoulders, the occasional strand still held in by pins. 'Jasmine's sorting it. They'll come and arrest the assailant.'

The assailant, Lauren thought. Why was he calling her that? Why not just say Kiera?

'She's gone, hasn't she?' Lauren asked.

'For now,' Adam smiled. 'I think I scared her away.'

Lauren nodded gratefully. 'Thank you.' He had saved her life.

They sat in silence for a moment, a million thoughts buzzing round Lauren's head. 'What happened between you and Tracey?' she asked, finally.

He sighed, stroking her hair. 'It was just a fling. It only lasted for the holiday, then it was over.'

'I never realised. Back then, I felt you and I had a connection.' She'd always told friends that her relationship with Adam had started in Thailand with the meaningful looks they'd shared on holiday. He'd never corrected her.

'I know,' he said. 'I should have told you about it long ago. But the longer I left it, the harder it got to mention it. We were happy. I didn't want anything coming between us.'

Lauren sighed. How much of their happiness had been built on lies and omissions, things Adam had failed to tell her?

'That was all it was – a fling? You haven't seen her since?'

'No, not until we came here. I wasn't interested. She wrote to me asking me to move over here, but I said no. I was with you by then.'

A rush of relief raced through Lauren. He had chosen her.

'Look,' Adam said. 'I've got something else to tell you.' Lauren's heart sank. What was it now? Was he in love with Kiera? Something worse?

'What is it?'

'Tracey kept something from me for years. Something she should have told me.'

'What?' Lauren asked, completely thrown by what it might be.

'I'm a father,' Adam said slowly. 'Jasmine's my daughter.'

Lauren stared at Adam in shock. It couldn't be.

But everything was slotting into place in Lauren's mind. The distance between her and Tracey, the way her sister had always seemed to be holding something back from her. She had never told Lauren about her pregnancy; never told her she'd given birth to a daughter. It must have been because the child was Adam's, because she didn't want Adam to know.

'When did you find out?' Lauren asked.

'Last night. Jasmine told me. She found my name on a document a few months ago, listed as her father. That's why she came to England. She wanted to meet me. She tried to talk to me at the pub, but I didn't recognise her, and she couldn't pluck up the courage to explain. And then I was away at the conference.'

'Oh,' Lauren said. 'I just can't get my head round it.' She shook her head. 'You're a father.' She thought of the baby they'd lost. She'd thought it would be their first child. But Adam already had another child. Jasmine.

'Tracey didn't tell either of you,' Lauren said slowly, trying to understand what had happened. 'That seems... almost cruel.' She flushed, suddenly seeing her sister through a different lens. Jasmine had seemed so lost when she'd come to England, so desperate to track down her family. But Tracey hadn't cared about that. She'd denied her daughter access to her biological father, denied Adam access to his own child. It seemed horribly unfair and selfish.

'What are you going to do?' she asked. 'About Jasmine?'

'Do about her?' he looked confused. 'Well, I want to build a relationship with her, be a proper father to her. We've missed out on so much. She wants to come to London again. I thought I could spend time with her then.'

'That sounds like a good idea,' she said. This was the Adam she loved, the Adam she had wanted to marry. A man who made mistakes, who sometimes avoided tackling things head on, avoiding confrontation. But also a man who put his family first, a man who was kind. A man who'd just smashed through glass to rescue her. Despite everything, she felt a warmth spread through her body as she leaned towards him, resting her head on his shoulder. She loved him.

But she wasn't willing to put her love into words. Not yet. He *had* lied to her. He couldn't get away with it that easily.

'I'm so glad you agree,' he said. 'I know this is a bit premature... but I'd really like it if we could all be a proper family. Without Tracey to support her, she'd be on her own and—'

'What do you mean, without Tracey?' Lauren asked, confused.

Adam met her eyes. 'Tracey will be in prison,' he said.

'What? Why?'

'She attacked you. Tried to drown you.'

Lauren frowned at him. He'd got this completely wrong. 'It wasn't Tracey that attacked me. It was Kiera.'

Adam sighed. 'I'm sorry, Lauren, but it was your sister. It's been her all along. Did you see who attacked you just now? I saw her run off. She was wearing a blue bridesmaid's dress. It was Tracey.'

CHAPTER SEVENTY-SIX

Adam

Adam sat close to Lauren on the sofa. He could see the torment she was going through, hearing that her sister had tried to kill her.

'It was Tracey?' she asked, her lip quivering, still disbelieving.

'Yes,' he said. 'She's been jealous of our relationship for years, although I had no idea. Jasmine told me that when she got our wedding invitation it sent her over the edge. It must have been her who sent the card with the picture of the doll. She'd have got it from the market here. And then, when she was staying with your uncle in Oxford, she must have taken his keys in order to get into the flat and steal your mother's bracelet.'

'No,' Lauren shook her head. 'She wouldn't have done it, not any of it. She wouldn't have tried to drown me.'

The doorbell rang and Lauren jumped.

'It might be the police,' Adam said, getting up to answer it. He opened the door, and Jasmine rushed in.

'I called the police,' she said, her face pale. 'They're on their way. I've left Mum in reception and asked the security team to keep her there until they come.'

He took her in his arms. 'Thank you. It must have been hard.' He couldn't imagine how painful it must be to have to call the police on your own mother.

Jasmine pulled away and looked at Lauren. 'I'm so sorry for what she did to you. For what she's been doing.'

'It's OK,' Lauren said. 'I'm fine. Honestly.' Adam knew she wasn't really fine, that she was still shaken by her experience in the jacuzzi, still shaken by the fact that it was her sister who'd hurt her. But she wouldn't want Jasmine to worry.

'Adam told me that you're his daughter.'

Jasmine nodded. 'Yeah,' she said, shifting from one foot to the other.

Lauren reached out and touched her arm, and Jasmine seemed to tense. 'It will be great to spend more time with you when you next come to London,' she said.

Adam felt a surge of love for Lauren. She was willing to accept Jasmine as his daughter, to welcome her with open arms. And she was still planning to be living with him in London. Which must mean she still wanted them to stay together.

'Are you hurt?' Lauren asked, looking at a cut that ran over Jasmine's shoulder. 'That's a nasty cut.'

'I had an argument with a palm tree while I was looking for you,' Jasmine said. 'The palm tree won.' She laughed.

Adam glanced over at his daughter. It would be easy to forget she had just learnt that her mother had tried to drown Lauren, and had had to call the police on her. He was impressed that she had been so calm under pressure. He felt a surge of pride that he was her father.

There was a pause, then Jasmine spoke. 'I came to give you this,' she said to Lauren. She handed her a small silver bracelet with a blue stone.

CHAPTER SEVENTY-SEVEN

Lauren

Lauren reached out and took the bracelet from Jasmine. Her mother's. The one she was going to wear for her wedding day. The only thing that had been stolen from her flat.

'Oh!' she exclaimed. 'Where did you find it?'

'Mum had it in her bag.' Lauren's heart stopped. Up until now she'd still wanted to believe that none of this could be Tracey. But this was the final proof. Her sister had stolen it from her flat in London. She felt heat rise through her body. Her sister had tried to kill her.

'Are you OK?' Adam asked, rushing over to the sofa. 'You look pale. I'll get you a glass of water. He fetched one and she sipped it gratefully.

'Jasmine!' A voice called from outside. 'Jasmine! Are you in there?'

The colour drained from Jasmine's face as she rushed to the door. Tracey must have somehow got away from the security guards who were supposed to be watching her.

Lauren's heart raced as Adam jumped up and followed Jasmine to the door.

'What have you done?' Tracey screamed at Jasmine. 'How could you?'

Lauren thought of how Jasmine had asked Tracey's own staff to retain her mother. She must have been furious.

'It was for the best, Mum.'

Adam jumped in front of Jasmine, trying to shield her from her mother's anger.

'Are you OK, Lauren?' Tracey asked, turning to her.

Lauren glared at her sister, uncomprehending. How could she ask that, after everything she'd done? 'Get away from me,' she hissed. Tears formed in her eyes. She didn't want Tracey anywhere near her.

'I'm so sorry. I never meant—' Tracey came closer to Lauren and she shrank into the sofa, afraid of what she might do next.

'Get away!' Adam shouted, holding out his hands to stop her coming nearer. 'Where are security?' he said to Jasmine, panic in his voice. 'We need to get them. Now!'

Jasmine picked up her phone and spoke rapidly in Thai.

'What are you doing?' Tracey shouted at Jasmine.

'You tried to drown me,' Lauren said, her voice louder than she expected. She couldn't hide from her sister any more.

'I didn't,' Tracey stuttered. A look of confusion crossed Tracey's face as she looked from Lauren to Jasmine.

'We know it was you. Adam saw you leave.' Lauren heard the chill in her own voice and she realised that in this moment, she truly hated her sister. Looking into the eyes that were so like her own, she realised it had been a mistake to ever trust her, to ever look up to her and admire her. All she'd done was hurt her.

'And the bracelet,' she said, holding it up. 'Jasmine brought it back. She found it in your bag.'

'Oh,' Tracey said, her eyes darting back and forth between them like a trapped animal. 'I'm sorry,' she said. 'It's not how it looks.'

'Then what is it, Tracey? What's your explanation?'

Tracey sank down to the floor in tears. 'I didn't mean for this to happen,' she mumbled.

Lauren was crying too, now. Both of them were shaking with sobs, but she'd never felt further apart from her sister. She'd so desperately wanted them to be close, like they'd been in childhood. She'd thought that the wedding had made them close again. But she had imagined it, thought that if she wanted it enough it would be true. It had never been true.

Just then two Thai men carrying guns burst into the room. Jasmine spoke in Thai, pointing to Tracey.

'Plain-clothes police,' Jasmine explained. They grabbed Tracey roughly and escorted her out of the room.

CHAPTER SEVENTY-EIGHT

Adam

'Do you think we should have gone with them?' Lauren asked Adam, after the police had taken Tracey away. Jasmine had left with them, talking to them rapidly in Thai, as they walked out of the room.

He shook his head. 'We should leave it to them. I imagine they might want to interview us later.'

Lauren nodded. 'I wouldn't know what to say.'

'Just tell the truth.' Adam ran his hand through her tangle of hair, now dried into a messy nest on her head.

'I didn't see her, though.'

He looked at her. He could see how much she wanted to believe that it wasn't her sister, even now.

'I did. I'll tell them.'

'What do you think will happen to her?'

'I don't know Thai law. But I imagine she'll go to prison.'

'But what will happen to Jasmine if her mother goes to prison?' Lauren said worriedly.

'I think she'll probably come to London, see more of us.'

Adam felt Lauren lean towards him, and he slid his arm around her. 'Our lives will be different from now on, won't they?' she said. 'Now you're a father.'

His heart leapt. Our lives. She still wanted to be with him. Even after all of this.

'Yes,' he said. 'A little bit different. But we'll still be in it together.'

'I'd like that,' she said. She reached for his hand and he gripped hers tightly. Their lips brushed against each other and he felt hope building inside him. Maybe they could continue as before. Maybe they'd still spend the rest of their lives together.

'Can I get you anything?' Adam asked her.

'I think I need a drink. Our wedding champagne would be nice. Maybe it doesn't have to go to waste.'

Adam sighed, thinking of all the plans they'd made for their wedding day. 'It would go down easily, wouldn't it? What would we be doing now? If we'd gone ahead…'

Lauren looked at her watch. 'Cutting the cake, I think.'

'I'm so sorry all this has happened.' He held her in his arms. 'I really wanted everything to be perfect.'

'Me too,' she said wistfully. 'But perhaps our wedding was never meant to be. So many things went wrong.'

'All of Tracey's making.'

'I still can't get my head round it, why she'd do that to me.'

'I don't know why anyone would do that.' He stroked her arm, feeling the warmth of her skin. She would have been his wife by now, if things had been different. 'If it's any consolation, I love you more than ever. For being you. For being willing to accept that Jasmine's my daughter, in spite of everything.'

Lauren smiled at him. 'I love you too.' His heart lifted, and he leaned in to kiss her. As their lips met, he realised what he'd said was true: that he'd never loved Lauren more than he did now.

They were still on the sofa, wrapped in an embrace, when they heard knocking on the door. Lauren glanced at herself in the mirror before she went to open it. Her hair was matted, her mascara smeared down her face. She looked dishevelled, as if she'd already had a very long night.

Adam got to the door before her. It was Noi.

'We've been wondering where you got to,' the wedding planner said politely, as if several hours hadn't passed since Lauren had been due to walk down the aisle.

'We…' Adam looked at Lauren, struggling to find the words.

'I know things have been difficult…' Noi looked at them both, and Adam wondered if she had any idea that her boss had been arrested.

She paused and then continued, 'I just wanted to let you know that the officiant is still here, and that if you do want to get married today, we can go ahead still. But it would have to be now.'

Adam looked at Lauren, his heart full of hope. It reminded him of when he'd first asked her to marry him, his heart pounding in his chest, unsure whether she'd say yes.

'We still have a chance to get married,' he said softly. 'To have our special day. To not let Tracey ruin it.'

Just then his phone started to buzz in his pocket. He tensed, wondering what it could be now. But it was just his mother, probably checking he was alright. He swiped to reject the call. Whatever she had to say would have to wait.

Lauren looked at Adam and smiled. 'Yes,' she said. 'Let's get married.' She turned to Noi. 'I just need fifteen minutes to redo my make-up and make my hair look OK. Then we'll be there.'

A beam spread across Adam's face and he hugged her so tight he thought he'd never let her go.

'Sure,' Noi said. 'If we go soon, we'll catch the sunset as you take your vows.'

'That would be perfect,' Lauren said.

CHAPTER SEVENTY-NINE

Lauren

Lauren hadn't taken her wedding dress off since she'd run away from her wedding. It seemed like a lifetime ago now. The silk straps of the dress were watermarked, and the train was sandy and dirty, but it would do. She ran her fingers over the stitching that concealed the tear, and thought of Tracey slashing through it with a knife.

But she couldn't stop her marrying Adam. Even after everything she'd done. Lauren quickly brushed her hair, hastily combing out the matted bits. She reapplied her make-up carefully. It didn't look anywhere near as perfect as when the make-up artist had done it, but it was good enough. Her wedding shoes were still discarded on the beach, from when she'd run away, so she slid on her flip-flops instead. For the second time that day, she walked down the steps over the rocks and onto the red carpet on the wooden pathway which stretched out over the white sand beach, leading to the ocean. But this time she was arm in arm with her husband-to-be.

A bird squawked above as the small crowd of guests came towards them and cheered as they walked down the aisle. Lauren grinned and met Adam's eyes as they headed towards the pier. The photographer must have left, but the guests were making up for him, snapping away on their mobile phones.

The sun had started to set and the sky was darkening. Someone had lit the tea lights on the pier and they twinkled, reflecting in the water below. It was magical. The restaurant rose up on its stilts, a shadow against the setting sun.

They walked down the red carpet to the white archway. Underneath it, Adam turned to her, took both her hands and smiled. 'Are you ready?' he asked.

'Absolutely.' Lauren had never been so sure of anything in her life. She loved him, and nothing would stop her marrying him.

He lifted her up in one easy motion and she wrapped her arms round his neck as he carried her under the archway and onto the pier.

Beneath them the pier creaked. She caught sight of the raging water below, the violent waves.

She felt safe in Adam's strong arms. No matter what had happened between them, she knew she could trust him now.

'I love you,' he whispered.

'I love you too.'

The officiant at the end of the pier smiled at them as she welcomed them to their wedding day. Adam put Lauren down and they stood side by side in front of the setting sun, its red and orange rays stretching out over the darkening sky and reflecting in the ocean below. The train of Lauren's wedding dress fluttered behind her in the light wind.

It took a moment for Lauren to recognise the sounds of shouts from the beach, above the roar of the waves and the sea breeze. Confused by the commotion, Lauren turned and saw Tracey running across the sand.

Her breath caught in her throat. Adam gripped her hand.

Wasn't anyone going to stop her?

She saw Jasmine in front of her mother, blocking the pier, still in her flower girl dress. And then Zoe was behind Tracey, grabbing her arm, holding her back.

'Let's just do this,' Lauren said.

The officiant started to read out the wedding vows, glancing behind them as she did, her face etched with worry.

'Do you take this man to be your husband?'

'I do,' Lauren said, smiling up at Adam, trying not to look at the beach, at Tracey.

Out of the corner of her eye, she could see a flash of blue coming up the pier. She turned. It was only Jasmine, holding the basket. She must still want to be part of the wedding, her father's wedding.

'And do you take this woman to be your wife?'

'I do.'

The officiant reached into her pocket for the rings, but then Lauren saw her gaze shift to a point behind Lauren further down the pier.

Lauren turned and saw Jasmine, walking purposefully up the pier behind them, holding something in her hand under the basket. A can dripping a dark liquid. She gazed in horror, barely comprehending what was happening.

Adam took the ring from the officiant. 'I give this ring as a sign of my love,' he said, and slid the gold band onto Lauren's finger.

But Lauren was looking at Jasmine. She was nearly beside them, her expression determined and angry. As she reached the end of the pier, Lauren smelt the petrol. She gasped. Suddenly, it was like time had slowed down. Everything was happening in slow motion and yet Lauren was rooted to the spot, unable to move, unable to stop it. She saw Jasmine turn over one of the tea lights into a puddle of petrol. A burst of flames shot up and in seconds the planks of the pier caught fire.

'Jasmine?' Lauren's mouth was wide with horror.

But Jasmine didn't reply. She was next to them now, trying to grab Adam, to drag him back to the shore before the fire took hold. But it was too late. The fire had shot along the old wood and the pier behind them was falling away, its stilts buckling and collapsing as burning planks dropped into the sea. There was no way back.

CHAPTER EIGHTY

Adam

Adam saw the stilts of the pier crumbling into the ocean, the flames hungrily devouring the rest of the pier as they rushed towards them. At first he didn't understand what was happening, but then he saw the can of petrol in Jasmine's hands.

He grabbed Lauren's hand and ran, dragging her towards the restaurant at the end of the pier. Behind them, he saw the flames had caught the end of the train of her wedding dress, devouring the lace in hungry gulps. It would reach Lauren's body in seconds. He wrapped his arms round her back and fumbled to find the clip that attached it, ripping it off. Then they ran into the restaurant, letting the train fall behind her, the whole piece of lace material gone in an instant, its ashes dancing in the air.

As they entered all the lights went out, the electricity lost. Jasmine rushed in behind them and then the officiant appeared, panting. In the dark, Adam could just make out the wedding decorations, the white congratulations balloons and the pressed tablecloths.

'You were supposed to get out,' Jasmine said angrily to Adam. 'It was just supposed to be her in here.' She jabbed her finger at Lauren.

'What have I ever done to you?' Lauren asked.

Out of the doorway, Adam could see the fire approaching from the pier. It had slowed. There was no longer a river of kerosene for it to devour. But it was creeping closer. They didn't have long.

'You denied me my father. He should have been bringing me up with my mother, but instead he was with you. I missed out on so many years. All because you wanted him for yourself.'

'I didn't know Tracey had ever even been with Adam. And I definitely didn't know you were his daughter.' Adam glanced at Lauren as she desperately tried to convince Jasmine.

'She didn't,' Adam said quickly, taking Lauren's arm. 'She really didn't. How could she? I didn't know myself.'

Jasmine laughed. 'What does it matter whether she knew? She deliberately took you from my mother. That left me fatherless. How can you take her side against me? How can you marry her?'

Adam shook his head. He couldn't believe this was who his daughter really was, so bitter, so angry. He stared at her blue dress. The dress he'd seen the woman wearing by the jacuzzi, who he'd thought was Tracey. It must have been Jasmine who planted the dolls, who tried to drown Lauren. He gulped, afraid. She was unstable. Dangerous. 'Jasmine – you're my daughter. Nothing will ever come between us.'

Jasmine grinned cruelly. 'She's the one who'd come between us. She took you from me. She stole my whole family. First she killed my grandparents. Then she stole my father.'

'She didn't kill your grandparents. That was an accident,' Adam insisted desperately, reaching towards her.

At that moment, flames burst into the restaurant with an angry roar. The officiant screamed as the heat forced them back into the corner of the room. On the stand in the corner, tiny bride and groom figures watched the fire from the top of their wedding cake.

Adam came to his senses. There wasn't time to talk. They needed to figure a way to put out the fire. He scanned the room, looking for something to throw on the flames. He noticed the door to the kitchen. Of course. There might be a fire extinguisher in there. If not, there'd be lots of water.

He ran to the door of the kitchen and pushed it open. The others followed. Without the flames to light it up it was pitch-black in there, huge shadows of industrial cookers looming over the room.

He reached into his pocket for his phone and turned on the torch.

A text message flashed up on the screen from half an hour ago, before the wedding.

A message from his mother. He read the words without thinking.

I need to speak to you. Jasmine's not your daughter.

CHAPTER EIGHTY-ONE

Lauren

Suddenly Adam took out his phone and went silent.

'Adam, what are you doing?' Lauren asked.

He looked up then. 'I've got a torch on my phone,' Adam said. 'We might be able to find a fire extinguisher in here.'

'There's no time for that,' the officiant said, desperately, pulling off her shoes. 'We should swim to shore.'

'No!' Lauren shook her head violently. She remembered the stories of the current below the pier, how the rip tide could carry you out to sea in an instant. She thought of her own parents, in their last moments. 'The current – it's too much.'

Adam shone his torch around, exposing the heavy grey industrial cookers that were perched on the planks of the restaurant. Jasmine was silent, still clutching the can of kerosene like a weapon.

'I can't see any fire extinguisher or blanket,' Adam shouted.

A flash of orange leapt past the doorway of the kitchen and Lauren saw the fire eating up the paper lanterns and white streamers in the restaurant, demolishing the tablecloths. They heard a creak below them, and she saw parts of the wooden structure of the restaurant breaking off and falling into the sea, the chairs and tables and Lauren's decorations sliding after them.

She stared into the hole where the restaurant had been. Now all she could see was the pounding waves below them. In the distance she could hear the faint sound of screams from the guests on the shore.

'We'll have to use water,' Adam shouted, desperately trying to turn on the taps. Nothing was coming out. The pipes must have broken when the restaurant fell into the sea.

'It's too late,' Lauren said. 'Jasmine – please – is there anything in here to help? An extinguisher? A fire blanket?' Jasmine was the only one who knew the layout of the building.

'There's ice in the freezer,' Jasmine said, rushing over to the huge freezer in the corner of the room. She must have realised that she was going to die here too, unless she did something. They were all desperate now.

But as she opened the freezer door there was a huge bang. The wooden planks beneath the cooking equipment gave way and the freezer tumbled into the sea, ripping a hole in the floor and taking Jasmine with it. They saw her body flailing through the air, the huge freezer hitting her head as she fell into the sea below.

'Jasmine!' Adam called out, jumping down into the dark, swirling water after her. Lauren caught a glimpse of Jasmine, her pale body and royal-blue dress buffeted by the sea.

She watched Adam wrestling the waves, trying to stay above the water and reach Jasmine. He was pushed away from her by the current, getting further and further out. Lauren saw a dark pool of blood by Jasmine's head. She was face down in the water; Adam wasn't going to reach her. She'd die down there.

Lauren thought of her parents. Jasmine was their granddaughter. Tracey's daughter. She jumped. She would reach her.

The cold water shocked her and she realised instantly that she had made a mistake. The thick silk of her wedding dress was weighing her down, the long skirt making it impossible to move her legs properly, to tread water.

The current was strong and she wanted to shout out to Adam, but when she opened her mouth she was slammed into by a wave and her mouth was filled with salt water. She was sinking now, losing her sense of which way was up and which way was down. All she could see was water, whichever way she looked. The sea violently pushed her from side to side as if she were its plaything.

She fought to find the surface. She broke up through the water for half a second and managed a gulp of air, before she was submerged once more. She was fighting to stay afloat, fighting for her life, her wedding dress wrapping round her ankles like bindweed. She tried to wave for help, but when she raised her arms above the surface the rest of her sank under. She couldn't catch a breath for long enough to scream.

And then she was submerged again, under the angry water, her lungs burning with the need for air. She came up for the briefest second and then sank again. This was what it had been like for her parents, she thought. She fought back to the surface. She wasn't going to go the same way. She wasn't. None of them were. But she sank under the water again, swallowing a mouthful. She kept fighting, her arms flailing desperately.

Lauren heard a creak above her. She tried to shield her head as the remaining structure of the restaurant gave way above her, beams of burning wood tumbling down, tables and chairs falling like confetti around her.

CHAPTER EIGHTY-TWO

Adam

Adam could see the burning orange embers of the restaurant. They were far away now, slowly extinguishing and disappearing. Once he'd jumped into the water, the sea had swallowed him and the rip tide had carried him far out. He'd fought to the surface and tried desperately to swim back, but the current had taken him further and further away. He thought of Jasmine, how she'd hit her head. She'd die in this sea.

He remembered his mother's text. *Jasmine's not your daughter.* His phone had been swallowed by the sea when he'd fallen in the water, and now he wondered if he'd imagined the text entirely. Why would she have sent that? Jasmine had shown him paperwork with Adam named as the father.

Something hard bashed into his leg and he turned to see a chair that had been carried out in the current with him. It still had its royal-blue sash wrapped around it, the one Lauren had chosen to match the bridesmaids' dresses. When he thought of Lauren, tears pricked his eyes. The restaurant was gone now and the area around it was completely black. She was out there somewhere, too, in the dark water.

He had to focus. He needed to stay alive. The only lights now were the distant ones from the shore. He tried once more to swim towards them, but his legs and arms felt too heavy. He sank below the surface for a moment. When he fought his way back up again, he saw torchlight. At first he thought it was a mirage, but then he heard the hum of an engine.

'Adam!' He thought it was Lauren, but surely it couldn't be. He couldn't tell if it was even a voice or just the whispering of the waves. She couldn't be here, not now. He must be confused.

'Adam!' He heard the voice again, screaming his name. The engine of a boat got closer.

He lifted his hands up and waved with every ounce of his remaining energy.

The boat was getting further away again, its torch scanning the ocean, going in the other direction.

He screamed out, 'Lauren!' and his mouth filled with seawater.

Then the light was on him. He waved frantically. They'd seen him.

Strong arms reached for him and pulled him into the boat.

He tumbled over the side and then looked up to see his rescuer.

It was Tracey.

His eyes adjusted to the dark and he looked around him. There was a body lying in the bottom of the boat. At first he thought it was Lauren, but then he saw the royal-blue dress. Jasmine.

Adam saw Lauren leaning over her and felt a rush of relief. She'd cut off a large chunk of the skirt of her wedding dress with a penknife and was wrapping it round Jasmine's head wound as the boat rocked in the choppy waters, flung about by the angry waves. Jasmine was still unconscious, but breathing. He could see her chest rising and falling rapidly. As he stared at her, he felt a rush of emotion: love, pity, anger, hate. What had she wanted from him? Was she even his daughter?

Tracey was steering the boat back to the shore. The officiant sat shivering in a blanket beside her.

He reached over and held the makeshift bandage in place for Lauren, helping her to wrap it tighter round Jasmine's head. When they were done, he kissed Lauren's cold cheek softly.

Then, shivering in his sodden wedding clothes, he stepped to the front of the boat towards Tracey. As the boat hit a wave he nearly flew back into the sea. But he steadied himself and reached out to touch Tracey's arm.

'Thank you,' he said, but his voice was lost in the crashing waves.

CHAPTER EIGHTY-THREE

Lauren

The day after the wedding

Lauren and Adam took a taxi to the hospital together. As Lauren watched the scenery go by, she fiddled with the wedding ring on her finger. It had survived the fall into the ocean, survived the fire. A symbol of their love. Everlasting.

In Jasmine's room at the hospital Tracey greeted them. 'Thanks for coming,' she said softly.

Machines beeped around Jasmine, who lay pale and expressionless on the bed, her face barely visible beneath the bandages. She'd slipped into a coma the night before.

Lauren put her arms around Tracey. 'I'm so sorry this has happened,' she said, tears pricking her eyes. She hated what Jasmine had done to her and Adam, but she didn't want to see her like this.

Adam went over to Jasmine and stroked her arm. 'I'm here,' he said.

Then he turned to Tracey. 'Thank you for rescuing us yesterday. You saved our lives.'

'I wish I could have stopped the whole thing,' Tracey said quietly.

'Is that why you wanted to meet me the night before the wedding?' Adam asked. 'To warn me about Jasmine?'

Tracey shook her head, confused. 'I didn't want to meet you.'

'I got a text from you, asking me to meet you in the hotel bar. But then Jasmine was there… that was her too, wasn't it?'

'It must have been. I never texted you, I don't have your phone number. She turned to Lauren. 'I didn't know what Jasmine had been doing until after you ran away from your wedding. It was when you confronted me about the bracelet that it really dawned on me.'

'Why didn't you just say it wasn't you, then?' Lauren asked. 'You didn't defend yourself, you let us think it was you.'

'I couldn't. I thought you'd tell the police, get her sent to prison. She's my daughter.'

'She told me she was mine, too,' Adam said, stroking Jasmine's hand. 'Is that true?' Lauren watched Adam. He'd told her about his mother's text last night, but neither of them had known whether to believe it. Sam had come to the hospital last night to see them, but once she'd seen they were well, she'd left them to recover. She hadn't mentioned the text, and they'd been so caught up in everything that had happened, they hadn't thought to mention it either.

'Sorry?' Tracey looked baffled. 'What did she tell you?'

'That I'm her father.'

Tracey shook her head. 'But you're not.'

Lauren's eyes widened. Had Sam been right?

'But the timings…' Lauren said. 'Jasmine's birthday is nine months after our holiday.'

'She was born early,' Tracey said. 'She was in the premature baby unit for a month. I got pregnant after the holiday.'

'Oh,' Adam said, his voice shaking. 'I thought that when you invited me out to live with you in Thailand, it must have been when you were pregnant with Jasmine.' Adam took a step back, away from Jasmine's bed.

Tracey sighed. 'It was. I was confused. I felt so alone, and I wanted to be with you. I thought if you came out to live with me, you might accept the baby even though it wasn't yours.'

'Why didn't you tell me you were pregnant?' Lauren asked. She could have helped her sister, supported her.

'I couldn't. I was too embarrassed. I found out quite late and I just… I wanted to stay in Thailand and pretend it wasn't happening. I knew if anyone at home found out they'd want me to come back to England. I couldn't do that. I needed a new life. But that's why I was so stressed when the inheritance didn't come through quickly. It took you so long to sell the flat, and I had a baby to feed. I really needed the money.'

'If you'd let me know I could have helped, sold Mum and Dad's flat quicker.'

'I didn't want to talk to you. A part of me blamed you for what happened to Mum and Dad.'

'So Jasmine was right about that,' Lauren said, tears in her eyes. 'You did blame me.'

'Maybe years ago, I did, but not any more. I told Jasmine once that what you did had meant her grandparents were dead. I was having a tough day, missing them, and it kind of slipped out. I didn't mean it. But she must have remembered.'

'I'm so sorry about what happened.'

'It was just an accident. Bad luck.'

They both looked at Jasmine in the bed. Their family seemed to be plagued by bad luck.

Adam interrupted them then. 'But I don't understand,' he said. 'Jasmine showed me a picture on her phone. Of my name listed as her father. You must have written that down.'

Tracey shook her head. 'I wrote Dr A. Glenister on all the forms. It could have been you. But it wasn't you.' She sighed and looked at the floor.

Lauren suddenly got the connection. 'Dr Antony Glenister,' she murmured. Tony. Adam's father. Suddenly the funeral flashed back to her. Tracey hardly speaking to her, downing glass after glass of wine. Tracey chatting to Adam's father.

'He was kind to me at the funeral. He'd known Mum and Dad for years. He was the only one who seemed to understand. The rest of you were there when the accident happened. I couldn't talk to you about it.'

'You slept with him?' Adam asked.

'You can hardly judge,' Lauren said sharply. 'You weren't even talking to her.'

'It's all a bit of a blur,' Tracey said. 'I mean, it was something I wanted at the time. Just to take my mind off things, I suppose. But the next day I felt so ashamed. I just tried to forget it. By the time I realised I was pregnant there was no going back.'

They all watched Jasmine, thinking of how different things might have been.

'I wanted her, though,' Tracey said, gazing at her daughter. 'As soon as she was born I fell in love with her.'

She turned to Lauren. 'I have something for you.' She rooted around in her bag and pulled out a phone.

Lauren recognised it as hers. The one she lost in the club.

'When I went to get a bag of Jasmine's things to bring to the hospital, I saw two phones on the side. I wasn't sure which one was hers so I grabbed both. I think this one's yours.'

Lauren nodded. 'She must have taken it in the club,' she said.

Tracey sighed and glanced at her daughter. 'That doesn't surprise me. She's had a fake ID for years. Easy to get round here. She must have come to the club on her own, instead of going back to the hotel. I'm so sorry. I should have realised she was so out of control.'

Lauren looked at the machines surrounding Jasmine and put her arms around her sister. 'Don't worry about any of that now,' she said.

The machine behind Jasmine suddenly beeped and Tracey rushed over. She touched her daughter's arm, and Lauren saw Jasmine's hand lift slightly off the bed in response.

EPILOGUE

One year later

Lauren walked into the church with Adam, cradling her new baby boy. Jamie. Named after her father. The golden August light beamed through the stained-glassed windows. This was the place they had decided to christen him, the place that had been so much a part of their lives, which had hosted her parents' wedding and then, years later, their funerals. The place where she'd been due to get married herself a year before.

A year ago they'd come back from Thailand and booked a registry office. They'd had a small wedding, just the two of them, with Sam and Zoe as witnesses. It had turned out that their wedding in Thailand would never have been legally binding, even if it had gone ahead. No paperwork had ever been filed with the Thai authorities. Lauren had thought Tracey was looking after it, but once again Jasmine had been emailing from her account.

In the church, they sat in the pew reserved for close family and waited as the place filled up, greeting friends and family. Tracey had flown all the way over from Thailand to join them, and met them at the church, sitting with them at the front.

'How's Jasmine?' Adam asked, out of both curiosity and politeness. They hadn't seen her since their wedding. They'd dropped the various criminal cases against her because Tracey had begged them to, insisting that Jasmine was repentant, that she'd just had a moment of madness. Lauren hadn't been sure she believed Tracey, but she knew her sister would be devastated if her daughter was put in prison, so she agreed on the understanding that Jasmine would never be a part of their lives again.

'She's fine, she's over in London at the moment, working in a hotel.' Lauren shivered at the thought of her being so close by. Jasmine claimed not to remember the wedding at all, and to be shocked by her own behaviour, but Lauren suspected she was just a good actress.

'We didn't know,' Lauren said.

'I didn't think you'd want to know.'

Lauren had no interest in seeing Jasmine. They were moving soon anyway, out of London to the country. Their flat was full of packed boxes, ready to start their new life. She'd always been so attached to this part of London, which helped her feel closer to her parents. But now she knew it was time to move on. She had her own family now, and she wanted to create the best life for her son. Her own life, not a repeat of her parents'.

'She's spending a lot of time with her father,' Tracey said. And as if on cue, Tony appeared next to them, Jasmine beside him.

'Hello!' he said, kissing Lauren's cheek. 'Lovely day for a christening.' Lauren winced.

'Why did you bring her?' Adam asked, indicating Jasmine.

'She's family.'

'Hi,' Jasmine said softly. The baby cried in Lauren's arms as if he sensed something was wrong and Lauren rocked him back and forth.

'Can I hold him?' Jasmine asked.

Lauren thought of the doll in the card, the hand on her back pushing her down the stairs, the fingers on her neck in the jacuzzi, the petrol on the pier.

The baby cried harder.

'No,' Lauren said firmly, standing tall and strong.

'But she's family,' Tony repeated. 'Your flesh and blood.'

She thought of how Tony had behaved towards Adam, ignoring him throughout his childhood. 'Family is more than blood. It's love. It's care. It's looking out for each other. People should earn the right to be called family.'

Tracey gripped her hand, and Lauren thought of all the years they'd been apart, how Tracey had rescued her from the water. They'd both made costly mistakes, and their close relationship now was hard won.

'I think you'd better go, love,' Tracey said to Jasmine softly. 'This is Lauren's day. She doesn't want you here.'

'I have everyone I need in my family right here,' Lauren said. She looked from Adam to Tracey, then to Sam in the row behind them. She held baby Jamie tightly. It was time to move on. A new beginning for all of them.

A LETTER FROM RUTH

Dear reader,

I want to say a huge thank you for choosing to read *The Wedding*. If you enjoyed it, and want to keep up to date with all my latest releases, just sign up at the following link. Your email address will never be shared and you can unsubscribe at any time.

www.bookouture.com/ruth-heald

What a strange time to have written a book about a wedding! Although I had the idea for the book several years ago, I didn't start writing it until December 2019. As we all know, things changed dramatically around the world in 2020 with the arrival of Covid-19 and the devastation that's caused. As the world was changing, it was a relief for me to escape into fiction, although Lauren and Adam's normal world has seemed further and further removed from life today. In the UK, weddings were banned, then allowed with limited numbers, then banned again. I can't imagine how difficult those of you due to get married in 2020 must have found it.

In Lauren and Adam's world, wedding planning was still pretty normal. Nevertheless, I hope you could relate to Lauren's dilemmas throughout the book, and her worries about her wedding being ruined and losing Adam. I managed to escape into this book at a time when the world seemed to be unpredictable and full of uncertainty. Whenever you're reading this book, and whatever's going on in the world and in your own life, I hope you've been able to escape into the novel too, and that you've enjoyed reading Lauren and Adam's story. If you did, I would be very grateful if you would write a review. I'd love to hear what you think, and it makes such a difference in helping new readers to discover one of my books for the first time.

Thanks,
Ruth

ruth.heald

@RJ_Heald

www.ruthheald.com

ACKNOWLEDGEMENTS

Thank you first to my wonderful husband, who supports me in whatever I do and is always there for me, celebrating with me when I'm riding high and the writing's flowing freely, and acting as a sounding board when I'm worried about a difficult edit. To clarify, none of the relationship between Lauren and Adam was based on us, or on our wedding! Thanks also to my family and friends, who have supported my writing career, cheering me on from the sidelines.

As always, my exceptional editor, Christina Demosthenous, has been instrumental in the creation of this book. Her editorial insight has been invaluable and her patience and understanding greatly appreciated. Thanks also to Laura Gerrard, my copy editor, and Jenny Page, my proofreader, who both really helped to fine-tune the book. And thanks to my audiobook narrator, Tamsin Kennard. I can't wait to hear how it sounds.

This book owes a lot to my brilliant beta readers, Charity Davies and Ruth Jones, who have provided great insight and feedback. I can't thank them enough for their help making the book the best it can be. Fellow authors have been a source of support during the pandemic. Rona Halsall, Vikki Patis and Lesley Sanderson have provided a wealth of encouragement during the writing process, and were the voices of reason when I felt like giving up. Sophie Hannah has supplied superb guidance on all aspects of writing and publishing. I'm also grateful for the informative conversations about publishing I've had with the members of the Savvy Writers' Snug and the Psychological Suspense Authors' Association.

This year, it's been exciting to get more involved in the local author community and to take part in panel discussions hosted by the Chiswick Book Festival and Ealing Library, with Marianne Holmes, Nicola Rayner and Eleni Kyriacou. I've been delighted to have the support of Pitshanger Bookshop, where I signed copies of my last book, *I Know Your Secret*.

I'm so lucky to be published by the superb team at Bookouture. Despite the stresses of 2020, they've never stopped working, going all out to give every publication the best chance of success. Thank you to the wonderful publicity team of Kim, Noelle and Sarah. And to Alex Holmes and the production team, as well as the marketing and promotion team, insights team and rights team.

Finally, thanks to my readers, whose kind reviews help spur me on. I wouldn't be able to do it without you.

57151293R00181